Beach Week

Beach Week

· · · · ·

SUSAN COLL

Sarah Crichton Books
Farrar, Straus and Giroux   New York

SARAH CRICHTON BOOKS
Farrar, Straus and Giroux
18 West 18th Street, New York 10011

Distributed in Canada by D&M Publishers, Inc.
Printed in the United States of America
First edition, 2010

Portions of this book first appeared, in slightly different form,
in *Bethesda Magazine*.

Library of Congress Cataloging-in-Publication Data
Coll, Susan.
  Beach week / Susan Coll. — 1st ed.
    p.   cm.
  ISBN 978-0-374-10925-7 (alk. paper)
  1. High school graduates—Fiction.   2. Beaches—Fiction.   3. Parents—
Fiction.   4. Washington (D.C.)—Fiction.   5. Domestic fiction.   I. Title.

PS3553.O474622B33 2010
813'.54—dc22

2009045682

Designed by Abby Kagan

www.fsgbooks.com

1   3   5   7   9   10   8   6   4   2

For our friend Chuck

How huge it is, how empty, this great space for which I have been longing all my life.
—*The Sea, the Sea*, by Iris Murdoch

PART ONE

The Meetings

1

. . . . .

When Leah reminded her husband at breakfast that they were hosting a meeting that evening to discuss the logistics of the forthcoming annual high school graduation celebration known as Beach Week, he kept his eyes locked on the sports section of the newspaper and made a plaintive choking noise that sounded like the bleat of a sheep. A few drops of coffee sprayed from his mouth, landing on his pressed white shirt.

Charles had reacted in a similar, if less theatrical, fashion when she initially informed him of this meeting a few days earlier. Still, she had hoped for something else, some sudden change of heart that might have made him warm to the idea of welcoming into their home this group of parents whom they barely knew, to discuss a subject that had, admittedly, caused him to bristle even when it first crossed their radar as a mere abstraction on a local NBC News segment entitled "Mayhem at Beach Week" more than a year earlier, before their daughter had begun her senior year. After viewing footage of underage drinking and lewd sexual behavior, Charles had quipped that the idea of packing one's child off for a week of presumed debauchery was akin to negligent parenting.

It was unlike Leah to act unilaterally in a matter concerning their daughter, and for a brief moment she felt a twinge of guilt disproportionate to having merely volunteered to invite a few people over to their home for a brief discussion involving child rearing. She could only regard this as a sad indication of how constricted her life had become since they moved to the suburbs of Washington, D.C., almost two years earlier. She had given up her job as a teacher back in Omaha and had since failed to find—or to seriously look for—another. Once, an act of daring on her part might have involved challenging a contentious school board on a ninth-grade reading curriculum; now she felt like a renegade for simply inviting the parents of her daughter's friends to their home and preparing to set out plates of cheese cubes and bowls of salted nuts without first consulting her husband.

Of course it was true that Charles might have other cause for annoyance; for one thing, it probably appeared that Leah was disregarding their plan to have a meaningful, considered conversation specific to the potentially loaded question of whether their daughter would even be allowed to attend Beach Week. But Leah wasn't disregarding it. They would have plenty of time to discuss this later. Tonight's meeting was purely informational, intended only to find facts, to meet their fellow parents and hear them out.

Leah might have tried to explain this now, but she felt suddenly afraid of what she'd done to disturb their increasingly delicate marital balance, and her instinct was to retreat. She walked over to the sink and wet a paper towel, which she pressed to the specks of coffee that were starting to merge above Charles's left breast pocket into an amorphous brown cloud. She regarded with some tenderness his hairline, which was receding incrementally each day. Charles was a gentle, easygoing man who only ever raised his voice to yell at professional athletes on television, but lately he'd become somewhat mercurial. Although there were outside forces that had altered the family dynamic, Leah knew that she was not without blame when it came to the matter of his changeable moods, particularly on this occasion.

"This was one of my best shirts," he said.

"I'm so, so sorry," she said, and she was. "It's no big deal. I can definitely bleach it out."

This was not quite true; she didn't have the talent to remove this spot. She was the sort of laundress who turned whites pink and inexplicably lost socks. Why now, even in assertions to do with laundry, she wondered, was she behaving with duplicity?

It wasn't as if Leah had invented the idea of Beach Week. Kids from this community had been flocking to the same stretch of the Delaware shore to commemorate their high school graduations for as long as anyone could remember, and although there were occasional minor incidents involving citations for possession of alcohol or cases of sun poisoning, nothing truly awful had ever happened. She had done a little poking around online to assuage herself with the knowledge that this sort of thing wasn't unique to the affluent suburb where they now lived. At high schools all over the country, graduation was marked by one sort of celebration or another. Some communities called it Senior Week, and activities ranged from barbecues to trips to amusement parks to presumably more raucous expeditions to such notorious party spots as Cancún. Sharing a house with a nice group of girls from good, solid families at a beach only a few hours from home—Leah could easily imagine worse ways for Jordan to cap her high school experience.

Besides, it was Jordan herself who had proposed the idea. Their seventeen-year-old daughter had come into their bedroom late one night the previous week to say that she and her friends had found the perfect rental for this coming summer, but they had to act quickly to secure the lease. Leah and Charles had at least been on the same page in groggily suggesting the need for a proper conversation about this at a more reasonable hour. That was the extent of their discussion to date, so it was not as if Charles had expressly said *no* to Jordan's participation, and it was not as if Leah had put forth her own completely out of character *yes*-leaning view.

After a difficult transition following a move halfway across the country the summer preceding Jordan's junior year of high school, compounded by a terrifying, high-impact collision on the soccer field that had left her sidelined with a concussion and its lingering—albeit mercifully dwindling—side effects, Leah wanted, above all, to have her daughter be a happy, healthy teen. That she set this goal intellectually didn't stop her from trying to protect Jordan at every turn. Since that disorienting moment when Leah had glimpsed her daughter unconscious on the 18-yard line, the blood from her nose brilliant in the afternoon sunlight as it trickled down her white jersey, she had become a bit overzealous in her mothering, and she knew that she needed to let go.

By all indications, they were over the hump: Jordan's postconcussive migraines had largely subsided, her concentration had returned, the bursts of vertigo were now rare. She did remain a bit moody and aloof, but Leah understood that these hardly qualified as signs that something might be wrong in a teenage girl. Given the scale of disasters that might befall a family, this was clearly minor; nevertheless, Jordan, Charles, and Leah herself had all lost equilibrium, recalibrating emotions in private, and not always linear, ways. Leah had started to have bouts of What Might Have Been, with the insidious sidebar crazy mothering issue of What She Might Do to Prevent This from Ever Happening Again. If only the dangers in this world could be confined to the soccer field! Leah now had a heightened awareness of the catastrophes that loomed at every turn. There were crooked bolts of summer lightning shooting randomly from the sky and distracted Beltway drivers swerving out of lanes, cell phones pressed to their ears. She had even just seen a newspaper photograph of a bear roaming their pristine subdivision, on one occasion walking right onto someone's deck and swiping the bag of hot-dog buns that had been left beside the grill. And the environment! There were toxins galore—in food, in plastics, in underarm deodorants, microscopic carcinogens in the water and the air. From what she'd read, it was possible that some of these might even be triggering Jordan's headaches.

Allowing Jordan to go to Beach Week was of course hugely inconsistent with Leah's recent neurotic style of parenting, but she thought it a good sign that their daughter wanted to go, that she was seeking to engage with her new Verona friends, about whom she at times seemed ambivalent. Leah wasn't completely naïve; she had some insight into teenage behavior, having been a high school English teacher for nearly two decades, but she trusted Jordan and had come to the conclusion that certain kids were going to misbehave no matter where they were, whether under twenty-four-hour guard or on their own at the beach. She'd seen bed-hopping by members of the wind ensemble she chaperoned at a school-sponsored band trip, had spied a National Merit finalist snorting coke in the bathroom at the local Dunkin' Donuts late one night, and had once walked in on two male students having sex after debate team practice—and this was in the supposedly more conservative, bucolic Midwest. If kids were going to get into trouble, they would, regardless of whether their parents kept them on a short leash. Leah understood as well that Beach Week was an important rite of passage, a dry run for the more wrenching letting-go that would by necessity take place when Jordan left for college in the fall.

Admittedly, there was something else to this whole Beach Week thing. Leah would say it was subliminal, except that she had easy access to the thought. She wanted to go to Beach Week herself. Not actually, physically go to Beach Week at the age of forty-two, of course, but symbolically, in an if-she-could-only-go-back-in-time kind of way. Having grown up in a small town, Leah had always wished for a richer teenage experience, which in her mind would have involved going to a large, coed, racially diverse public school that was the stuff of television dramas—the kind of school her daughter now attended, minus the diversity part. In addition, Leah had grown up dreaming, quite literally, of the beach itself. She wanted crashing waves, funnel cakes, boardwalks with video arcades and Skee-Ball. She wanted to build sand castles and collect shells and look for jellyfish and sit at restaurants that served crabs with Old Bay seasoning. She was twenty-three before she'd stuck a toe into the ocean, and that was on her honeymoon. What could be better for her daughter, more healthy and natural, than relaxing at the beach with friends, breathing in the fresh sea air?

Would Leah dare say that in some private corner of her mind she longed for the bad stuff that Beach Week was known

for, too? Although she and Charles weren't physically estranged, a thick layer of resentment hung over them in bed
like plane-grounding fog. Marital tension might have made for
better sex in theory—the release of pent-up anger and whatnot—but in their case it did not. That might have been
because there was nothing very arousing about the other
source of anxiety in their lives, which was money. She wondered if it might have given her a charge to contemplate problems of infidelity: Charles having an affair with his severe,
pretty department head with whom he played tennis twice a
week, for example. More likely, not: the thought only made
Leah want to impale him with the racquet—and maybe impale
her, too. But that wasn't the point. The point was that they
were still fielding hospital bills from increasingly arcane sub-
specialists whom they could barely recall encountering after
Jordan's injury. Their insurance company had yet to pay a
claim without rejecting it first, requiring countless hours of
aggravating, haranguing phone calls. On top of this, they had
given up trying to sell their house back in Omaha, which had
languished on the market for months before they decided to
take it off and rent. Now their mortgage's balloon payment
was coming due. They had also brought Charles's mother,
Florence, with them and installed her in a nearby overpriced
nursing home. But the mother of all money tension had to do
with Charles's new job, the very thing that had brought them
to the East Coast. A large bonus that constituted the bulk of
his compensation was tied to the commencement of a project
that now seemed hopelessly stalled.

After the coffee had been blotted as best it could, Leah imagined that Charles would check his Blackberry and discover

some work conflict that would preclude his participation this evening, but before he had the opportunity, Jordan appeared in the kitchen.

"Oh my God, I had no idea how late it was," she said. Even though she was in an apparent rush, she didn't seem especially panicked as she moved through the room gathering her belongings. It took her a moment to locate her wallet, which Leah finally spotted on the counter by the telephone. Her keys proved more elusive, but they found them on the seat of one of the kitchen chairs that had been pushed into the table, making them hard to spot. Jordan with great deliberation studied the selection of bananas ripening in the fruit bowl and finally ripped one free from the middle of the cluster.

"I stayed up way too late working on my history paper, and I guess I overslept," she said.

She dropped into a chair and pulled on her boots, then bunched her hair into a sloppy ponytail—a wild, thick mass of dark ringlets, as hopeful and unruly as a shaggy lawn in spring. Leah could soak in the sight of her daughter, her only child, for hours, and delight, and draw inferences from details as slight as the hungry, aggressive way she peeled the skin from the fruit and took a bite. Her appetite was good! Leah was further encouraged by the sight of her daughter's rosy cheeks, which seemed to be a sign of health, although it was equally possible that her color merely reflected the thermostat, which Leah had begun to tune low in attempts to be both energy- and cost-efficient.

"Dad, can you give me a ride to school on your way to work?"

Charles looked up from the paper and mustered a smile for his daughter. "Sure. Can you wait a sec?"

"Not really, Dad. School starts in . . ." She pulled her cell phone from her pocket to check the time, even though the clock above the stove was clearly visible. "Seven minutes."

He put down his paper and grabbed his coat, and they were on their way. He forgot to give Leah a kiss, but she felt a swell of warmth all the same at the sight of her family heading off for another productive day. Or maybe what she felt was just relief that she had managed to pull this off, although why she wanted to host a Beach Week meeting was a question she had difficulty answering, even to herself.

Once the parents began to arrive that evening, Leah realized that their house was not spacious enough to accommodate this group comfortably. She had given no thought to where she would put their winter coats, which she began to heap on the bed in the spare room upstairs. She had also failed to consider that those who had come straight from work would be hungry, determined to cobble together a meal from the simple and not very elegant spread of light hors d'oeuvres set out on a couple of side tables. She had worried she was overdoing it on the hospitality front, given that this was meant to be a brief meeting of the sort that she was pretty sure didn't call for food at all. Now she wished she had ordered some platters from Whole Foods, even chilled a few bottles of wine.

Leah felt like she could never quite get it right in Verona. Distance-wise it was a relatively straight line, a thousand measly miles from Nebraska to Maryland. The language was the same, the local customs no different, people looked and dressed in a mostly similar fashion, and yet. And yet . . . *what*, was what she was still struggling to figure out. Omaha was a cosmopolitan city, and she and Charles were hardly hicks. Not to put too fine a point on it, especially since Leah considered herself an antisnob, but they were cultured, educated people. They listened to NPR and saw foreign films, and Leah had belonged, simultaneously, to two different book groups back home and had immediately upon arriving joined one here. She and Charles went to the occasional opera and enjoyed the theater, too. So why was it she felt she didn't belong in this town? Was it simply that everyone was almost absurdly accomplished? Leah was too intimidated to mention to the neighbor next door that his teenage son frequently blocked access to the Adler driveway with his haphazard parking after she discovered that the man had recently won a Nobel Prize for pioneering research in enzymes—or something. Another neighbor had just returned from a stint as ambassador to Norway, and the woman directly behind them was a senior State Department official. Leah never knew for sure who anyone was, which could be downright mortifying. At a recent dinner party hosted by Charles's former college roommate, who lived nearby, she had asked a world-famous author *what he did*, and then, moments later, asked a two-term U.S. senator *where he was from*.

Perhaps she was overstating this, and was merely feeling displaced. Moving was right up there on the list of major life stressors, alongside death and divorce, after all. On top of this, she was unemployed for the first time in her adult life, and now an empty nest loomed. And she and Charles, once the best of friends, had drifted into some distant, difficult-to-define space. She was in a fragile place emotionally, probably just getting her signals crossed—surely that's all that was going on. It was almost certainly the case that she had only imagined a snicker, for example, when she casually inquired of another mother on the soccer field where the nearest Walmart was, and there was surely no subtext when the woman replied that while she didn't know the answer, it was probably in another state.

Janet Glover, the mother who was organizing this event, walked through the door carrying a heavy stack of folders. She had prepared a PowerPoint presentation, she explained to Leah, but just that morning her computer had crashed, so she'd spent much of the afternoon, with the help of her assistant, xeroxing and assembling these materials to hand out to the parents. Janet had photocopied a meeting agenda onto sheets of fluorescent yellow and affixed these with a single staple to the front of each folder, which made for the soothing sound of papers rustling in the wake of the ceiling fan Leah had just switched on in an effort to ventilate her living room, which got stuffy even in winter, with all the piped-in, stale heat. One of the folders blew open; the contents scattered on the floor. Leah turned the fan to a lower speed and gathered the strewn papers, finding among them a map of Chelsea Beach, a Chelsea Beach area information and transportation guide, a statement from Corporal Winston White of the Chelsea Beach Police Department, a list of frequently asked questions, and two pages of helpful tips compiled by parents who had started a blog called Beach Week Survivors. Leah set the folder back in the pile wearily, with a sudden sense of foreboding. Maybe Charles had been right and she had been too quick to agree to even considering this idea. She was apparently not alone in this sentiment.

"I think this entire idea is a travesty," said Alice Long, who was next to arrive. "What kind of irresponsible parents would allow a bunch of young girls to go to the beach for a week, unsupervised?"

This was an unfortunate way to begin the evening. Alice was widely regarded as difficult, but more to the point, she was the mother of Cherie Long, who had been charging toward the arcing soccer ball when she butted heads with Jordan. One girl walked away unscathed; the other wound up in the hospital and was still on the mend almost a year later. Who could explain these things? Assigning blame was useless; no one had been at fault, unless you were petty enough to point out that Cherie Long had been out of position and was generally considered a ball hog. These things happened in competitive sports, yet a word of apology or even of genuine concern from Alice Long, either at the time of the accident or in its aftermath, might have gone a long way to appease Leah.

Alice was arguably Verona's most famous citizen, if you took out of the equation the many politicians and journalists who lived there. The source of Alice's fame was at least amusing: she was a former television actress, best known for her long-running title role in *The Winged Wife*, a shamefully derivative drama about a crime-fighting suburbanite whose flying superpowers kicked in when she tapped her toe to the ground as certain serendipitous meteorological conditions collided (there seemed to be an unusual amount of hail and gale force wind in the fictitious California suburb where the show was set). A self-righteous style of parenting combined with her former acting gig had earned her the derisive nickname the Flying Nun.

Now she was better known as a helicopter mother extraordinaire, the sort that teachers feared: her daughter, Cherie, was Ivy League–bound, she told them in late-night calls to their homes to complain about grades or a too-heavy course load, and nothing was going to come between her and a 4.79 weighted GPA.

Her stunning daughter was a nearly exact replica of Alice, and side by side they looked like they belonged in tweed ensembles in a *New York Times* fall fashion spread, leaning against a split-rail fence. In addition to her physical elegance, Alice put herself together well, creatively accessorizing, as evidenced by the lovely strand of coral around her neck that contrasted nicely with the long blond hair, which appeared, against all odds, to be natural, even as her peers mostly slogged, with varying degrees of grace and coherence and semipermanent color, through middle age. (Leah had stopped highlighting her hair, having read something, somewhere, about cancer-causing dye, and had since become acutely aware not only of the little strands of gray creeping into her increasingly dull shade of brown, but of the coloring, bleaching, and frosting habits of others.)

Leah wondered why Alice had bothered to come to the meeting if this was her view. Also, didn't Leah deserve some sort of hello, or perhaps even a thank-you, for opening up her home? On top of which, wasn't the very fact that these ten sets of parents were assembling some five months prior to the event to discuss logistics an answer to the question itself? These were *concerned* parents, not irresponsible parents. But she didn't say as much.

Fortunately, she was alone with Alice Long only for a moment, as the others arrived behind her in one parental clot that had trouble squeezing through the narrow entryway. Leah recognized most, but surprisingly not all, of these people, even though she had diligently turned up at every school event this past year. One of the fathers looked familiar. He had thick, curly dark hair, and he wore a pink cable-knit sweater that looked fresh from the Brooks Brothers box, with no fabric pilling in sight. He had the aura of someone famous, and Leah wondered for a moment if he was that political commentator on cable television, the guy who had been somehow involved in the Clinton administration. His foreign policy adviser? Or maybe not—maybe he was that local insurance agent whose face was plastered on the backs of grocery carts and buses. Behind him was a couple Leah recognized as the parents of one of Jordan's friends, but which one?

Leah had always been acutely aware of the passage of time, but now that she was facing the prospect of Jordan's leaving home, she was becoming a sentimental basket case. Interactions with her daughter lately seemed fleeting and precarious, set against the backdrop of the fraught emo music so frequently emitting from Jordan's room. Leah had once taken pride in having struck a good balance between teaching and mothering that, although perhaps not ideal, had felt right at the time, but now she found herself dwelling on every missed opportunity. If she could rewrite the past, she would have worked less, as if more time spent with Jordan in the formative years might have prevented her from having that concussion.

Now she wished she had signed up to supervise every field trip, had managed sports teams, had indulged her daughter's request at birthdays and holidays to decorously wrap every gift and adorn it with colorful bows and yards of ribbons that they would fray and curl, no matter how long it took or how late the hour. If she could only have a do-over, they would make cookies from scratch at least once a week and frost and sprinkle them with every sugary accoutrement on offer in the grocery store cooking aisle. And she'd be more indulgent: she wouldn't have tossed the American Girl catalog in the trash before Jordan got home from school in an effort to discourage materialism. In fact, given a second chance at mothering, maybe she'd even go back in time and splurge on a hair appointment and a set of skis for Jordan's one and only Molly doll that time they'd visited the flagship store in Chicago. Then Jordan might have turned out to be the sort of kid who told her mother who her friends were.

There were only about twelve people at first, but it still felt crowded in Leah's living room, and there were more on the way. A few stray spouses, including her own, were going to arrive a little late, she was informed, and the Linds had sent their regrets as they were currently in Canada scouting a hot goalie prospect to possibly sign to the hockey team they owned. It was one thing to have this many people for a cocktail party—not that she and Charles ever had cocktail parties—but in order to hold a meeting, presumably everyone needed to sit, yet one more item to add to the punch list of things she should have thought about earlier. Fortunately, no one seemed to notice, since the atmosphere had in fact begun to feel like a happy hour, albeit one with only soft drinks and lemon Perrier and her mediocre spread of snacks.

It was getting late—half an hour after the appointed meeting time. Was Leah responsible for actually calling the meeting to order? This was a terrifying thought. She had offered to host for the largely selfish reason of integrating into this community of parents, admittedly a little late in the game. She had very little actual knowledge of the subject at hand, such as the details of the beach house. Still, someone needed to take charge, or they'd be here all night and she was already running low on nuts.

She looked over at Janet, who had her back turned to the group; Alice was leaning into her, whispering in her ear. Janet was one of the region's most successful divorce lawyers, a no-

nonsense woman who walked out on her own philandering husband years earlier with two toddlers in tow. She was the mother of Jordan's best friend, Dorrie, and although Leah liked and admired Janet, she was also a little afraid of her. She looked like one of those important Washington women Leah sometimes noticed on C-SPAN, women who wore tailored suits and had nicely coiffed hair. Leah forced herself to rise above the fleeting thought that, like mean girls in high school, Alice and Janet were talking about her. She was too old for this sort of thing. They were here for a meeting, and the point was to move this thing forward. She considered clinking a spoon to a glass or ringing a bell, as if she were about to clear her throat and make a speech.

"Welcome," she managed to say, barely audibly. Fortunately, this lame attempt at moderating at least captured Janet's attention, and with a single sharp command Janet got everyone quiet and situated, with folders in hand.

It was Janet who had called Leah a week earlier to say that she had followed up on the house their daughters had found online, and that if they wanted to act, they needed to move quickly. Evidently most groups of kids had secured rentals as long ago as October, and it was late to be starting the process in January. Janet had already spoken to the Chelsea Beach Realtor, and she had the lease in hand. All they needed were two signatures and a security deposit. Then Janet had called again to report that a preliminary sampling of parents indicated the desire for a group meeting. The plan was to meet initially without the girls present. There would be additional meetings later, in the spring, which the teens would attend. It was during this phone call that Leah rashly offered to host, if Janet would take charge.

Leah took stock of her living room, marveling at the way

the place seemed transformed, with people everywhere, including on the arms of the love seat, on the floor, and on the fireplace hearth. She hoped her aged sofa wouldn't collapse under the weight of one father who was morbidly obese. She planted herself near the back of the room and leaned on the windowsill to provide quick access to the front door should latecomers straggle in.

"As your kids have probably told you," Janet began, "a couple of the girls have taken the initiative and found a rental at 7221 Seascape Lane. This is a single-family house that sleeps twelve and is in a quiet cul-de-sac right off Route 1. The house is within walking distance to the beach . . . I'm basically reading to you straight from the listing here . . . with parking for two cars only . . . I suppose that could be a problem."

"It's not *my* problem—I'm certainly not letting *my* daughter bring a car to the beach," Alice announced. "I think that any parent who allows a teenager to drive with other passengers is completely irresponsible." She was seated on an ottoman, her long legs extended and crossed at the ankle.

Janet skillfully cut the woman off, as if she were managing a difficult client. "Let's not worry about that right now," she said. "Let's just do the needful and discuss the lease . . . The rent for one week, June 5 to June 12, is three thousand dollars. They are asking for a security deposit of fifteen hundred, and parking permits"—she turned toward Alice as she spoke, perhaps to discourage another outburst—"are twenty dollars per vehicle."

Leah winced. It wasn't an outrageous amount, yet when you considered the various end-of-year costs—the graduation parties and gifts and related clothing needs—and factored in such Beach Week incidentals as food, gas, and pocket money, it added up. At least they were being spared the expense of a prom, which had been canceled this year as punishment for a food fight in the cafeteria that had turned violent when a group of senior boys attacked the small contingent of vegans who were protesting the implementation of sushi day; Jordan had come home stinking of the raw fish that had gotten mashed into her hair and on the soles of her shoes. Leah was among the parents who had seen this as an unfair response by the school administration, but in truth she was grateful to be spared what she'd heard could be an astronomical expense, hundreds of dollars by the time one finished paying for the dress, the boutonniere, the limousine, and dinner out.

"Jeez, that's an awful lot," said Courtney Moore's mother. Leah was relieved to learn that she was not alone in this sentiment. Millie Moore and her husband were tax attorneys who shared an office in downtown Verona. They looked more like wannabe artists than tax attorneys, both thin and ghostly pale, clad this evening in black T-shirts and Keds, and Courtney's father wore expensive-looking eyeglasses with chunky frames. They struck Leah as people who were clinging hard to a vision of themselves as bohemian; both Moores seemed eager to weave into any conversation the fact that they were just doing time in their boxy colonial in order to partake of the good public schools. Their daughter was a quiet, studious girl, an accomplished pianist who seemed to be on the fringe of Jordan's core group of friends, although given that Leah was decidedly out of the loop, she wasn't completely sure this was still the case.

"It says it sleeps twelve, and we're currently just ten, so what about defraying the cost with another two girls?" Millie Moore suggested.

"I'm not so sure about that," Arthur Moore replied. "Two more girls and you are exponentially increasing the chances of trouble." The couple exchanged a fractious glance, and Leah was glad to see that she and Charles were not the only household in disaccord on this subject.

She felt a subtle vibration, an indication that the garage door, directly beneath where she stood, had just opened; Charles had arrived home. She quietly exited the room to intercept him in the kitchen and remind him, in case he might have forgotten, or somehow failed to notice the cluster of cars parked in front of their house, that there were more than a dozen parents, at least one of them highly contentious, assembled in the next room.

She was relieved to see him looking his normal self and was suddenly overcome with gratitude. She didn't care if his nonchalance reflected a sometimes maddening ability to compartmentalize, or even just complete oblivion. She gave him a longer than usual kiss on the lips and playfully traced her finger over the faded spot of coffee on the shirt he hadn't had time to change that morning. He looked at her strangely.

"That bad, eh?" He threw his coat on a chair and went over to the refrigerator and retrieved a bottle of Corona.

"Mea culpa. You were right," she said. "This was probably a bad idea."

Leah half expected him to seize on "probably" with a snide quip, but he didn't. Instead he switched on the television. "You do realize there's a big game on tonight," he said. "The Wolves play the Wizards."

"Oh God! I'm so sorry!" She actually did feel bad. Charles was juggling two jobs right now and was under a lot of stress: in addition to his troubled development project, he was a visiting professor at the University of Maryland in the department of urban studies, where his one class sometimes seemed more trouble than it was worth, between the commute and the amount of paperwork. He unwound from all this by taking his sports playing and viewing seriously. She tried to give him a wide berth, but lately it seemed as though every game was important, and he had come to embrace any activity that involved a ball with equal amounts of passion and fierce evening- and weekend-consuming dedication. He was the pitcher on a faculty softball league, and he sometimes rose early to play racquetball, and of course there was that biweekly indoor tennis game with his boss. He had played golf in high school and college but had given it up on the grounds that it was both too time-consuming and expensive. He was a committed spectator, too. He'd grown up in Minnesota, and his family had held season tickets to the Vikings' games for three generations; he'd splurged on tickets the last time the team came to town to play the Redskins. There was pretty much nothing Charles wouldn't watch on television, and there was always something on. Fencing, cricket, boxing—Leah had recently found him up in the middle of the night watching volleyball broadcast live from the University of Hawaii.

She couldn't really gauge his mood and hadn't been able to for some time now. She had recently begun to entertain the thought that the longer they cohabitated, the less well she knew him. Just a few days earlier, when she picked him up at the Metro, Leah had failed to recognize him as he approached from the top of the escalator, just a few yards away. This had less to do with failing eyesight—she still had perfect vision—than with some subtle change in his carriage. This small thing seemed profound in its implications, but it was too much to take in, so she had pushed the possible meaning to the back of her mind.

A well-timed flash of a smile interrupted this flow of negative thought, suggesting that he was not really angry, just mildly annoyed, and that they were in this particular unpleasant parenting task together.

"It's almost over," Leah lied. "But do you want to grab a quick bite first?" she asked, with a nod toward the refrigerator.

"No, I'll wait until after." He rolled up his sleeves and glanced once more, longingly, at the television. Leah hesitated when she saw him ready to enter the meeting with the bottle of beer, and she considered suggesting that he at least pour it into a glass to disguise the contents, since she should have offered everyone a good, stiff drink, but she didn't want to lose what there was of her husband's goodwill.

She was about to follow him back inside to the meeting when something at the window, a flash of movement, caught her eye. She pressed her face to the pane. It took a moment for her eyes to adjust to the darkness, but so far as she could see, there was nothing there. She stared out at the rusting swing set for a minute and allowed herself a schmaltzy thought about midwestern cornfields, and then a more worrisome one about the wayward bear. Then she followed Charles in.

"So what exactly needs to be done tonight?" a father was asking, somewhat impatiently.

"Really, all we need to do tonight," Janet replied, "is collect money to send in to reserve the place, which is the security deposit. And then we need to decide who is going to sign the lease. The Realtor said that typically, for Beach Week, two sets of parents sign the lease."

"Uh-oh. I didn't know that we had to pay anything tonight," said Courtney Moore's mother. "We didn't bring our checkbook."

"I didn't realize we were going to act this quickly, either," said the father of Amy Estrada, whose third-generation Chilean ancestry was the only nod toward diversity in the room. "Are we going to have any discussion of the pros and cons of Beach Week? I've heard a lot of bad things happen. I'm not completely sure that I want to let Amy go."

His wife chimed in. "I think we should talk about proper behavior at the beach. We should be sure they have a buddy system so they are never on their own, and we should also talk about drinking, sun poisoning, and . . . I know this may sound a little psycho, but I've heard reports of shark attacks at Chelsea Beach."

"Hear, hear!" said Alice. "I was beginning to wonder if I was the only responsible parent in this room!"

Leah wondered if, as the host of this meeting, she ought to do something about Alice's obnoxious behavior—to intervene, maybe even adjourn for a brief cooling-off period. But no one else seemed bothered by her remarks. Leah tried to catch Charles's eye for a brief exchange of sympathy, but he was staring toward the television, which he could see through the open kitchen door.

"And as I was trying to say before," Alice went on, "I think it's a bad idea for these girls to be driving while they are there. What if we drove them to the beach, then picked them up again? Does anyone agree with me?"

The possible Clinton foreign policy adviser was the first to reply. He spoke with a trace of an accent that Leah couldn't quite place, which sounded vaguely Eastern European. "Personally, I don't think that makes much sense. But here's a thought: I have a house at the beach, and I'd be willing to let any parents who are willing to chaperone stay there for free."

For free? Leah was confused by this—might he have actually considered charging his fellow Beach Week parents who volunteered to chaperone? She wondered why, if he had a place at the beach, he wasn't offering it up as lodging for the girls. A few moments of murmuring ensued. She was sure this proposal would be rejected out of hand; it seemed to contradict the very point, which was for the kids to go off and have a taste of independence. By summer, most of the girls would be eighteen—although Jordan had a late birthday and wouldn't be of legal age until the following December. Leah had some vague recollection of a theory suggesting that the kids who went off to college and partied the hardest and displayed the most egregious behavior were typically those whose parents had hovered the closest throughout high school. She was aware that she was guilty of hovering rather closely herself, although she liked to think it was in a different way, and was justifiable in her case, given Jordan's medical issues.

"I'd be willing to go for part of the week," Courtney Moore's mother offered. "But I don't have my checkbook with me tonight," she reminded them.

"Sure, I'll go," Courtney Davidson's mother agreed. "It will be a nice break!"

Although Leah didn't know all of her daughter's friends, she was reminded that a disproportionate number of them were named Courtney.

A few others volunteered, too. Leah looked guiltily toward her husband as her own hand began to levitate upward. Although she was generally pretty good at decoding Charles's expressions, she had no idea what the look on his face meant on this occasion. It might have been *Have a nice time chaperoning at the beach, darling,* or it might have been *Have you lost your fucking mind?*

"Excellent," Janet said. "I've brought a sign-up list, so I'll just start circulating this and you can note what days suit you best. Be sure to put your phone numbers down so I can call you to sort this out if the dates overlap. Also, speaking of phone numbers, I'm going to send around this other sheet, and I'd like you to put down all your contact information. Home phones, cell phones, work phones, e-mails, pagers, faxes, emergency contacts, et cetera."

As if Janet had made it so by merely speaking the word, a phone somewhere began to ring. Several people checked their cell phones, embarrassed, before Leah realized that it was her own landline. She excused herself once more and ducked into the kitchen. Why she still hadn't trained herself to check the caller ID was a mystery, since the vast majority of calls, including this one, were from telemarketers, and she was unable to just hang up, often taking pity on the poor person who was trying to earn a living at some call center somewhere. When she returned to the living room after a couple of minutes, she could tell that the conversation hadn't advanced very far.

"Hang on . . . What do you actually mean by *chaperoning*?" Courtney Greene's father asked. "I mean, obviously if the chaperones are staying at the Krazinski place, they aren't going to be there twenty-four seven. And I suspect if there is any trouble to be gotten into, it's going to happen in the wee hours of the night." *Krazinski,* Leah thought . . . was this a name she ought to recognize?

"Of course that's true," Mr. Krazinski replied, "but the point is really more to just have some adult presence down there. If anything bad were to happen in the middle of the night . . . *particularly* in the middle of the night . . . someone would be close by, and we wouldn't all be scrambling to drive three hours."

"Two and a half hours," Mr. Davidson corrected.

"I've actually made it in two hours, without traffic," Mr. Estrada countered.

"It depends how you go. Obviously there's no avoiding the Bay Bridge, and that's always a crapshoot, traffic-wise, but once you are on the Eastern Shore, you can avoid Route 1 and cut through the back roads and . . ."

Jordan's entry into the room silenced the debate. Everyone turned to look at her, as if they were students caught with a bottle of Jack Daniel's.

"Sorry!" she said, clearly mortified to be the sudden center of attention. "I was about to start my homework and realized I left my backpack in here." This appeared to be true—it was in the corner by the window. No one said a word as she made her way through the crowded room to retrieve it. She had changed after school into a hooded black sweater and sweatpants, and even in sloppy, baggy clothing she looked quietly ravishing. Leah hated that a roomful of people were noticing this, too. The relief she felt each time she glimpsed her daughter looking so vibrant after these difficult months nearly mitigated the loss she felt for her own youth, but not quite.

"Hi, Jordan," one of the mothers said as Jordan crossed back through toward the kitchen, her heavy bag now slung over her left shoulder.

"Hey, Mrs. Cooper," she replied. "Tell Courtney hi from me!"

Leah was momentarily confused—was there yet another Courtney in the group? But no, it seemed that Mrs. Cooper was probably married to, or at least partnered with, Mr. Greene.

A few other parents greeted Jordan as well, and Leah felt proud of the way her daughter responded to each one politely, despite the fact that she clearly wanted out of the room. She hadn't even reached the kitchen when she pulled her cell phone from the front zipper of her bag and began tapping at the keyboard.

"Okay. Well, this sounds like a good start," Janet continued. "Now, really all we need to do before we adjourn is get two volunteers to sign the lease. If you open your folders and thumb through to page seventeen, you will see a xeroxed copy of the agreement. You might all want to take a moment to review this."

Leah glanced at her watch. The meeting had already lasted ninety minutes and they hadn't even begun a proper discussion of trip logistics. How many more meetings might this possibly involve?

"If we're having chaperones," Alice Long interjected, "then I really don't see the need for the girls to drive." The room was silent except for the turning of pages as everyone skimmed through the document. "Certainly I don't trust *my* daughter to drive. She's a complete space cadet. A total moron when it comes to traffic."

Leah thought she could detect some surprise at this public derogation of her daughter.

"I know exactly where Seascape Lane is," Mr. Krazinski replied evenly, "and there's really no way the girls will be able to get anywhere without a car. They can't even walk to the grocery store from there, never mind to the boardwalk. I for one have no problem letting Marta take her car. She's a good, safe driver, and I'd prefer to have her behind the wheel rather than worrying that they might wind up stranded somewhere, hitching rides from strangers or some such."

"I agree completely. I'm speaking hypothetically here, since I'm not convinced that I want Jordan to even go to Beach

Week, but if she were to go, I'd rather have her driving than hopping into cars with less responsible drivers."

It took Leah a moment to process what she had just heard. Was this really Charles speaking? Indeed it was. His jaw was clamped tight and his chin slanted forward like an angry child's; he was staring purposefully at Alice Long. Leah felt a jolt—of what, she couldn't quite say.

"Okay, this is good," said Janet. "We are off to a good start. Already we've got two drivers, which, depending on the size of the vehicles and how much stuff the girls bring, may be all we really need. Now there's just the lease and the security deposit."

Silence ensued, which struck Leah as the only reasonable response. Who in their right minds would put their names on this lease, assuming legal and financial responsibility for whatever might occur?

"I'm certainly not signing the lease," Alice said, which seemed a good thing; surely no one wanted her in a position of control, even if it absolved the rest of them of responsibility.

"I'll sign the lease," Krazinski volunteered. "Marta and Deegan—Deegan's her twin brother—are my second and third kids to go off to Beach Week, so I've been through this before. Honestly, I think this is much ado about nothing."

Leah looked across the room to Charles, somewhat worried. Now that he was riding a wave of Beach Week cooperation, or maybe just a surge of Alice Long agitation, perhaps he'd second the offer before they could discuss it. Mercifully, he seemed to have lost interest and was back to staring into the kitchen at the basketball game.

"That's great. Perfect. Thank you," said Janet. "Any other volunteers?"

"What are the legal ramifications if, say, something really

awful happens, like the house burns down?" Amy Estrada's mother asked.

"Then we're all screwed," a Courtney mother replied. This remark was followed by some nervous laughter.

"No, really. I'm serious. I mean, let's say the house is worth one million. There are ten of us. So is the extent of our liability then one hundred thousand, give or take?"

"No, no, no . . . I mean just imagine if someone was injured, or God forbid died. What if there was a party at the house and it burned down and there were multiple injured parties? The litigation could go on for years. Decades. I know, I'm a partner at Weiss and Schraub," said Faye Andrews, Courtney Davidson's mother.

"Well, at least we'll have free legal counsel," Amy Estrada's mother joked. "Of course John is a lawyer, too, so we're in doubly good shape," she said, evidently referring to her husband.

"No, she's absolutely right," said Mr. Greene. "I'm an attorney as well, and I mean, we don't want to get carried away here, but I do think we need to really impress on the girls that this is serious business. I agree these are good girls, and I don't see them behaving badly, but we need to be realistic about the kinds of things that can happen even if they aren't at fault. I heard a story where, at Beach Week somewhere in New Jersey, a balcony collapsed during a party and three kids died. Never mind the liability—three kids died!

"Before the girls go off, I think we should have a meeting with parents *and* girls and kind of scare them straight," he said.

"Look," said Mr. Krazinski. "I'm a lawyer, too, and I think you are all making too much of this." Leah wondered if his being a lawyer negated her foreign policy adviser theory. Probably not. She also wondered if it would be completely inappropriate to ask for a show of hands to tally the number of lawyers in the room. It wasn't irrelevant, given the possibility that, from the sound of things, they might be sued.

"This just doesn't add up," Alice Long said. "If this whole Beach Week thing is so bad that we're sitting here talking about kids dying and parents being sued, why are we letting our kids go? This just seems irresponsible to me."

"You've mentioned this a number of times, and while I confess that I have my own reservations, it leads me to wonder, if you don't mind my asking, what you are doing here? You seem a little . . . negative." Again, against all odds, this was Charles speaking.

"What do you mean, *what am I doing here*? I'm being a responsible parent," said Alice.

"Yes, but you haven't come here to discuss so much as to accuse. You are clearly opposed to the whole idea of Beach Week. As I said before, I can't say I'm sold on it myself, but it seems that you've come here with your mind made up, to judge the rest of us . . ."

"Who are *you* to judge *me*? I mean, look at you, so eager to let your daughter take responsibility for the lives of others, behind the wheel . . . And you—standing there with a beer in your hand while your daughter walks in and out of the room! What a fine example!"

Leah listened, slightly stunned. Had parenting mores grown so severe that a father was no longer supposed to drink a beer in front of his child? But it was more than this that Leah found confounding. Here she'd been trying so hard to fit into this place, to gain acceptance, and now when she looked around at this group, what she saw was a roomful of bickering, overregulating, overindulging parents. That said, here she was among them, and she couldn't say that her own behavior, or concerns, were really any different.

"I don't feel the need to explain to you that we have certain policies in place for our daughter regarding her driving, as well as rules about drinking," Charles retorted, "and I'm quite comfortable with those. I don't need to be told what's responsible parental behavior by someone I've never even met before."

Increasingly, Charles made pronouncements that puzzled her. When she recently pondered aloud whether their money tensions had led to what felt to her a subtle disconnect, he had made some elliptical comment about how any long-term marriage involved patches of distance, as if this were a known fact. And now here he was referring to some driving policy, and some particular set of rules having to do with alcohol, that she was unaware of. Was he privy to information, aware of great truths that she was not? Or did he just make this stuff up as he went along?

Alice Long unfolded herself from the ottoman and walked across the room, her eyes locked on Charles as she theatrically poured what was left of the Perrier into her cup. She then dropped a melting ice cube into her glass, creating a small splash. The room was uncomfortably silent. *Awkward*, as Jordan would no doubt say.

"Oh . . . *kay*," said Janet. "It's getting late. I think we've covered enough ground.

"So let's just get another parent to sign the lease, and I'll collect the checks—actually, make them all out to me so that I can write one to send to the Realtor, and then we can reconvene in a few weeks."

Courtney Moore's mother reminded them for the third time that she did not have her checkbook.

"I'll cover for you," Leah heard herself say,. "and you can drop a check off tomorrow." She avoided looking in Charles's direction as she made this offer; surely they were the last couple in the room that should be volunteering Beach Week bridge loans, but she was tired and willing to do just about anything to move this meeting toward conclusion.

"That's great. Thank you so much! I'll stop by on my way to work tomorrow," Millie Moore said.

"Okay, the lease . . ." Janet repeated.

This was truly beginning to feel like a bad dream. Who would ever sign this lease without duress? Although actually the whole evening was a subtle form of duress.

"Look," said the Weiss and Schraub partner, "here's what I think we can do to alleviate everyone's anxiety, at least as it pertains to the lease . . . I'll go ahead and cosign just so that we can get this show on the road, and then I'll draw up an addendum to the lease, spelling out our shared responsibility. All of the remaining parents will sign the addendum, and then there is no issue of anyone getting stuck or being financially or legally responsible on their own. I concentrate on family law, but I'll ask one of my colleagues for advice. It's pretty straightforward stuff. How does that sound?"

There was a bit more back-and-forth on this subject, the upshot of which was that there were at least two more lawyers in the group, bringing Leah's informal tally to eight. Eventually there seemed a consensus that this was a reasonable solution, but Leah couldn't help but think that really, everyone was just worn down. Hungry, tired, and bullied by Alice Long, they'd sign any piece of paper if it meant they could just go home.

2

· · · · ·

Jordan had been at the party for only a few minutes when she noticed two things: Dorrie had just pulled a bottle of rum from her purse and was pouring it into her Coke, and there was a very cute guy leaning into the wall, looking slightly bored. Jordan glanced in his direction and they briefly locked eyes. She turned away, embarrassed.

To think her mother had sent her here! Leah had come into her bedroom earlier that evening and practically ordered her to put her book down and go out with Dorrie and Paul; her friends had left her multiple text messages, and when she hadn't replied, they stopped by the house to see if they could coax her out. Her mother evidently agreed that it was better for a girl to go out to a party than to study on a Friday night; her father never seemed to offer an opinion on such things, or at least not directly. If her mother only knew what went down at a typical Rene Palmer party! On this occasion Rene's father was in Europe, her stepmother's whereabouts were unknown, the housekeeper had the night off, and someone, probably one of Rene's many stepbrothers, had procured two kegs. Beer sloshed onto the expensive-looking carpets, and someone had just inexplicably thrown a shoe across the room, shattering an enormous porcelain vase that Rene shrieked was some sort of heirloom. The more lasting damage, however, seemed likely to come from Deegan Krazinski, who had his video camera trained on Rene as she danced seductively on the pool table. There were rumors about Rene, suggestions that she'd been in a Girls Gone Wild video and also possibly in something even more lurid that had found its way onto the Internet, engaging in a sex act that Jordan had not previously heard of and had to look up. It wasn't in the dictionary, but she'd found it on-line, making Jordan wonder if the act itself was new, or just the decision to give it a name. No one was completely sure whether it was Rene or just someone who looked like Rene; regardless, people joked about getting in on this, too, making their own directorial debuts, and the truly surprising thing was that Rene seemed to find it all amusing and did nothing to discourage the cameras or the gossip.

Jordan looked back at the guy and decided that he looked a bit older. He was clean-shaven, with curly dark hair and flecked brown eyes. He wore khaki pants and a slightly tattered blazer over a white T-shirt, which—compared with the way most of the guys at the party were dressed, in baggy jeans or weather-inappropriate shorts and in some cases even flannel pajama bottoms—was practically the equivalent of business attire. She saw him catch his own reflection in the windowpane and run his fingers through his hair. The gesture indicated a little narcissism perhaps, but who could blame him for wanting to look at himself? Jordan thought that given the chance, she'd stare at him nonstop.

The music was so loud that the walls were vibrating, and things were starting to get a little rowdy as groups of boys, clustered like primates, spilled onto the front lawn. They were worse than girls with their cliques: soccer players, basketball players, football, hockey, and lacrosse, in a generally descendant order of acceptable human behavior. They weren't all animals, of course, but alcohol didn't tend to bring out anyone's better side. Rene's parties were always well attended, and with the line of parked cars now stretching three blocks, it seemed a good bet that the police would soon be on their way, if they weren't already. Jordan had only just noticed this scrum surrounding Rene, so she wasn't sure of the sequence of things: Was Rene dancing for the video camera, or was the camera trained on her because she was dancing? Jordan watched, mostly as a way to pass the time. She had no way to get home, since she had driven with Dorrie and Paul—Paul, whom Jordan had once had a brief, ill-defined, mortifying *thing* with, and who was now Dorrie's boyfriend. Given that Paul had pushed his way up to the front of the crowd gathered around Rene, and that Dorrie, despite her promise to control her drinking this evening, seemed headed for another blackout (although she insisted that she only ever *browned* out and never went completely dark), Jordan got the feeling that she'd be stuck at this party for a while.

Most of her other friends in attendance, including Mindy, Courtney D., and Cherie, were in the basement cheering on Zack Norton and Mike Seltzer in an intense game of Guitar Hero. Zack was the reigning Verona champion, or so he claimed. Jordan had no idea whether this was a real title or a joke. Mike was the lead singer in a popular high school band. He had an amazing voice—gravelly and full of range, and he also played guitar, bass, violin, and piano. He aspired to go to

Juilliard in the fall, and it was widely believed that he had a shot; it therefore made him a little crazy that Zack, who wasn't the least bit musical, could usually beat him at this stupid video game. Zack didn't even play with his eyes open—he claimed he just "felt the beat, man," which seemed like a weird thing to be able to do with a fake plastic guitar.

At the same time, Jordan found the boys' fascination with the game weirdly compelling. She wondered if, for example, you could get any genuine pleasure out of keeping a robot dog as a pet or tending to a garden of synthetic roses. It made her think about that Radiohead song "Fake Plastic Trees," with its fake Chinese rubber plant in plastic earth in a town full of other rubber plants. It made her think about her parents, too. How was it that they just kept at it day after day, living a sort of plastic life in a plastic house in a plastic suburb? She got that this was a bit of an overstatement—one of those things you can't really understand until you reach that phase of life yourself, where you find sitting on the couch and watching shows on HBO every night fulfilling—yet ever since they'd moved here, she'd begun to think differently, in what she could only describe as a more expansive way. Perhaps more accurately, she'd begun to think differently ever since she found herself flat on her back on the soccer field having the cosmic, otherworldly sensation of floating up above the goalpost, looking down on everything, and suddenly understanding—although what it was she understood she could no longer remember, let alone explain in any meaningful way. If she had to distill the experience, what she'd say was this: briefly, she had seen things from a different angle and had known that there was more.

Ultimately, though, this amazing moment had become embarrassing. They'd had to stop the game and call an ambulance, and everyone made a huge fuss and someone even wrote about it in the school newspaper; now this bit of history seemed to hover in the background of every conversation she had. She wasn't considered the new girl anymore. She was the kid who'd had a concussion, who not only had to sit out the rest of the soccer season and effectively give up the game, but who spent the next six months plagued by headaches, as well as by preheadache auras that were both magical and frightening in their intensity. She'd see strange lights and shapes, things in the room rearranging themselves in Technicolor, and she'd have to hold on to something to keep from spinning. It was almost impossible to explain, so she'd stopped really trying. On top of this, under doctor's orders she'd spent the rest of her spring semester junior year putting in just half days at school. Not only had she missed a lot of classes at a critical academic moment, but she had to endure long afternoons with her mother, who on the one hand kept a respectful distance, but also seemed to obsess over Jordan's every bite of food or changed facial expression. Her mother was seriously getting on her nerves.

Still, Jordan was as worried about her mother as her mother was about her. Leah had changed since she stopped teaching; all she seemed to do all day was cook and clean, like some 1950s housewife, and her life seemed to revolve around Jordan's and her father's comings and goings. She really wished her mother would go back to work or somehow get a grip. It seemed like her mom had been more wigged out by the concussion than she'd been. She'd had this completely irrational reaction that now extended to every nuance of health and safety, the most extreme being that she had become completely obsessed with carcinogens. Once, in front of Dorrie and Courtney D., she reminded Jordan that she had breast-fed her until she was sixteen months old and that she'd then gone straight to a sippy cup, bypassing baby bottles altogether. And when Jordan had asked (admittedly somewhat coldly, in retrospect) what the hell she was talking about, her mother said, simply, "Plastics!" (Again with the plastic!) Really, all Jordan wanted from her mother was to see her move on and maybe even buy some good, old-fashioned junk food for the house, because no matter how strange the universe, how interconnected things might be, there was absolutely no relation between banging heads on the soccer field with Cherie Long and a diet rich in green, leafy vegetables.

Of course, having her mother all involved in her life was not necessarily what Jordan had in mind when she'd hoped to see her snap out of her funk. Her mother was completely overcompensating, like calling Dorrie's mom to talk about Beach Week logistics, hosting the stupid meeting at their house, and, now, volunteering to *chaperone*. Jordan had actually appreciated that previously her mother wasn't meddlesome, wasn't hugely annoying like some of the other mothers she'd observed, but lately she was always trying to talk, asking really embarrassing questions about boyfriends and sex and college plans, and getting irritable when Jordan didn't want to come downstairs for dinner or go out with her friends.

Maybe there were depressing aspects to life in her parents' house, but was it really so awful for a kid to have wanted to avoid this party, to prefer to stay in on a Friday night? It was her senior year, and she had a ton of work to do, not that she'd actually been doing any of it when she was practically ordered to go to Rene's party, and not that it mattered, since she'd already applied to college and her forthcoming grades were unlikely to factor into any decisions. She was ambivalent about college and couldn't get all worked up about it the way her friends did. It wasn't that she was feeling gloomy or morose—

quite the opposite. She couldn't wait for her life to actually begin, and the prospect of sitting in school for another four years failed to excite.

"Just send off a bunch of applications," her parents had urged, "and then you don't have to think about where you'll go until the spring." Her guidance counselor had said the same thing. "Choose a range, give yourself options. Big schools, small schools. You can always defer. " At least this last bit made sense, and she'd decided to appease them in the short term by applying, even though she wasn't entirely sure if she'd go. Gap year was what she found herself thinking. Someplace crazy and far away.

The only thing she knew for sure was that if she did go straight to college, she wanted to attend a big school in a big city. Partying in the woods pretty much summed up weekends at some of the smaller schools in the middle of nowhere, from what she'd heard. She was already going crazy here in Verona, and this was hardly the woods (and it was at least more urban than the suburb of Omaha where she'd lived most of her life). Although, with its sprawl, Verona was probably worse than the woods, as suburban geography perpetuated its own set of rituals involving not just drinking, but drinking and driving and then drinking some more. It was invariably the boys who did the most stupid things, like driving through McDonald's plastered, placing bogus orders, saying really stupid stuff to the poor person working the night shift, vulgarities about Happy Meals—Happy Meals and happy endings—that weren't even remotely funny. Or going into the pizza parlor with a toy gun, like one of their friends had done, wearing swimming goggles and flippers. Even though it was a prank, he'd been expelled from school and sent to juvie, and no one had heard from him for a while. Most recently, some of the boys she knew had broken into the principal's house while he and his family were on vacation and left a goat inside, which they had stolen from a nearby petting zoo. The goat had chewed through the sofa and torn out the stuffing, and he'd eaten the mail that had dropped through the slot. The boys had been suspended, lucky to have avoided prosecution for breaking and entering. They still talked about this like it was some major achievement. Really, she had to get out of here. It may have been this instinct that had led her to briefly get excited about Beach Week. She had agreed to share a house with Dorrie and the Courtneys, et al., mostly so that they would stop bugging her about it, although she supposed that she had fleetingly been excited about the prospect of escape. But she was now back to her original position: the prospect of a seven-day party didn't hold much appeal.

There were a few things she didn't mind about high school, though, and one of them was watching Mike perform. Seeing him play a real guitar was even better than the plastic one. She wasn't in love with him the way most of the girls at school were—she wasn't trying to hook up with him or anything, she just thought there was something fundamentally sweet about him, something solid and true that made her want to be around him, even if all those good qualities were still mixed up with the usual stupid stuff of being a teenage boy. The teachers, and apparently even some of the moms, adored him, too. There was something startling about his physicality, particularly when he played—like in the middle of a song he'd take his hands off the guitar and reach for something, and it looked to Jordan like longing. She supposed she might be transforming what were simply good looks and charisma into something more profound, but evidently others agreed. His band drew large crowds to the coffeehouses held at local churches and whatever small auditoriums they could talk their way into for an evening, and there was always the prospect of some lucrative recording contract looming in the background. Mike was tall and lanky, and like a puppy with big feet, he looked like he hadn't finished growing into his own body. Whenever Mike challenged Zack to a rematch, crowds formed, and the current number of girls jammed into the Palmers' basement was just about equal to the number of boys upstairs watching an eighteen-year-old practically pole dance.

Jordan looked back at the cute guy once more, and this time he smiled.

His name was Khalid, he was a senior at Georgetown, and he hoped to become a marine biologist. Jordan learned this by pretending she was the sort of person who could walk up to a strange man at a party and start chatting him up. The weird thing was that all you had to do to become this sort of person was, evidently, to decide that you were.

"A marine biologist?" she said, not sure how you followed up on that. "So where are you from?" Already she thought she was in love with him, the idea of a marine biologist seemed so intriguing. (Dorrie would later tell her she was completely delusional, that she was inventing some great dramatic narrative to explain what was only a banal attraction to a cute boy, nothing more mysterious than a mouse liking cheese.)

"I'm from glamorous Knoxville, Tennessee," he said. "And never going back." It was only then that she was able to place the accent. The way his words rang thick and sweet spoke of someplace warm, but his name had thrown her off, had made her think of more exotic places. (Ditto on Dorrie's analysis of this: *"Puh-lease.* Give me a fucking break," was what she'd actually said.)

"Well, I'll go back to visit my parents, of course," he continued, "but I'm not planning to live there after I graduate."

"So what *are* you planning, then? Grad school?"

"Maybe grad school, but not right away. I'm going to Carthage this summer on an exchange program. I hear they have some funky, run-down little fish museum there—fish heads in formaldehyde, that sort of thing. I've never been, but that's where my grandparents were from, so I feel like I should at least pay a visit."

Now she was absolutely in love, although where Carthage was, she had only the vaguest idea.

"I'm currently interning at the aquarium in D.C., and I'd like to bring some ideas back to Tunisia, to sort of spruce up what they have there, which I gather isn't much."

Ah, of course, Tunisia . . . Carthage was in Tunisia. She'd have to go home and find that on Google Earth. Find the fish museum. Find a street café. Walk along some promenade with him, holding hands. She was getting ahead of herself; he hadn't even asked for her name.

"I'm doing my senior-year project on the question of whether a lobster can feel pain," he said. "Last summer I interned for a while for a company called Lobsta-Stun—we were trying to determine the most humane way to end a lobster's life and preserve the taste of its meat." Tunisia, lobsters, even Knoxville, Tennessee—all of this was so outside the realm of your typical high school conversation that Jordan felt herself swoon.

"That sounds kind of Orwellian," she said, proud to be able to make this mature-sounding reference. Just last week they'd finished reading *1984* in English.

He laughed. "Unfortunately, that's completely right. You should see this machine they've devised. The idea is to kill lobsters en masse with high doses of radiation."

"How awful. It sounds like a lobster concentration camp!"

He laughed.

It was one of those conversations where everything clicked, like in a romantic comedy or something, without the killing lobster bits. She felt like she'd become some other girl, bold and flirty. "How do lobsters . . . even . . . you know?" she asked, giggling. "I mean, I don't want to be gross, but I've never thought about it before!"

He gave her a long, technical, scientific kind of answer that made her sorry she'd asked, except that it did get him talking about his favorite lobster, a large, spiny specimen named Minnie, which he'd named for the mouse; apparently he loved Disney World and had been there five times. He'd rescued Minnie from an experiment in which she'd been slated to die during that summer stint at Lobsta-Stun, which was headquartered on Cape Cod. He'd smuggled her out of the lab one night, stuck her in a portable tank, and ferried her back to the cove from which she'd been harvested; then he waded out in thigh-high boots to set her back gently in the sea. Jordan found this to be the most irresistible thing about him so far—both his affection for the lobster and for the stupid girl mouse—even though she hadn't much cared for Disneyland the one time she was there with her family on vacation in Los Angeles.

Lobster sex actually sounded kind of base and brutal, one step shy of rape, with the whole molting thing going on, the poor female a naked hunk of meat cowering on the ocean floor waiting to be mounted by this hideous thing with claws. Even if she was sorry she'd asked, at least her question kept him talking, and it led to a few more personal revelations.

"So, do you live on campus?" she asked.

"No. I've got an apartment in Dupont Circle, with a couple of roommates. It's actually better, since I'm spending so much time at the aquarium. It's helpful to be near the Metro."

"I went to that aquarium once, on a field trip to D.C. when I lived in Omaha. It's the most amazing place." She was shouting over the loud music, and even though they had moved into a corner, they kept getting jostled by people coming and going. She was holding a beer, but she wasn't drinking; she only wanted to make herself look older. The last thing she wanted to do was go looking for a morning-after headache.

Even this limited disclosure contained more personal information than she'd intended, since she was already planning a lie that had her in college, too, and she didn't want to get tripped up by her own timeline. She figured she'd claim to be a junior at the University of Maryland, as this at least put a little geographical distance between their otherwise possibly colliding social worlds. Of course that meant she'd have to avoid having any of her high school friends come over and blurt out inane references to the likes of Beach Week while she was standing there talking to him. Unbelievably, just a few minutes earlier, she'd found herself listening to a conversation in which a group of the boys, including Deegan and Paul, mentioned that they'd formed a Facebook group called "4212," which was the address of the house they had rented on Ocean Breeze Lane at the beach. They had announced plans to glue these numbers to their mortarboards at graduation so that you could identify members of their Beach Week group from the upper levels of the auditorium, the way a helicopter can pick out rescue vehicles in an emergency.

Jordan needn't have worried. Her friends were all preoccupied. And Khalid had yet to ask her a single question about herself. "Surely you're thinking of the Baltimore Aquarium. We're the poor relation. It's a little shabby down there in the basement of the Department of Commerce. It's kind of hard to think of a less romantic spot."

She was leaning in close in order to hear him; bits and pieces of his words were being swallowed by the blaring music. "It's too noisy here to have a proper conversation," she said. "Maybe we could have a coffee sometime?" She couldn't believe she'd just said this.

He looked at her for a minute, like he was unsure.

"Sorry. I didn't mean to be so . . ."

"No, no. It's fine. It's just . . . I have a girlfriend, but she's away . . . she's doing her junior year abroad, in Barcelona. But . . . well, coffee is just coffee, right? Why don't you come to the aquarium sometime? I'll show you around and introduce you to some starfish, and maybe we could have that coffee afterwards."

Jordan wasn't sure what to make of this. She didn't even drink coffee, but of course that was hugely beside the point. This didn't seem the best first impression she could make, and she was already embarrassed by her own behavior. Then again, with Rene Palmer swaying to the music like a stripper a few feet away, asking a guy to have a coffee didn't seem like the sort of thing that ought to keep her awake at night.

If she was ready to move on to the next phase, why not have some sort of exit strategy while she muddled through the last few months of high school. That was the positive spin on this sudden, fierce attraction. The more worrisome part was that already, after only twenty minutes or so, Khalid had some sort of grip on her. She felt weirdly like she wasn't fully in control, so she let the bad part of this slide into the part that seemed promising and even educational: she'd visit the aquarium. She'd meet some starfish and have coffee. It was practically a date, and this had its own appeal, given that everyone in her group seemed to travel only in a herd, except when they peeled off in couplets to hook up.

She'd try to swing by sometime, she said.

Later, when she tried to tell her friends about him, she could see the alarm in their eyes and knew right away the sorts of assumptions they were probably making.

"*Khalid?*" Dorrie asked, incredulous, as they left the party. Jordan offered to drive Dorrie's car, a tiny new Lexus that was an early graduation present from her dad. He lived in Virginia with his second wife, and the car had apparently been the source of an ugly blowout between her parents, as her mother thought a Lexus too ostentatious for a kid. Her dad had countered with something about its great gas mileage.

Paul insisted that he was completely sober, and he grabbed the keys from Jordan's hand. Sober was a bit of a stretch, but at least Dorrie wasn't behind the wheel. That she was even upright and semi-coherent was itself impressive.

"His name is *Khalid?*" Dorrie repeated, laughing. She climbed into the front seat and opened the window as Paul pulled the car out of the spot with a lurch.

"Your point?" asked Jordan.

"Are you serious? First you tell me that you spent the whole time talking to some guy about lobsters . . . I mean,

God, that is so gross. Do the males really have two penises? That's disgusting! Like something out of a horror movie! And now you're telling me that he's a . . . Khalid? Isn't that a terrorist name?"

"What's wrong with you, Dorrie? How can you say such a stupid thing? He's from freaking Tennessee! And could you close the window, please? It's February, and it's freezing back here!" This was one of the many problems with high school—you wound up hanging out with people for completely random reasons, like you had lockers next to each other or you were in the same homeroom or you were on the soccer team together, all of which happened to be the case with Dorrie, which Jordan had to admit was too many coincidences to really count as random. Dorrie had been very kind to her when she'd first arrived in Verona: she had noticed Jordan sitting alone in the school cafeteria on her first day of school and had invited her to join her and the Courtneys, who had since become her friends. And Dorrie was sweet and extremely, almost painfully pretty, with long white-blond hair and blue eyes the color of sapphires. She was also one of those kids who was as smart as she was dumb, this latter quality evidenced by the fact that she seemed to be in love with Paul, a potentially lethal combination of immature, oversexed jock and science genius, who had only come out of a select magnet program in order to play on the Verona lacrosse team. Like Paul, Dorrie could ace any standardized test; she had a transcript full of A's but zero common sense and no interest in anything going on in the world outside of Verona. Jordan felt a real affection for her, yet it had never seemed an intimate friendship, and this racist comment helped to highlight why.

"God, Dorrie. How can you say something so awful? He

was just telling me about this one really cool spiny lobster, and we got to talking about it—I was the one who asked how they reproduce, and it wasn't lewd or anything, it just kind of came up in the conversation."

"Okay Miss Lobster Sex. Tell me where this Khalid is from."

"I just told you. Knoxville!"

"Well, before that. He's obviously not American."

"I think he was born here. I didn't ask him that specifically, but he's spending the summer in Carthage, which is where his family is from originally."

"Carthage? North Carolina? I have a cousin who lives there!"

"No, Tunisia."

"Carthage sounds like a long-lost city, like Atlantis," Paul said irrelevantly.

"Okay. Well, moving on, girlfriend, how old is Khalid-from-Carthage? He looked older."

"He's from Knoxville," Jordan repeated. "That would be in the United States of America. And yeah, he's a little bit older."

"Did you happen to tell him you're in high school?"

"It didn't come up."

"I cannot believe this. He's like, twice your age, and Muslim. Could it get any worse? I suppose it could, actually. Maybe he thinks women should wear chadors or burkas or whatever you call those things. Or who knows, maybe he's married!"

"You're so awful, Dorrie. He's not that old. And I don't know that he's Muslim, but if he is, who cares? Besides, are people from Carthage even Muslim?" She clearly had some homework to do. Granted, Dorrie's instincts weren't entirely wrong, even if the problem wasn't religion: he was too old, he was self-absorbed, and he'd admitted that he had a girlfriend. Still, it was seductive, the way he was looking at her when everyone else was busy staring at the spectacle that was Rene Palmer having had a little too much to drink, pushing a football player up against the wall.

3

* * * * *

Leah and Charles had not spoken of Beach Week since the meeting adjourned six weeks earlier. They had straightened up in silence that night, collecting paper cups and crumpled cocktail napkins, hunting for the toothpicks that had been used to spear cheese cubes and were strewn haphazardly about the living room. Leah had found a few of the wooden picks inside the sofa cushions, as well as one embedded in the armrest, sticking up like a flag. After the cleanup, Charles had gone down to the basement and planted himself in front of the basketball game without further comment. Like certain other matters in their lives, Beach Week seemed a subject best avoided.

Yet here Leah was, about to bring it up again. She had called for a family dinner meeting this evening. Jordan and Charles generally resisted these events, the announcement of which invariably produced groans and eye-rolling. Her husband and daughter shared the opinion that one ought to just deal with life as life arose, let issues unfurl in a natural way, and not make a federal case, not formalize every little thing with an agenda. Perhaps it was the legacy of her years as a teacher—all those parent conferences and departmental meetings and back-to-school nights—but Leah liked to manage in an orderly way. She liked outlines and bullet points and highlighters. She liked to see things spelled out on paper. Besides, it seemed to her efficient to consolidate into one conversation the things that needed discussion, to get it all over with in one go.

It wasn't satisfying for her to be the family shrew, but they had matters in need of resolution! The meeting wasn't meant to be just about Beach Week; there was also the unpleasant topic of the upwardly spiraling cell phone bill. Between Charles's Blackberry and Jordan's sudden proclivity to communicate prolifically—and with regard to her mother, almost exclusively—in texts, they had just received a bill for $327.83, which was nearly $200 more than the norm. She would save for last the sweetener, a discussion of the graduation party for Jordan that Leah hoped to begin planning.

At least the announcement of a dreaded family meeting generally had the upside of bringing everyone together for dinner. Except that in this case it did not, because Jordan had failed to show up, the prospect of shredded beef tacos, her favorite meal, notwithstanding.

A hunk of beef emerged from the bottom of Charles's taco as he put the other end into his mouth and took a bite. The piece of sour cream–slathered meat hovered at the end of the shell for a moment before oozing onto his thigh, down the leg of his trousers, and onto the floor. Leah stared for a moment as the food melted into the green swirls on the linoleum. Three years ago the dog would have struggled to her arthritic feet to slurp this up, and even though she was long gone, they were both still primed for her response. They talked vaguely of getting a new dog, but never did anything about it; they no longer even skimmed the classified ads or stopped to admire puppies they saw on the street.

Leah stared at the floor for a moment, then rose from the table and went over to the sink and rummaged around in the cabinet until she found a bottle of Lysol spray cleaner. She held it aloft, studying the label.

"I wonder if this contains triclosan," she said. She had recently discovered a blog called nomoretoxichouse.com and was on a quest to rid the house of possible contaminants. She anticipated Charles's response to this. He thought she should stop reading these nutcase blogs. She had accordingly refrained from telling him what she'd learned earlier that day about a local incidence of *E. coli* and had instead forced herself to embrace the thought of healthy protein. She thought this was pretty big of her. A sign of forward progress.

"You already bought it, so you might as well use it," he said of the spray cleaner.

"It's not like a fur coat, Charles. It's not like the animal is already dead. It's an active poison, the release of which pollutes the environment. *Your* environment, I might add."

This hadn't come out in quite the right tone. Why was it that, in some practically quantifiable way, when she was feeling the most vulnerable, her words conveyed the most venom? There was probably some obvious Darwinian explanation for this—some analogy to be drawn to turtles and protective shells, or perhaps, more accurately, to porcupines and quills— that wouldn't require too much probing.

"You're absolutely right. And I'm sorry I'm such a slob. I'm happy to clean that up, and we can just use organic soap and water. Let me do it . . ."

She shot him a look, aimed the spray bottle at the floor, and pulled the trigger. It only made it worse when he pretended to agree. She got down on her hands and knees and began to scrub. This was overkill, yes. Things in the rented Adler split-level colonial were shipshape, even though she suspected that they had all been a lot happier when she had been working and they'd lived in dusty chaos. At the same time that she was busy obsessing about things like putting healthy food on the table and keeping the floors clean, however, she understood that she was failing in more important arenas. The last time Charles had suggested that she finally register her car in the state of Maryland, as well as get herself a local driver's license now that they had lived here for nearly two years, she had burst into tears.

It was true, at every turn she was resisting sinking into this place. The sentiment, at times, appeared to be mutual, and she wasn't feeling a particularly warm embrace. When she first put out feelers for a job, for example, she was told by the secretary in the county hiring office that teachers in the area typically had Ph.D.s, her eighteen years of experience notwithstanding. And maybe it irked her in a purely selfish way that while most Veronians seemed practically oblivious to the recession—there were reports of a hobbled real estate market, and people spoke anecdotally of stock losses—the Adlers alone appeared to be pinched. On her better days she was able to say that it was possible, and even quite likely, that Verona was in fact the perfect place to live and raise a family, the Platonic ideal of a good and just society, and that she had simply failed to integrate or to really even try. Leah wondered if she had begun to lose her center and was slowly collapsing inward like one of her daughter's flaccid soccer balls.

She wondered how much of her own moodiness, and the recent marital chafing, could be pinned directly on the move. Yes, they were under pressure. Financial and health issues that had not been formerly present were now in the fabric of every exchange, but lately she wondered if these were merely symptoms of a larger problem. If their marriage couldn't withstand relocation, did that speak to something structural, like a house that gets lifted off its foundation only to discover beneath it massive rot?

It had been on something of a lark, a couple of years back, that Charles had shown her the job posting on the Urban Planning Association website and then, at her urging, sent off an application and his résumé. A prestigious real estate development company in northern Verona County was in need of a planner with Charles's particular skill set, which involved the ability not only to interpret byzantine zoning regulations, to charm and soften government bureaucrats and liaise with sometimes contentious neighborhood committees, but also to devise the right concept for a unique parcel of land that incorporated a blighted warehouse district and an underutilized harbor area. This was a good opportunity for him. He would be the chief planner on this highly visible project.

Charles was an urban planner with a specialty in combating sprawl. He'd been part of the team that had so successfully redeveloped Omaha's downtown and riverfront areas, attracting more than $1 billion in public and private sector investments. *Smart growth, mixed-use development,* and *sustainable, walkable communities* were among the buzzwords of his trade. This job posting wasn't just weirdly up his alley, it practically qualified as karma, since he already had applicable blueprints in his drawer. He sketched these sorts of urban centers just for fun. Or at least he used to. Now Charles seemed as emotionally depleted as Leah, and while they got through the days with some semblance of cheer, *fun* was not a word in the Adler family lexicon. Part of it was just a spiritual anemia from this constant hemorrhage of cash, but admittedly there was some subliminal anger, too. Lately Leah found herself shooting down all of Charles's whimsical ideas, which was particularly sad since his endless supply of these had been one of the defining characteristics of the man she'd fallen in love with. Now she was liable to scowl before he could finish any sentence that began with "How about . . . ?" or "What if . . . ?"

She wasn't proud of these sour moods, but it was one of his fanciful propositions that had brought them here, and so far that wasn't turning out so well. She had to sometimes remind herself that she'd been a big enthusiast of this project at one time. Grocery stores, affordable housing, movie theaters, schools, playgrounds, recreational facilities including a public solar-heated Olympic-sized swimming pool, everything an easy stroll, the cornerstone being access to public transportation. There would be no need for cars in this self-contained urban center. The North Verona project would be called "Downtown." Jordan said the plans were a little *too* perfect, and that they reminded her of the Sims game she used to play where you created virtual communities and then sent the virtual people to virtual shopping malls and bars and even stuck them in virtual hot tubs in the hope that they might meet others and virtually reproduce.

Charles was flown out for a series of interviews, then quickly offered the job. In karma begetting karma, a colleague of his at the University of Nebraska, where he taught a few urban planning classes, happened to know of an open slot at the University of Maryland. Everything clicked, or at least it did at first. Now Mirage Development was encountering opposition at every turn. One anti-Downtown coalition protested that the height of the proposed apartment buildings would ruin the aesthetics of the neighborhood. (That there was no neighborhood, just empty warehouses and the remnants of a munitions factory, seemed beside the point.) Another group had filed a petition with the county planning board fearful of the additional traffic Downtown would pose to the region. Then just last week, seemingly out of the blue came a bunch of people in bird costumes, claiming, with no hard evidence, that owls would lose their habitats should construction commence.

Although these objections were slowing things down, they were generally considered the sorts of to-be-expected nuisances that would eventually be massaged away. The larger problem was the unanticipated vociferous and litigious opposition to the new Metro line meant to connect northern and southern Verona County, the existence of which was critical to the overall vision as well as to the commercial viability of Downtown. Assuming that the Cobalt Line, as it was called, got approval, it was still unclear where the actual Downtown stop would be, which was one more obstacle preventing them from breaking ground. Reviews were now under way by the transportation planning board, the county planning board, and the governor, too. Leah and Charles talked about this at dinner just about every night, but Leah had to confess that somewhere along the way, between discussions of the Capital Cost Estimating Methodology Technical Report and the Architectural History Survey and the Air Quality Assessment and the

Travel Demand Forecasting PowerPoint presentation, and now with these people wearing feathers and strapped-on beaks, she'd begun to lose track of the status of things.

"When did you last hear from Jordan?" Charles asked, chewing, after Leah refilled his plate. She was aware that she was not the world's greatest cook, and the extra time the food had sat on the stovetop while they waited for Jordan hadn't done much to enhance either flavor or texture. Yet even if a bit of deliberate mastication was required in order to get the meat into swallowing condition, it seemed possible that Charles was being a bit dramatic in grinding his jaw. "You did tell her about dinner, yes?"

"I did, when she came home from school. She asked if she could borrow my car for a while, and she said she'd be back in time to eat with us. She was really looking forward to a family dinner!" She said this last part in a cheerful voice that she knew sounded a little forced. "This isn't like her, to not even call," she added as she heaped more beans and rice on her own plate.

Leah squeezed back into the chair across from Charles. Their table was the wrong shape and size for this kitchen, and it was difficult to access the side that was closest to the wall. When a larger person, such as Charles, attempted to sit, the table needed to be pulled out, then pushed back into position once he was situated. That their table didn't belong in this kitchen, a rectangular peg in an ovate hole . . . she forced herself to stop there; it was pointless to assign meaning to every little thing.

"Look, she's eighteen, we'd better get used to this," Charles said.

"She's seventeen."

"Practically eighteen. And better that she's out running around with friends than nursing headaches, acting all morose."

Leah refrained from pointing out that he was the one who had raised the subject of her absence, and now he was defending her right to be AWOL. "True," she said. "Although she's actually been out a lot lately. She's seemed kind of upbeat the last few weeks, but of course it's hard to tell with her, she's so up and down . . . But nine months away from being eighteen is not 'practically eighteen,' at least not when you're still a kid in high school."

"You need to take the long view," he said. "You're always getting stuck in the ruts of the here and now." It drove her crazy when he began philosophizing, but he had a point.

"I suppose you're right," she said. "Still, it would have been nice if she'd at least have let me know she'd changed her plans. I would have made something . . . else. But it's par for the course, I guess. It's been kind of a frustrating day around here."

"Why?" he asked, pushing the food around on his plate. "What's going on?"

"It's too aggravating to discuss."

He cocked his head and took another bite of the taco while waiting for her to answer.

"It's petty, I know," she said, "but, well . . . it has to do with Beach Week."

She thought she could see the wedge of meat move down his throat, as if he had swallowed an eraser.

"I thought we were basically done with all this for now," he said. "What could have possibly come up already? We coughed up the money. They can have as many meetings as they want.

Our work is done. At least mine is. As far as I'm concerned, Jordan isn't going anyway! We gave the security deposit just to pacify you. If anyone needs a week at the beach, it's me!"

"Um, okay. Wow. Sorry to bring it up. Never mind!"

She knew she didn't sound the least bit sorry. This wasn't a decision he should be making on his own, even if, with sober second thoughts, she couldn't say that she disagreed with him entirely.

"No, it's fine. Sorry. Tell me."

"Forget it. It can wait."

"Just tell me. Please?" He sounded almost sincere, but it was probably just that he didn't want to generate a secondary thread of resentment about whether he genuinely wanted in on a slice of this irritation.

"No big headline I guess, but we're kind of back where we began. Evidently the people who agreed to rent to us had a change of heart, or they double-booked, or they were foreclosed on, or . . . something—I didn't really follow that part, but they tore up the lease, so Janet and the Realtor scrambled and managed to get a new place, which is actually kind of interesting. Do you know that book *Peeper*?"

"No."

"Really? It was kind of huge. The author went on *Oprah*. There's been a lot of talk about it locally because Clara Miller, the author, lives in Verona. I read it for my book group and it gave me the creeps. It's about a guy who's a perv, but there was some controversy because it's based loosely on her husband, and he's not *actually* a perv. Just a Peeping Tom or something, but not in a bad way? I didn't catch *Oprah*, but I saw the author on the *Today* show once, trying to explain that it's fiction."

"Well, what about it?"

"It's her house! Also, it's right on the beach, which is a real find—the other one was about a block away."

Leah got the impression that she was losing Charles's attention; he was staring longingly at his Blackberry, just out of reach on the kitchen counter. Leah harbored an intense, almost irrational hostility toward his Blackberry. She had seen the results of a survey that suggested she wasn't alone in this sentiment; some notable percentage of women found it more offensive to have their partners reading e-mail at dinner than to have them ogling the waitress. The sound of him scrolling was the last thing she heard before falling asleep and the first thing she heard each morning. She planned to suggest that they drop the service when the contract expired next month, or at least get Mirage Development to foot the bill.

"Whose house?"

"Charles, are you listening to anything I'm saying? The house belongs to the author of *Peeper*. She lives in Verona. And that seems really good, in the sense that if anything happens, we know how to reach the owner."

"That sort of cuts both ways, don't you think? We don't necessarily want the owner to be able to reach *us* if something happens! If, of course, Jordan even goes. Needless to say, you know my position on this. And wait, what did you just say about a perv? Does a perv live in the house?"

"Really, could you possibly be any more negative about this? I didn't say that. It's a novel anyway. Fiction. You know, a made-up story?"

"I'm just being realistic. If the kids trash the house, it's not necessarily a good thing that the owner lives in our community."

"Well, that's not why I brought this up. There's something else—a bit of a catch."

"I'm afraid to ask."

"Yeah. Actually, you *should* be afraid to ask, as it involves more money." She tried to make this sound light, and even somehow funny. "Janet needed a new deposit."

"The same amount?"

"Basically."

"So no big deal, then. Which I say hypothetically, of course, since . . ." At least he had the decency to not finish the sentence.

For reasons Leah could only partially comprehend, this whole Beach Week thing seemed to be throwing all of their problems into sharp relief. She couldn't say why she was putting pressure on this right now; they had enough on their plate, and there was a part of her that understood how irrational it was that she, of all people, should be advocating that their daughter even go. She was prepared to rethink her position—she just didn't want to be bullied into it by Charles. Still, it wasn't the time or the place for this conversation. She could see that Charles was tired. He typically left for work in the morning looking bright and crisp and optimistic in his starched shirts, but lately he'd been returning home a little crumpled. They were all beginning to sag under the weight of the last two years.

"Except that the first deposit has already cleared the bank and has yet to be refunded," she heard herself explain. "But Janet said there's no problem, we'll get it all back. It just may take a little while."

"Super!" he said. "I don't even want to do the math."

"Yeah, but it's less about the money than the way it was handled," Leah said, truly mystified by her own relentless pursuance of the topic. "This time the Flying Nun agreed to take care of the new security deposit, but she refused to cover for us. I don't know, maybe I'm being overly sensitive, but evidently there've been a bunch of e-mail exchanges about this, and for some reason our names weren't even on the list, so we missed all the back-and-forth, and we were the only family that hadn't been consulted and then the only ones who hadn't turned in a new check, and they were on the verge of cutting Jordan out of the house. I know it's dumb, but I feel so . . . I don't know, *ostracized*, I guess. Maybe I should have put out more food. Or maybe you shouldn't have brought in that beer."

"The Flying Nun?"

"Yeah, surely you've heard that Alice Long was some superhero on TV, like in the nineties."

"That woman who was arguing with me?"

"Yes. Don't you remember her from Jordan's accident? Although I guess you weren't there, at the game that day . . ." This was an unfair low blow. They had divided the soccer schedule evenly, and it had been Leah's turn that day. Although they both loved watching Jordan play, the amount of distance involved, coupled with games that could last more than two hours, had sometimes eaten up half the weekend.

"That woman is a nun?"

"No, Charles. She's an actress who plays a superhero, and everyone calls her the Flying Nun as a joke, since she's so holier-than-thou. I've never seen the show," Leah added, "but I hear it's still on late-night cable."

"Is it?"

"So I've heard, but as I was saying, the point is, there was a group e-mail going around about Beach Week and we didn't get it."

"One thing I don't really understand," he said, "is why that woman is letting her daughter go to Beach Week if she's so negative about it."

So they were still stuck on Alice Long, it seemed. "That's a reasonable question. I asked Janet about this myself. Apparently Alice made some sort of bargain with Cherie, that if she got straight A's and got into Princeton, she could go to Beach Week."

"Excellent parenting."

"Exactly."

"So, wait, if she doesn't get into Princeton, she's going to be punished? Well, if you consider not going to Beach Week a punishment . . ."

"I agree it's horrible, but that's not our problem."

"Doesn't she have a husband weighing in on this?"

"Someone said he had a stroke a few months ago, and he's still out of it. He's older. Like a lot older. Anyway, why are you so focused on this? My only real point here is that we're the only parents in the group who didn't get the e-mail."

"I understand that, Leah." Now he sounded genuinely annoyed. "Look, don't get me started on this again, especially about that goddamned beer. I know I was rude to that woman, and I don't particularly care. It takes a lot to make me angry, and I rarely speak my mind like that, but she was really out of line, and I have no regrets about anything I said, apart from suggesting that Jordan drive, because, as you certainly know, I'd really rather not see her go at all."

"Well, it's a little late for that."

"Is it? If we are writing a new check?"

"The thing to do is just secure this spot for now. I wouldn't underestimate how hard it can be to get a bed during Beach Week. If she bails out later, I'm sure someone will take her place and we'll get reimbursed. Maybe we can sell her spot on eBay. Or StubHub."

Charles didn't laugh or even smile at her attempt at a

vaguely sports-related joke. "I truly can't believe we are having this conversation," he said at last. "You know, Leah, we've gotten through so much tough stuff in the last couple of years, and I can't help but wonder if you are, for reasons I can't understand, pouring all of your frustrations into this ridiculous situation—"

"I might say the very same thing about you!"

Jordan seemed to appear in the room from nowhere before Charles could offer a defense. "Sorry I'm late—traffic!" their daughter said. Her backpack hung from her shoulder and the car keys dangled from her hand, the nails of which were painted a shade of red so dark it looked almost black. She made a jangling sound as she moved, the result of wrists full of silver bangles. They both looked at her, surprised. Neither one of them had heard the garage door open or her key turn in the door. "Are you guys fighting about Beach Week?" she asked, sounding oddly cheerful.

"We're not fighting, sweetheart!"

"Not at all," Charles agreed, forcing a smile.

Jordan didn't seem particularly concerned about whether or not this was true. She stuck her head into the refrigerator and rummaged around for a minute. "Jeez, Mom, could you *please* buy some diet soda?"

"Yeah, sure," Leah joked. "Why don't I just sprinkle particles of enriched uranium in our air ducts instead!" When no one laughed, she added, "Aspartame," by way of explanation.

"There's juice," she continued. "Passion fruit and guava, behind the milk. Orange juice with omega-three something or other. There might be some cranberry back there, too."

Jordan studied the selection. "What is omega-three, anyway? I'll just have water."

Leah didn't actually know what omega-3 was, but she did

consider blurting out the word *perchlorate*, the most recent of several contaminants discovered in their local water supply. She also considered sharing the contents of an e-mail she had received that morning from a friend back home, connecting dots between breast cancer and drinking from plastic water bottles that had been left in hot cars, but she forced herself off this awful topic.

"Where have you been? Don't you want some dinner? I made tacos."

"Tacos?" Jordan said. "Yum! But too bad, I ate already, sorry. Oh God . . . I'm so sorry . . . I missed the family meeting!"

"Where did you eat?" Leah asked.

"We grabbed a sandwich at Union Station."

"Who is *we*? And *Union Station*? What were you doing downtown?"

Charles raised his eyebrows in an apparent signal to Leah to stop grilling their soon-to-be-eighteen-year-old daughter. What was his central thesis on Jordan's movements, anyway? Give her all the room she needs, except when it comes to Beach Week.

"I have a friend who works nearby. Well, he's technically interning nearby."

"A friend? A new friend?"

"Yes, Mom. A new friend. If you insist on knowing every little thing, his name is Khalid. Okay? We just had a quick bite because he had to get back to the aquarium. I had a salad. He had a panini with grilled chicken. Anything else you need to know? Beverage selection?" But she wasn't saying this in a hostile tone at all; she seemed to be glowing as she relayed the details of their meal, and she was smiling, as if she was happy to have this secret pried from her, to have a reason to speak his name.

"*Khalid?*"

"Jesus, Mom. Are you ever going to fix this ice maker? And I beg you to leave any bigoted comments to yourself," she said, struggling to pop a cube out of the plastic ice tray. Jordan brought it over to the tap and ran hot water over it until they could hear the sound of ice cubes falling into the sink.

"I didn't say anything bigoted!"

Jordan dropped a couple of cubes into her glass and left the tray sitting on the counter. If things weren't already so tense, Leah might have asked her to please refill the ice tray. Everyone was always leaving the empty ice trays on the sink for Leah to replenish, along with the Brita water filter.

"You didn't have to. I heard it in your voice," Jordan accused. She left the room in anger, forgetting her glass of water.

"Honey," Leah yelled after her. "Wait . . . I wanted to talk to you about a couple of things." She understood that this was not the best time to introduce the topic of the cell phone bill, and Beach Week was already proving conversationally toxic, but everyone loved a party. "I thought this might be a good time to talk about your graduation party. I know it's early, but if we're going to buy tickets for Grandma and Grandpa to come in, and also, if we want to get anything, like . . . oh, I don't know, a tent, or a cake, or a photographer—"

"A *tent?*" Jordan repeated. Leah couldn't see her daughter's face from the other room, but she detected incredulity.

"Well, not necessarily a tent. I'm just thinking out loud here, you know. If we have a large crowd spilling out into the yard, and the summer weather is so unpredictable . . . But we don't have to have a tent. I'm just saying we should just start brainstorming, is all—"

"I don't want a party, Mom," Jordan said. Her voice was moving farther away; it sounded like she was on the upstairs landing, or maybe it was just that her words hit Leah with such velocity that it felt like they'd been lobbed from the top of the staircase.

"Just a little party?" Leah heard herself say pathetically. Why should it matter to her if her daughter had a graduation party? It wasn't as if Leah had a whole lot of friends in Verona. Nevertheless, she could see them all in the backyard (she was already airbrushing out of the resulting photographs the over-grown azaleas, the wobbly fence, the aged, broken swing set), toasting Jordan and her hard work, wishing her well at . . . well, wherever she decided to go to school was fine, and paying for it was achievable—somehow. They'd wear floral summer dresses and get a big white sheet cake and embed in the frosting one of those cheesy plastic figures in cap and gown. Maybe she should propose having a joint party with Dorrie. Perhaps that would hold more appeal. Leah hadn't realized how invested she was in this idea until Jordan abruptly pulled the plug.

Leah and Charles sat in silence, staring at the blue tumbler their daughter had left behind. The ice made small crackling sounds.

"Why doesn't she want a graduation party?" Leah asked. "There's no prom this year, and Beach Week . . . well, that's just for the kids to celebrate. I feel like *we* need some way to com-memorate this—I don't know, this phase of life. To salute her hard work, her tough spirit, to send her off into the world . . ."

Charles shrugged his shoulders. "You've got to give her a little space."

"I'm trying to give her a little space by letting her go to Beach Week."

Apparently exasperated, Charles flipped his hands over so that his palms were facing upward, as if he were looking for help from above.

"Okay, look, I really don't want to have a fight about this," Leah said. "I only brought this up originally, this thing about the new house and the new check, because I was feeling kind of hurt; we went out of our way to host the meeting, and then we're randomly cut out of the loop."

"Yes, right. That's what I was about to explain." He took a deep breath, as if anticipating her reaction. "I got an e-mail, and I confess I didn't really pay any attention to it. I should have forwarded it to you, but I—well, I just figured you got it, too, and since this is your thing, I thought I'd just let you deal with it."

"*My* thing?"

"Okay, well *our* thing. I didn't mean it like that. I give up. I'm just digging a deeper hole here."

"I don't understand how you got the e-mail and I didn't. Was my name on the list?"

"Honestly, I didn't notice. I know I made a mistake. I should have forwarded it to you."

"I'm trying to remember . . . is it possible that the e-mail list came around while I was in the kitchen maybe? On the phone?"

"Probably that's what happened," Charles agreed, seeming relieved to have an explanation. "Honestly, Leah, I don't remember. It's really not a big deal, not the sort of thing we ought to have a fight about. Let's let it go."

Perhaps he meant this, but now that his memory was refreshing, he had another question.

"Did that Courtney mother ever pay you back?" he asked. "Didn't you cover her original deposit?"

"Millie Moore, you mean? No. I'll follow up," she said. This was a lie, although just a white lie, meant in the spirit of aggravating him a little less. She had in fact called Millie Moore already. Three times. Millie had not returned the calls.

"What about that lawyer? Did she ever provide her addendum?"

"I'm sure she will, soon."

"I'm not entirely comfortable with—well of course, as you know, I'm not comfortable with any of this, but I'm particularly unhappy about basically agreeing to sign a legal document that I've not yet seen, even if ultimately it's all just hypothetical, since we don't know if Jordan will be allowed to go."

"It's only going to say that we all agree to share responsibility. I mean, how complicated can that be? I could draw that up myself! And look, if you don't agree with what it says, we don't have to sign it. I'm well aware of the fact that we haven't reached a decision about whether Jordan will be allowed to go. We're just—"

"Securing her a spot. Yes, I know."

"Okay, look, you don't have to be so mad at me! I'm trying my best here. It's not like this whole thing was my idea . . . You want me to be a part of Verona, to stop being unhappy here, so I'm trying. Cut me a little slack."

"Oh, so we're back to this again? How could I forget, this is all my fault!"

"Are you guys *still* fighting about Beach Week?" Jordan yelled from her room.

"No," they replied in unison.

"Good. Please don't bother. I don't want to go anyway. I

was thinking I might go to Tunisia with Khalid during that
week we have off between exams and graduation."

Leah refrained from claiming victory, from making a pro-
nouncement that their daughter was now going to Beach Week
whether she wanted to or not. Silently, she walked over to the
sink and began scraping the remnants of the taco dinner down
the drain.

4

· · · · ·

Noah had seen a lot in his day, but watching Mrs. Bergstrom getting ready for bed was the last meaningful thing that he saw in Verona. His fall from the tree he had climbed to get a view inside his neighbor's bedroom window effectively concluded his investigation into the goings-on across the street, the details of which he was recording in a small spiral notebook.

"It's a little undignified to decide to become Harriet the Spy at age thirty-five," his wife had said. Noah wasn't sure what she'd meant. He had only some dim knowledge of this Harriet person—some school-age memory of kids toting books with a bespectacled girl on the cover—but since this was actually one of the nicer things Clara said to him in the aftermath of "the incident," as they had come to know it, he hadn't pressed too hard for clarity. Some of her other comments he tried not to think about at all. If he'd been more adept at interpreting his wife's facial expressions or at hearing nuance in her voice, he would have understood that Clara was telling him this Bergstrom business was a pretty big deal, that this girl named Harriet, or his relationship with her, was somehow responsible for the beginning of the end of his marriage.

It began with the walkie-talkies.

He had bought Oliver a set of walkie-talkies for his seventh birthday, and Noah had just inserted the batteries and they were doing a test. Oliver was on the back porch, and Noah was upstairs in the master bedroom. Clara, as always, was busy writing, although this was before she had begun writing about *him*. If no other good had come from this Harriet business, at least it had proved good material for her book. Not that she'd ever thanked him.

"Testing, testing, one, two, three," Noah had said. When he pushed the button for reply, instead of his son's tiny voice he heard an unexpected ethereal cry rising from the static. A woman seemed to be choking out the words "He's killing me."

Then he heard a male voice reply, "I keep telling you, you need to get out of that house."

Noah had looked out the window and seen Mrs. Bergstrom pacing around on her front lawn with a cell phone. Did it look like she was crying, from the distance of across the street? Yes. He was pretty sure this was her voice he was hearing, in real time. Noah was certain that this was what she'd said, even all these months later when he asked himself if he might have misunderstood or imagined the entire episode. But if there was one thing in the world he knew with any certainty, it was this: Mrs. Bergstrom thought that "he," whoever he was, was trying to kill her.

Later that night, Noah had volunteered to walk the dog. (Clara's dog—Noah had never truly warmed to the thing, and the feeling appeared to be mutual. He was *not a dog person*, was Clara's diagnosis.) Accidentally on purpose the dog slipped off her leash, and the next thing Noah knew, she was scampering toward the flower beds that framed the Bergstrom house, and in accordance with his half-baked plan, Noah went chasing after her. That was the first time he'd ever looked in a window so deliberately, and it proved extremely interesting. After a couple of weeks of similar observations, he made some notes:

1. Professor Bergstrom had not one, but two cell phones.
2. Mrs. Bergstrom cried a lot.
3. The teenage Bergstrom boy sometimes leaned out his bedroom window and smoked cigarettes. (Or maybe he was smoking something else. But the nature of what he was smoking was not critical to the investigation.)
4. The Bergstrom girl, who looked to be about fourteen, kept mostly to herself.
5. The curtains on the basement windows were always closed.
6. The Bergstroms seemed to get a lot of deliveries. UPS, DHL, FedEx, and once, the postman even made two drops at their house on the same day.

His research continued for about a month. Before he was able to collate and interpret his field notes—his original plan had been to load them onto an Excel spreadsheet, but he never got that far—he had fallen from that tree, and then his wife, after doing the needful for him legally and medically, shipped him off to the Delaware shore. He sometimes worried that no one was keeping an eye on the Bergstroms in his absence, or on Verona for that matter.

Chelsea Beach was a hybrid of new and old—of fabulous, incalculable wealth and people barely scraping by. There were multimillion-dollar mansions built precariously close to the sea, some of them sprawling compounds on which one could imagine generations of Kennedyesque clans tossing footballs in the sand. These were interspersed with a handful of ramshackle homes built early in the twentieth century, lacking in the upkeep that might have lent them a little prewar charm. Most of these older homes had been torn down, replaced by modern McMansions with pink stucco facades.

Beach castles, was how Noah thought of some of these grander homes. Many of them did, in fact, have turrets from which sprouted figurines— insignia of fish or whales or birds, or other whimsical, aquatically themed creatures. Noah came to regard the occupants of these homes as somehow related to their symbols, as if they were family coats of arms, expressions of personality—like the kids he saw with hoops through their noses or the ones with purple hair. On his block lived the Seagull family, as well as the Dolphins, and his friend Jill, the Blowfish, next door. In accordance with his agreement with his ex-wife, however, Noah tried to limit explorations of his various neighbors' fishiness or possible birdlike behavior.

One thing he absorbed without looking into any windows was that around here, real estate was some kind of sport. Who was putting his house on the market, how much he was asking, what kinds of rents one could charge, and whether Noah was willing to sell so that they could tear down his house and build something more in keeping with the community were popular topics of conversation. Another thing they took seriously in Chelsea Beach was rules. Some old, skinny guy in a Marlins hat who lived at the end of the block once knocked on Noah's door to tell him that it was against community bylaws to leave his towels hanging off the front porch railing. Another time he was scolded for substandard recycling practices, putting cardboard and plastic in the same bin.

Grouchy neighbors aside, apart from missing Oliver with a fierceness that sometimes approached desperation, things weren't so bad at the beach. Not only had he found a job straightaway, but thanks to the divorce settlement, he owned his own beach house now. Never mind that he no longer owned the home he had actually purchased with his hard-earned money back in Verona, but at least he had a roof over his head, even if the paint was chipping, the siding was rotting, the garden was overgrown and weed-infested, and vines had strangled the once-gorgeous rosebushes and were now twisting up around the rainspout, angling for an assault on the drainage system. Cobwebs formed an awe-inspiring canopy over the front porch, resembling one of those plastic habitats where a person could observe ants building sand colonies, except that this one was the real McCoy, the spiders and their prey right out in the open, a mini–Lion Country Safari but with bugs, a few still writhing, most of them dead. And that was just the outside! Noah's mother-in-law had apparently died on the couch and had lain there for four days with the television blaring before Jill, the Blowfish neighbor, had broken down the door. You could still smell death in the living room, which was filled with musty antiques, more Gothic than beachy, with crystal chandeliers and heavy velvet drapery. After Clara's mother died, she'd inherited the place, then essentially traded it to Noah in the divorce settlement, a process in which he'd had little say.

The condition of the house didn't bother him that much; what Noah loved best about the beach was the boardwalk, and he had the good fortune to land a job there, manning the counter at Joseph's Famous Salt Water Taffy. The Chelsea Beach boardwalk wasn't the most impressive on the Eastern Shore, but it held its own with its amusing mechanized miniature golf courses, bumper cars, and video arcades, its abundance of sunburned children vomiting from one too many spins on the roller coaster, and a full range of junk-food concessions. Joseph's had the best spot, and it was also a landmark, the anchor at the key intersection where the beach met the part of the boardwalk that turned into the small downtown area of Chelsea Beach. The neon sign for Joseph's Famous loomed so high and large that it was visible from the coastal highway, and Noah felt a certain pride in being part of this important enterprise.

Although it was true that selling saltwater taffy could get a little dull, especially in the chilly winter months when boardwalk traffic was sparse, Noah devised a little game to pass the time on his shift. He'd try to guess where his customers were from, and then, for double bonus points, he'd take a stab at predicting their orders. When the first wave of tourists arrived in spring, trailing beach towels and floppy sun hats and scuba gear and screaming sunburned kids clutching pails and shovels, he got the impression that his customers enjoyed these interactions. One girl, clad in a skimpy yellow bikini even though the weather that day really called for sweats, said she'd been coming to Chelsea Beach for three years and had never encountered anyone so friendly working behind the counter at Joseph's Famous Salt Water Taffy.

By mid-June, however, he was instructed to stop being so chatty and just make change. Evidently a few girls had complained to Maury, the grandson of the long-dead Joseph, and hence his boss, that Noah's manner was *leery*. Noah wondered if anyone had actually used that word, or if Maury had poured all of these supposed complaints into one overwrought adjective, the way the sugar and corn syrup and the natural and not so natural flavoring got stirred in the giant vats into one sticky amalgam and squeezed out as taffy. *Leery*. Perhaps the relentless, scorching sun made everyone kind of irritable, or maybe these girls were just cranked up from too much sugar, but he didn't see how asking someone where she was from could really be construed as *leery*—or, for that matter, whether *leery* was technically even a word.

He wasn't having much success with the guessing game anyway. He had worked with numbers all his life and was certain that consumer behavior, like Bergstrom family behavior, must be quantifiable somehow. Before coming to the beach, he had spent ten years in a dusty cubicle in an accounting firm tucked behind a mattress store in a strip mall. Clara had always seemed troubled by his lack of trajectory; she had higher aspirations on his behalf. A degree from MIT apparently meant that he should be doing somehow . . . better. He hadn't really understood this: Was there something wrong with liking your job, even if it seemed stultifying to the rest of the world? Noah was proud that he had never considered himself above the work, even though crunching numbers for the likes of Kramer's Discount Furniture Depot was a frequent source of complaint among his colleagues.

Now that he was pulling in the minimum wage, money was tight, but beyond the essentials, his needs were few. He didn't really want the cell phone Clara had given him for his birthday, for example. She had gone and put him on her family plan for only $9.99 per month, which seemed to him kind of a sad, insulting joke, since now she had a *new* family, a new husband and a couple of step-kids. And she had Oliver. Noah had no real interest in this whole American blended family thing. He was not a violent man, but he still thought the healthier instinct was to want to murder the man who was currently reading bedtime stories to your kid and screwing your wife, rather than to peacefully coexist with him on a Verizon family plan.

Compared with untangling the often sloppy books of small businesses, his work at Joseph's should have been easy, but this refusal of the taffy input to behave less erratically really bothered him. Categorical values, disaggregation, dependent variables—even the most basic statistical concepts had lost meaning. Naturally there would be anomalies, results that surprised, but he still thought there simply ought to be some way to get a formula going, such that the people with crooked teeth and thick legs and raw pink burns on the fleshy, tender parts of their arms ought to hail from the sticks. And yet this wasn't proving true. Just as many of these types came from cities as the ones with perfect teeth and movie-star tans came from straight off the farm. He found this hard to fathom. It had been less than two years since his fall, but in that short span of time, it seemed like everything had turned upside down.

At least he had a higher success rate when guessing people's orders. There was a huge amount of variety on offer— long sticks and kisses, sugar and sugar-free, boxes of assortments, single flavors, or even individually selected mixes that might include any ratio of chocolate to molasses, vanilla, orange, lime, banana, cherry, peppermint, strawberry, lemon, licorice, spearmint, or peanut butter. So far he had clocked a 95 percent likelihood that his customers—no matter what their appearance or even their sex—would study the list of choices posted on the sign above his head, staring with great seriousness, deliberating for considerable lengths of time, and then finally just order the one-pound box of assorted taffy kisses. This was the first option on the list, and it was also a relative bargain. It was a comfort that this much about the world remained true: people generally leaned cheap and took the path of least resistance.

Noah settled into one of the antique wing chairs he had dragged onto the front porch a few days earlier, when the last two slats of wood holding the Adirondack chair together had finally split. There was a reason you didn't put upholstered furniture outside—his Blowfish neighbor, Jill, had told him as much. The seat was damp, and he could feel moisture begin to seep through his jeans. Still, this was a small price to pay for being so close to the water that he could feel the ground shake each time a wave slapped against the shore.

Jill wandered by with a platter of fish encrusted with pistachio. On the side were baby carrots with a green garnish and salad. She did this a lot, all casual, as if she were just in the neighborhood—which of course she was, given that she lived next door—and she happened to have with her some fried chicken and corn on the cob. And there was always some explanation: her kids didn't like it, or they were eating out with their dad, or they weren't hungry, or she'd accidentally made too much and really Noah would be doing her a favor by just having a little bite. He felt funny relying on her kindness night after night.

He couldn't quite get a grip on Jill, like who she was before she'd taken over The Bank, which was the nickname the locals had adopted in referring to her house. The National Bank of Chelsea Beach. Jill's house was a pox on the neighborhood on account of its being too new and gaudy, whereas Noah's house was too old and squalid and sat a little crooked on the lot.

"I've solved the problem," Noah said, passing an envelope to Jill. "Well, the money one, anyway."

"What do you mean?" she asked, pulling out a sheaf of papers. "What is this?"

"A lease. Actually, four leases. Mitch—you know, the Realtor, Mitch Mingus, the guy who founded Mingus Realty?— said he's even got a couple of other possibilities in the works."

"What're you talking about? Leases for what?"

"For renting my place. I can pay all the back taxes if I just get out of the place for the summer." In the brief, confusing period when Noah was recovering from his fall and Clara was settling her parents' estate and divorcing her husband, the mortgage on the beach house got paid off, but no one seemed to pay attention to the fact that this meant the taxes were no longer coming out of escrow. Under normal circumstances, ones in which he had not recently fallen from a tree, Noah would have seen this coming. He was the numbers person; Clara was the so-called *artist*.

"*This* place?"

"Why do you sound so surprised? Everyone rents in summer."

Noah had heard about this thing called Beach Week, where you could make a ridiculous amount of money in a short span of time—not quite as much as buying a winning Powerball ticket, but at least it was a surer thing. When he'd first inquired about this, Mitch Mingus, who looked like he'd eaten a few too many Boardwalk Fries, said he didn't do Beach Week rentals. He said this as if it were some kind of manifesto. He told Noah a few horror stories to bolster his position: "You know Bonnie and Mike Reiner, up at The Cove?"

Noah shook his head no, but Mitch continued anyway.

"Their house *flooded* last summer, on account of someone left the water running in the bathtub, and the drain was closed, since they'd been using it to keep the beer on ice. No one knows how they could have left the water running for that long without noticing, but they had about fifteen thousand dollars' worth of damage. And the Bransons, at the end of your road?"

Again, no. Mr. Mingus Realty seemed to be under the impression that Noah was out mixing it up with all the neighbors, bringing cupcakes and lemonade to block parties or something.

"They rent every year, but they now ask for a huge security deposit because they've also had a lot of trouble. Doorknobs missing, cigarette burns in the carpet. Someone put a fist through the drywall last summer. Every year it's something different."

But then, a week later, Mitch had come by Joseph's Famous with the amazing news that some lawyer from Verona, Maryland, had called, looking for a Beach Week rental. She'd sounded slightly hysterical and said they'd had a place that had just fallen through. Because it was late in the season, they couldn't find a thing. Mitch had hesitated, he said, because Noah's place wasn't quite up to their usual standard; he'd begun to explain the circumstances, but as soon as he mentioned Clara's name, the woman got all excited and it was practically a done deal. Apparently she'd seen Clara on *Oprah*, or had heard about it anyway, and that was good enough. Without asking any further questions—apart from whether the place could sleep ten people and ascertaining the proximity to the beach—she said they'd take it. Mitch realized that all he had to do was drop Clara's name, and people were prepared to sign the lease, sight unseen.

This was good news, yet anything that involved either Verona or his ex-wife felt tainted. Everyone seemed to be obsessed with Clara now that she'd written her book. The book that was about him, although she insisted it wasn't. The book with the sad-sack protagonist who lived at the beach and had to commute three hours to see his own kid—except that in real life he wasn't even allowed inside his former house. Clara had made such a mess of his life that he wasn't sure what was true anymore. He got that the man in *Peeper* wasn't *really* Noah, because this guy—Jim, she'd named him—had blond hair and was short and had a bad complexion, whereas Noah was tall. Tall was his defining feature, although Clara had always said that what she loved about him, back when she loved him, was his elegance. He had long, thin pianist's fingers (a pity no one had paid enough attention to him as a kid to arrange piano lessons), a long, chiseled nose, and even his eyebrows were long, thin lines of charcoal. Clara had also said that the first time she'd seen him, a lone man on the Metro reading a book, she had fallen in love. He looked like someone's son, she'd said, and this thought had overwhelmed her: someday she might have a baby, and he might grow up to be a beautiful, sad-looking man, alone on a train. This, too, was pure Clara. She never stopped trying to make boring stuff like a guy on a mildewy subway car reading a book about personal income tax somehow poetic. She'd also made the character who was not really Noah kind of creepy, a bit of a perv who had a problem with his memory. Noah certainly wasn't a perv, and he didn't have a problem with his memory, but he supposed that if he did, he might not remember.

Jill studied the leases, although Noah wasn't entirely sure why he had given them to her, why he supposed she might have anything particularly useful to say on the matter. She was a pretty woman, but he didn't get the impression that she was a financial or a legal whiz.

"Really, Noah, I'm not sure this is the best idea. Do you want all these strangers in your house? Kids drinking, partying, making a mess? You're going to have to fix this place up, even if it's just a Beach Week rental. And where will *you* stay?"

He hadn't thought this last part through. But the strangers in the house part he kind of liked. He imagined himself coming over, making sure things were okay, shooting the breeze, offering to make them breakfast or taking out the trash. He'd be careful not to break the rules and do any formal observing, but he could at least bring them taffy once he ascertained what flavors they liked. Which made him think of something. "Did you know that there isn't actually any salt in saltwater taffy?" he asked Jill.

"You've got to stop talking about taffy all the time, Noah. You're starting to give people the creeps. And you didn't answer my question. I asked you where you'd sleep."

"I can sleep on the beach. I'll get a blender and a long extension cord and make drinks, like frozen mojitos, and sell them to the tourists. Ha! Not such a bad idea, you know. They do that somewhere. I forget . . . Oh yeah, Clara and I saw that once in Spain, on our honeymoon. Would you believe that we once saw someone clipping her toenails on the beach? And she was topless!"

Jill didn't look very impressed. "Don't be ridiculous," she said. "You aren't going to sleep on the beach."

He couldn't help but note that her concern didn't translate into an invitation to sleep in the National Bank. Still, even if she seemed to keep her distance—she frequently brought him dinner, but she'd never once asked him in—he felt a little less lonely when he caught sight of her and the boys. He could see them through the big bay window in their kitchen. Maybe he wasn't right there at the dinner table with them, talking about stuff like the weather or the progress of their homework, but he was pretty close.

"Really, you should let Clara—"

"I'd rather sleep on the beach."

"That's absurd, you know. She cares about you. She's almost certainly got the money."

"I don't want her money. I'd rather keep my dignity."

"If you want to talk about dignity . . ." She let the sentence hang, unfinished, then got up and took his empty plate.

This change in tone usually signaled that it was her turn to start venting about *her* marriage, and she seemed to think she had the moral high ground in this department on account of the fact that she'd been left for an age-inappropriate super-model. He supposed this was her stab at being glib, because in reality Noah had heard that the girl wasn't really a supermodel but a poet, a professor out at the University of Delaware. Whatever was going on, their divorce proceedings, which had begun amicably, had recently escalated into such an ugly affair that the court had put a freeze on all of her husband's assets, forcing him to stop work on his biggest project, the redevelopment of an outlet mall down the road that had come to resemble a ghost town as the shops went out of business one by one. The half-demolished buildings and the idle construction equipment were at such a prominent spot that their marital problems now seemed to blight all of Chelsea Beach; a bull-dozer with its blade poised midair sat practically adjacent to the sign proclaiming that you had just entered the city limit.

Probably Jill had just aggravated herself thinking about her ex, and she needed to go clear her head or cry or something (this he knew about—women weeping). She said she'd be right back, explaining that she had to check on one of her sons, who was supposed to be doing his homework. Noah tried not to let it show, but he felt jealous whenever Jill tended to one of her kids, even if she made it sound like a hassle sometimes. He thought about Oliver every time he saw a nine-year-old boy, which was kind of a problem, since they were all over the place. Everywhere you looked, there was a kid, collecting shells in the surf, eating ice cream on the boardwalk, and soon they'd be spread all over the beach, as thick as swarming fire ants, these little children.

5

. . . . .

Cherie Long rose from her chair at Starbucks and held her grande latte aloft. It looked, at first, like she was going to make a toast—*To Beach Week!* Jordan thought she might say. Or maybe it was someone's birthday. Instead, Cherie stared at the cup as if it were radioactive.

"This is totally not skim," she said. "I can taste the fat. There's no way I'm drinking it." She ran her tongue along the roof of her mouth, a gesture apparently intended to scrape away the scum of whole milk.

A cold front had just moved in from the Midwest, bringing snow and causing everyone to start buzzing about global warming the way they did any time the temperature fluctuated more than a few degrees. They'd start going on about disappearing honeybees, and then they'd get all misty-eyed about the possible extinction of polar bears, even though so far as Jordan knew, none of her friends really understood the correlation, on top of which, it wasn't all that unusual for it to snow in early April. At least Cherie's mini-tantrum was made picturesque by the thick, fat flakes that fell behind her as she stood with her back to the window. A person might reasonably expect someone like Cherie to rebel against her mother by trying to be different, by being quiet and thoughtful, the sort of girl who went through childhood hoarding material for a devastating memoir. Instead, Cherie seemed to Jordan to be a chip off the old block, the only twist being that she heavily self-medicated. Maybe Jordan was just being mean; it was true that she was predisposed to a certain negativity concerning Cherie ever since that game. It was bad enough that Jordan had been knocked unconscious, but adding insult to the literal injury, about twenty minutes after the ambulance had taken Jordan away, Cherie scored the tie-breaking goal.

"So take it back," Courtney Davidson said. "Tell them to make you a new one." Jordan didn't know Courtney D. very well, but she'd always been impressed by her confidence. She was one of those girls who seemed happy with herself; she didn't obsess about her hair, or spin herself in circles at the gym every day working off her lattes, or go home after school and fret that she might have botched a verb conjugation when she was randomly called on in Spanish class.

"I don't know, I hate to make a fuss," Cherie said, which struck Jordan as pretty comical since she was already making quite a production. "But I can't drink this. I started my diet yesterday. I've got eight weeks to lose ten pounds." Cherie was at least five feet ten, and although she wasn't sickly thin, she didn't appear to have a spare ounce on her frame, never mind an extra ten pounds. Clad in jeans so tight it looked like they'd been waxed to her skin, one could see that she was already bikini-ready.

"Stop whining, will you?" Courtney D. said. "We've got to

get this meeting over with. I told Mike I'd stop at his house afterward—Deegan and Zack are hanging out over there—and it's already nine-thirty." She grabbed the cup from Cherie's hand and marched over to the counter to broker the exchange.

"Make sure it's decaf!" Cherie instructed as Courtney walked away.

"Oh my God, if *you've* got to lose ten pounds, what does that mean for me?" asked Courtney Greene. Jordan wasn't one to notice weight, but it was true, Courtney was already heavy to begin with, and she'd put on another twenty or so pounds this year. No one even tried to respond to her rhetorical question. Jordan wished she could think of something nice to say, like size doesn't matter, or Beach Week isn't about how good you look in a bathing suit, or Courtney looked just fine as is, but she knew any of this would sound disingenuous. Jordan didn't spend a lot of time thinking about her own weight—she wasn't even sure she could accurately recite her current particulars, and she didn't much care as long as her clothes fit—but this conversation was making her anxious, all the same.

"Enough whining," Dorrie said. "We've already taken this place over as it is, and they're going to kick us out if we don't settle down." This was true: Cherie and Rene had rearranged the tables without asking for permission, and then they'd dragged over extra chairs, creating a makeshift table for ten.

"I wouldn't worry about it. We're the only ones in here," Amy Estrada pointed out. "And anyway, I talked to the manager about it and she said it was fine." Amy had selected the meeting spot and consequently must have felt some need to defend the arrangement.

"Okay. Well, moving on," Dorrie continued, "my mother talked to a few other moms, and they made up this pledge. It's kind of dumb, I know, but I'm going to pass around copies.

You need to sign on page two. I also promised I'd read this aloud, just so that the moms know you've at least heard it . . . Can you hear me over there?" she yelled to Courtney D., who was waiting for the barrista to concoct Cherie's new drink.

"Loud and clear," she said.

"I mean, if you think about it, our parents are letting us go, and they're paying for it, so the least we can do is pretend—"

"*Your parents are paying?*" asked Courtney Moore. "*Seriously?* My parents are making *me* pay. I've been saving up for a few months from babysitting money, and then the rest is coming out of my graduation present from my grandparents."

There was a moment of silence as the others absorbed this news, but apparently no one could think of anything comforting to say. Jordan felt bad about this expense, too, but since she was pretty sure she wasn't even going to Beach Week, she figured it wasn't an issue. Another friend of theirs, Zoe Shapiro, was begging to be a part of the beach house, so it would be easy to replace herself. She was at this meeting only because she hadn't worked up the nerve to share the news with Dorrie.

"There's also a list of what we need to bring, but we'll get to that after we go through the pledge," said Dorrie.

"I'll sign up to bring the tequila," Courtney Greene volunteered.

"What kind?" asked Mindy. "I only like Patrón. It's totally worth the splurge. It tastes really clean. I did, like, five shots last week and I didn't even get a headache afterward."

"I'll bring the Percocet," Cherie said before Courtney could reply. Courtney laughed, but it appeared that Cherie was serious. "I've actually got a bunch. I've been saving up for months, stashing away a pill a day. My dad has more meds in his bathroom than they've got at CVS. You name it, I can probably get it."

"Your drink, madame," Courtney Davidson said, returning to the table and setting the new latte on the table in front of Cherie. "Grande decaf skim latte." She gave a fake curtsy.

"Thanks . . . that was quick," Cherie said. She smiled, but she seemed to regard the drink with suspicion, like maybe Courtney was trying to pull a fast one and this, too, was teeming with calories.

"Okay, look," said Dorrie again. "We don't have to make a huge deal out of this. Like I said, I promised my mom I'd read through this list, and we have to sign, and then when the parents have their stupid meeting next week, we just have to show up and say we had our meeting, et cetera, and then we're good to go. So the sooner you guys stop messing around, the sooner we can get out of here. Plus it's really starting to come down hard out there, so it would be good to wrap this up."

"I know—look at it! How freaky is this weather?" asked Mindy. "I mean, it was like eighty-five degrees just two days ago. I'm still wearing summer clothes." She wasn't wearing just summer clothes, but *new* summer clothes. She'd gone on her annual spring shopping spree the previous week, and Jordan had been present for the brief segment of it that had involved the purchase of two Kate Spade purses at the handbag department at Nordstrom. Mindy had an American Express gold card and a monthly allowance that was more than Jordan spent on clothes each year. When Jordan asked her if she'd had to cut back at all, given the recession, she said that no, her parents' investment portfolio had actually increased, plus the hockey team was turning a profit, so she felt it was her civic duty to stimulate the economy. Jordan didn't think her parents

even had an investment portfolio, although she couldn't be
certain, as she didn't actually know what one was.

Mindy's cell phone rang; she answered and began talking
loudly. "No way . . ." she said. "No way! You're kidding . . .
Lizzie and Ben Newmark? Are you sure it was her?" She got
up from the table and walked to the other side of the café to
continue the conversation.

"This is really ridiculous," said Dorrie. "I'm just going to
read this, and I don't care if you're listening or not. You'll sign,
and then we're out of here. Ten minutes tops . . ."

As Dorrie read, Jordan followed along on the handout:

BEACH WEEK PLEDGE

I promise to obey the following rules to ensure a safe,
police-free, eviction-less week in Chelsea Beach.

1. We will create a daily house manager rotation that will be
   agreed upon in advance of arrival and posted at the beach
   house.

2. I will be a house manager one day during the week to
   ensure that the house is in good condition. I will be
   responsible for the key and locking the house when
   everyone is out. I will handle any problems that occur that
   day . . .

"Oh, cool . . . Can I make the chart? And can I be the first
house manager?" asked Amy.

"Amy, you can be the house manager every single day, if
you want," said Dorrie. "And you can own the chart. Go for it."

Amy beamed. Everyone loved Amy, but they also had a lot
of fun at her expense. She was going to make a good sorority
president someday, the sort of girl who would plan theme

dinners with appropriate matching paper plates, maybe carry around one of those oversize Filofaxes that she'd annotate with different-colored pens.

"You might as well be the house manager," said Cherie sarcastically, "because there are ten of us and only seven days of the week, so we don't want to get in some big fight about who gets left out."

"Okay, shut up, you guys, and let me finish," said Dorrie.

3. I will keep track of where at least one other girl is at all times . . .

"Wait. Why only one other girl? And like, at all times? What does that mean? Like what if someone is hooking up? Do we have to stand outside the door?" This was Courtney Moore speaking, and she appeared to be serious.

"One other girl just means, like, someone is always looking out for you," said Dorrie. "It's not the worst idea if you think about it. That way no one will actually disappear or anything . . . Look, I'm not defending any of this. I agree it's really dumb. But if it makes our parents feel better, where's the harm? Let me just finish . . . Okay, some of this is self-evident and kind of repetitive. We'll have a buddy system, we'll stay in Chelsea Beach, we'll—"

"I didn't know we were promising to stay in Chelsea Beach. What if there's a party up in Dewey Beach? Or Rehoboth?" asked Rene.

"Don't worry about it," said Dorrie. "Okay . . . no parties at the house, no overnight guests, no boys . . ."

A few of the girls were cracking up. *As if!* seemed to be the implication of their laughter.

"And then, again, the rest is just obvious stuff. We'll pay for any damage, we'll leave the house in the same condition that we found it in . . . So just go ahead and sign. And now, let me just read from the list of things to bring. Please, hold your laughter and applause. My mom can be a little, um, shall we say . . . anal?

"Soap/shampoo/conditioner
Cleaning supplies
Dish detergent
Laundry detergent
Bounce
Iron
Ironing board
Water bottles
Beach blankets
Beach chairs
Beach umbrellas
Pails and shovels (for sand castles)
Rafts/boogie boards, etc.
Deck of cards
Board games
Books and magazines
Notepad and writing utensils to leave each other notes and
    make shopping lists
First-aid kit
Tylenol
Sunscreen
Sunglasses
Prescription eyeglasses and/or contact lens solution
Sun hats
Benadryl

Pepto-Bismol
Bug spray
Personal medication (antidepressants, etc.)
Beach towels
Bath towels
Washcloths
Sheets/pillows
Pajamas
Slippers
Toothbrush/paste/floss
Cosmetics
Hair dryer
Swimsuits
Cover-up
Flip-flops
Real shoes
Pants
Sweatshirt
Shorts
T-shirts
Underwear
One or two nice outfits
Jewelry (nothing too nice!)
Rain jacket
Umbrella
ID
Change for vending machines, laundry, parking meters

Food: Real and snack
Decide this with your roommates. You might save money
   buying in bulk before you go."

"What about cell phones and chargers?" said Courtney Moore.

"Yeah, besides a bathing suit, that's about all we really need anyway," said Rene.

"I'm bringing a laptop," said Cherie.

"Is there Internet?"

"I don't know, but we can always find a café. Or find someone else's wireless."

"Don't forget the lime and salt for the tequila."

"This is more than I used to take to camp when I'd go for two months!" said Mindy.

"This is more than I'm taking to college!" said Rene.

Cherie was staring into her latte, stirring artificial sweetener into the cup with a wooden stick. "This is extremely illuminating. Are we finished yet?" she asked. Even Jordan had to confess that she was only half there, and to the extent that she was listening, she couldn't believe how snarky her friends were being. She didn't really want to be a part of this, either right now or this summer at the beach.

She sent a text to Khalid, asking what he was doing later that night.

"We're almost done," Dorrie said. "But we're supposed to divide up the grocery list. I know this is ridiculous, but look, it's not just my mom who wants us to do this. A couple of the mothers . . . I won't say which ones . . . want to be sure we've got some healthy food in the mix here, so I'm going to pass this around and you can sign up for what you want to bring. Some of it's pretty standard—you know, milk, orange juice, grapefruit juice, paper towels, napkins—"

"Do we really need paper towels *and* napkins?" asked Cherie. "I mean, can't we use one for the other? It's not like we're going to be having a dinner party."

"Oh, a dinner party!" said Amy. "We should definitely have a dinner party! Wouldn't it be fun to cook? Maybe we could do seafood, something beachy? I'll start looking for some recipes tonight. And also, I saw the most beautiful arrangements at Anthropologie last week, a bunch of seashells and stones in giant glass vases, with sand. We could do something like that for a centerpiece."

"Seriously, Amy, what planet are you from?" asked Cherie. Although there was a tinge of affection in her tone, Jordan thought you'd have to be listening pretty carefully to isolate it from the part that was just plain mean.

"Oh my God, I saw the cutest bag there last week," said Mindy. "It was covered with seashells, too! It totally made me want to go to the beach."

"Okay. Can we please get back to business?" Dorrie said. "All I was going to say is, if you sign up to bring, say, breakfast cereal, can you just be sure to write down that you're going to get some raisin bran or something, and not Cap'n Crunch, so a certain mother won't have a coronary? That's all I'm saying."

Was it her own mother Dorrie was referring to? Jordan wondered. This was more than a little embarrassing, but that said, it wasn't like any of the other mothers were particularly relaxed. The only mellow parent in the bunch seemed to be Mr. Krazinski, Marta and Deegan's dad, and it was only just occurring to Jordan that she wasn't sure she'd ever even seen their mom. She wondered if they even had a mom.

"I can't believe we're having this conversation," said Courtney D. "We're going to Beach Week. The only food-related issue is going to be whether we have enough beer . . ."

"Actually, I can't believe we're having this conversation, either," said Jordan, surprising herself. "I mean, can't we at least *pretend* to take this seriously? A lot of bad stuff happens at Beach Week, and our parents are just trying to do the right thing. Let's at least be mature about this. Let's not be total morons . . ."

This was more radical even than her flirty behavior with Khalid at the party. She couldn't explain her own shift in personality lately. Sometimes she pulled out the MRIs and CT scans the doctors had allowed her to take home, and she spread them out on her desk beneath the halogen lamp to study the ghostly echoes of her brain. There was nothing there, or at least nothing outside the norm. That's what the doctors said, anyway, when they'd tried to evaluate the cause of her headaches to be sure there wasn't anything going on besides the normal post-concussive symptoms. Jordan couldn't see anything there, either, although she had no idea what it was she was supposed to be looking for. Some specific clump of matter that she could point to and understand all of a sudden why she was behaving like such a moron, chasing after Khalid? Or why she was so intolerant lately of the vacuous musings of her group of girlfriends? Why she didn't get all excited when she received the acceptance letter last week from NYU? Why she'd balked when her mother suggested that they all go out for Chinese food to celebrate?

Her cell phone began to vibrate in her pocket, which was a well-timed distraction. It was Khalid, replying:

U can come over if u want.

It went without saying that she wanted to come over, particularly now that she'd just humiliated herself and probably pissed off her friends. Still, she wished that his invitations might occasionally sound more heartfelt. It had been two months, and she'd seen him only a handful of times. He always spoke about his girlfriend quite openly, but that didn't stop him from treating Jordan like she was his girlfriend, too, which was pretty confusing. He never took the initiative, but whenever Jordan suggested that they get together, he always replied affirmatively, even if his clipped texted answers weren't exactly the stuff of love letters. She knew this was somehow wrong, but she wasn't the one at fault. He was the one cheating! On the other hand, she supposed that lying about her age didn't exactly make her innocent. Her friends clearly disapproved, but why did they have to put her in the position of feeling like *she* was the one who'd gone off the reservation simply because she had a boyfriend who was outside their immediate circle? Maybe her friends were so worked up about Beach Week because they had no place else to go, whereas she had Khalid as her escape. Wasn't this actually more commendable behavior than consciously planning to obliterate oneself with drugs and alcohol at the beach?

She could rationalize this all she wanted, but the reality was that this relationship wasn't exactly making her happy. Was there such a thing as an even keel when it came to love, or was it always going to be the case that something wasn't quite right—like even when you were married, would there still be complications, grown-up versions of girlfriends on their junior years abroad?

Still, it seemed the thing to do was just stop thinking and embrace what was good. Khalid was very sweet to her when they were together, and he'd cleaved to her so tightly the few times she'd spent the night at his apartment that it felt like love, although it also felt a little bit like desperation, like he was looking to be absolved.

"Put your phone away, Jordan," she heard Dorrie say. It seemed rude to single her out; it wasn't like Jordan was the only one who wasn't paying attention. Clearly this had to do with Dorrie's visceral dislike of Khalid. Jordan put the phone in her pocket, but not before texting Khalid to say she'd be there soon.

"I know this is really lame of me," said Rene, "but I agree with Jordan. I feel kind of bad about all this. I promised my parents that we were going to behave responsibly. I spent a lot of time trying to convince them that this is a good group of girls and that we aren't going to Beach Week just to party. I'm not saying we won't party, just that there's more to it than that. I mean, I thought we were going to spend some quality time hanging out together. I know this list is really dumb, but we're all going our separate ways, and this could be a good bonding time. Wouldn't it be fun to play board games? We could get a great game of Monopoly going. Or there's a new team Trivial Pursuit. Or we could do a big communal jigsaw puzzle."

Jordan was grateful for this and, weirdly, not as surprised as she might have been that it was Rene speaking. As crazy out-there as Rene could be, hosting her parties, being more than a little loose, she was also very nice, and eager to please.

"Yeah, I agree," said Amy. "I mean, I know there will be drinking and stuff, but I also was thinking we were going to be a little more mature about this. I promised my mom that we were going to take this pledge stuff seriously."

"Well, we *are* going to take it seriously," said Dorrie. "That's why we're here. There's no great contradiction going on. We're going to behave responsibly—and we're also going to have the party of our lives. So let's just move this forward . . . Oh, wait. I was supposed to add two things to the pledge, so can you just write these down at the end of the list, and maybe initial them before you sign? No going into bars, and no talking to strangers . . ."

"Hey, Cherie—do you remember that unit we did in second grade about not talking to strangers? 'Stranger Danger,' it was called?" asked Courtney D. "And you were afraid of witches?"

"That was hilarious," said Courtney Moore. "She was always petrified at Halloween. So funny . . ."

"Yeah, totally hilarious," Cherie said, but she wasn't laughing.

Jordan was reminded at such moments that these girls had a common past that she didn't share. Rationally or not, this heightened her ambivalence. She'd never truly be part of this group. "Can't you guys be serious?" she asked. "I mean, I'm not entirely sure that I'm going, but if I do go, it would be nice if we could do stuff besides just get drunk every night."

"What do you mean, you're not sure you're even going?" said Dorrie.

"I mean, I'm just waiting to see what's going on. I might . . ."

"Don't start talking about going off to some stupid fish museum again."

She couldn't believe Dorrie was embarrassing her like this, in front of everyone. "Can we talk about this later?" Jordan said.

"There's nothing to talk about. You're going to Beach Week, girlfriend, whether you want to or not."

It was 10:30 p.m. by the time everyone quit mocking the pledge, by which point it was clear that no one intended to abide by even the most benign of parental suggestions. Even the idea of bringing citronella candles to keep potential bugs at bay had come up for ridicule, causing a twenty-minute sidebar debate about whether or not there were mosquitoes at the beach. Since it was getting late and Jordan had given Dorrie a ride, she asked her friend to come with her to Khalid's place downtown.

"We won't stay long. I promise—I've got a midnight curfew anyway. I just want to stop by and say hello. Besides, I want you to see his apartment and meet his roommates. I know you'll like him if you get to know him." Apart from glimpsing him at Rene's party that first night, Dorrie had met Khalid only once, when he'd picked Jordan up after she and Dorrie had gone to a movie downtown. Dorrie had agreed to cover for her, to pretend they were having a sleepover, so that Jordan could spend the night at his place.

"That's highly unlikely," Dorrie said. "Khalid and I will never like each other, because we're the only ones who totally get that all he wants is a piece of your sweet young ass." But she said this with levity, as if it were just a statement of fact rather than the passage of judgment. She opened the glove compartment and pulled out a pipe and a little plastic bag. "Hurrah! I *thought* I'd left it here!" Dorrie said.

"What? Are you kidding me?"

"What's the big deal?" Dorrie asked, sounding genuinely puzzled. She sniffed the weed and declared it a bit stale but serviceable before pinching some and packing it into the bowl of the pipe. She then rolled down the window.

"No way—don't you dare light that! This is my dad's car! He just got it a few months ago and he's like, totally in love with this thing. How long has that been in there?"

"Your dad's in love with a Honda Accord? That's kind of sad. I don't know, when's the last time you gave me a ride?"

"I have no idea, but a pretty long time ago. Like a few weeks ago maybe? Which means my dad's been driving around with drugs in the glove compartment. What if he got pulled over or something? He could have gotten arrested. And don't diss my dad's car. This was a big splurge for him. His old car was about twelve years old and the engine had to blow up before he agreed to get a new one. This is really nice. It's got leather seats, and you can even turn on a switch and heat them up. Not everyone gets a Lexus when they turn sixteen."

"Cool. Heat those seats up, baby. And Jesus, relax. It's only marijuana. It's practically legal. He could just say he has a medical condition or something."

Jordan's cell phone rang. She pulled it from her pocket, glanced at the screen, and sighed. "Hi, Mom!" she said, trying to sound casual.

Dorrie lit a match and held it to the pipe.

"Yes, yes, I know it's getting late. We're still at Starbucks and we're in the middle of the meeting . . . What? Yeah, I don't know when it closes, but they're being really nice, they're staying open late for us I guess . . . Would it be okay if I stayed out a little later? I mean, I just want to hang out with my friends for another hour or two . . . What? Yes, Dorrie's right here! Dorrie, say hi to my mom!"

Dorrie hesitated a moment to allow the smoke to curl out of her mouth; then she let out a little cough before speaking. "Hi, Mrs. Adler!"

"My mom says hi, back," Jordan reported, shooting Dorrie another angry look.

"Yes. Mom . . . Yes, I promise I'll let you know if I'm going to be any later than that . . . Okay, Mom. Yes, I promise . . . No, really, we're just at Starbucks . . . Honestly . . . No! I'm not going downtown to see Khalid. God, I wish you'd trust me a little more than that! Yes, I love you, too."

She set the phone in the cup holder and looked at Dorrie without expression. She supposed she didn't have grounds to act superior; lying to her mother mitigated the fact that her friend was smoking dope in her father's car—sort of. Besides, what was there to say? Sometimes a person had to lie. She didn't enjoy it, but these were extenuating circumstances. She needed to see Khalid, if only for a few minutes, just to settle her mind, or really her entire being; this was almost physiological in its intensity.

She kept dredging for some rational way to explain what was going on with Khalid. On the one hand it was pretty transparent, the sort of thing that was so pathetically obvious that it didn't require much analysis: he wasn't that invested in her, ergo she was hyper-invested in him. Simple cause and effect: Fucked Up Relationships 101.

The better question was, Why was she doing this to herself? Particularly at this juncture, when what she really needed was something to help her heal. If it was just a fling she was looking for, a nice distraction, something to make her feel good about herself, why seek out someone who was quite obviously going to bring her grief? She didn't *think* she had a self-destructive impulse. If she did, maybe she'd be having more fun drinking and planning the likes of this Beach Week blowout. Along those same lines, it would be easy enough to get something casual going with someone easier, someone age appropriate and in her group. Maybe it wouldn't turn out to be the great love of her life, not even something memorable, but she could surely distract herself happily with someone like, say, Mike Seltzer. She could probably find a way to make that happen, too. Mike didn't have a girlfriend, and from what she'd heard, he was the go-to guy for this sort of thing, in that he was actually nice. So nice that he'd hook up with anyone who hit on him just so that he wouldn't hurt her feelings, but also nice enough to not talk crap about her, after. Which was only to reason that there was obviously something else going on here, with this Khalid infatuation. Could it be simply that he seemed exotic, even though he wasn't, really, at all? So he had grandparents from Tunisia, a place he'd never even been. Big deal.

Maybe this wasn't even about Khalid, but about her mother. Maybe she was looking, subliminally, to irritate her mother by presenting a boyfriend with an unsettling name, the way a cat might bring a dead bird to the front door. Or maybe not, since the dead bird was a heartfelt gift, whereas the presentation of a boyfriend whom she was unwilling to talk about in anything other than a superficial way was possibly malevolent. If that was the case, she had real reason to feel bad. What had her mother done to deserve this, apart from driving her a little nuts lately with all her hovering? On top of which, Jordan knew that shirking this maternal concern, being rude and snide to her mother, even when she was at her most cloying, was dishonest: of course she wanted her mother to care, to rush through the door with a thermometer and a box of Kleenex anytime she sneezed, to bring her soup and those dumb old Nancy Drew books of hers when she was home sick. On the other hand, it was also a little annoying to have her mother ready to rush her off to the emergency room every time she said she had a headache. She knew it would actually be easy to appease her mother. All Leah seemed to really want was to be intimate the way they once had been, for Jordan to tell her about her friends, to fill her in on some harmless gossip, to talk to her about school. It wouldn't kill Jordan to open up a little more, even if it was only to tell her mother that she was feeling confused about the future, that in her heart of hearts she was starting to feel like she wasn't ready to go straight to college, to lock into a classroom for the next four years without some sort of break.

She might be seriously overthinking this. Maybe there was no reason to connect up her mother and Khalid. Khalid was simply about time and place. Like Dorrie said, she'd seen him at a party and he was cute, and now she was creating a soap opera out of what was essentially an extended one-night stand.

Whatever it was that was going on, it had turned her into someone who lied to her mother. She rationalized this by supposing that there might be an upside; an unintended consequence of her lies might be that she was making her mother happy by causing her to think Jordan was out with her high school friends, being a normal kid. Jordan had manipulated this to her advantage to extend her curfew on several recent occasions. Her mom always acted like the request was outrageous, but she'd ultimately agree. Then she'd make Jordan promise to either call or send a text if she was going to be later than whatever time they'd negotiated, so that she didn't stay awake all night worrying that Jordan had wrapped the car around a tree. Jordan was familiar with her mother's nocturnal patterns, however, and had learned the hard way that it wasn't always in either of their best interests to comply. If she woke her mom up by calling in her coordinates, Leah would proceed to call Jordan every twenty minutes or so until her key finally turned in the door.

Oddly, her driving was one thing her mom probably didn't need to worry about: Jordan was extra-cautious, although she had heard from a friend who had recently been pulled over that there was such a thing as being *too* cautious, since the cops seemed to assume that the sorts of people who bothered to obey stop signs on empty streets late at night probably had something to hide. What the cops probably didn't consider was that behind some of these overly cautious drivers were simply some neurotic mothers who had nearly paralyzed their daughters with frightening tales of black ice.

"Look," said Dorrie. "I'm happy to cover for you. But I'm just saying, as your best friend, you should really get a grip. He's not only too old for you, but he has a serious girlfriend! Not to mention, what does that say about him that he can't be faithful to her? And look at you. You're practically jailbait."

"You're so rude," Jordan said. "You'll see when we get to his apartment that it's not like that at all."

"It's just a fact that he's too old for you. Don't you know about the rule?"

"What rule?"

"Half plus seven. That's how old you have to be for it to be acceptable. So if he's twenty-two, you'd need to be . . . nineteen."

"Eighteen, you moron. Are you stoned, or drunk?"

"I'm a little of both!" Dorrie reported gleefully. She lit the pipe again and took another toke.

"Seriously. Put that thing away now!"

"Just chill! You are so uptight. Anyway I meant to say eighteen. It's not like I can't do basic math! But you aren't eighteen, are you?"

"No, but I might as well be. I mean, you are, and so is everyone else we hang out with. I just happen to have a late birthday. Besides, that's a really stupid rule. It's not like it's a real rule, like paying your parking tickets or not plagiarizing off the Internet or something." She put on her directional and looked over her shoulder and then switched lanes very slowly. "If two people love each other, that's all that matters."

"You're so cute—look at you! It's like you're steering a giant boat! Could you possibly drive any slower? You're like an old lady!"

"You should be grateful that I'm a safe driver. Anyway, you're not exactly sober enough to be giving advice!"

"I am! And I'm one hundred percent sober enough to ask you if he knows you're in high school."

"I told him I'm in college. Which means you're in college, too, don't forget—UMD, junior year. We're roommates!"

"Well, good thing we have our IDs, then!" Dorrie said. She had recently insisted they both get new fake IDs. Probably she'd been thinking about them being able to go to bars downtown or buy liquor for parties. But knowing Dorrie, it was possible she'd already been thinking ahead to Beach Week when just a few weeks earlier she happened to mention to Jordan that she had a friend who was making a small fortune working out of his parents' garage churning out fake IDs with a laptop and a laminating machine. Jordan said she didn't need a new one, given that she wasn't much of a drinker, but it was nevertheless refreshing to be rid of the old one she had: the girl in that picture looked nothing like her, and whenever she used it, she had to remember to pretend that she was from Elizabeth, New Jersey. She'd almost blown it once, when a bouncer asked her where she'd gone to high school, since he was from Elizabeth, too. Also, she'd heard that her alias had died on I-95 near Baltimore in a head-on collision with a truck. This had always felt like bad karma, but Dorrie said no, no, the girl would surely be happy to be doing some posthumous good, kind of like an organ donor, enabling someone to party from beyond the grave.

"Excellent big parking space!" Jordan said, pulling into an empty metered spot. She hadn't tried to parallel park since taking her test, which meant she wasted a lot of time driving around looking for places that were large enough to pull in headfirst. When she had her mother's big Subaru wagon, she avoided driving into the city altogether. "That's his apartment right there. See, it's meant to be! We won't stay long."

"Whatever," Dorrie said, stepping out of the car. "Your mom is the one who's gonna freak out. My mom's out of town on business this week." She pulled a faux fur hat over her white-blond hair, and Jordan thought she looked a bit like an Arctic princess, regal with those piercing eyes, although currently a little wobbly on her feet.

"You'll really like his roommates. And you're going to melt when you see the pictures of his niece and nephew—he's very attached to them. And there're some pictures of his favorite lobster. Her name is Minnie. Like for the mouse. He loves Disney World." Jordan had to wonder what it was that made her think this was so endearing.

"Adorable," Dorrie said. Judging by her flat reply, her friend evidently agreed.

The door to Khalid's apartment was ajar when they got off the elevator. Jordan knocked, unintentionally pushing it open a bit more just as Lewis, one of his two roommates, yelled for them to come in. She'd met Lewis a few times before. He was a scientist, too, an aspiring astrophysicist from Los Angeles, working on something Jordan didn't completely understand that had to do with asteroids and satellite technology. Or magnets. Or something. He'd told her, but now she couldn't remember and was too embarrassed to ask again. This was so outside her realm she felt like she was in another universe sometimes, which she understood was part of what made it all so appealing. The third roommate, a sweet, soft-spoken man from India named Hari, was doing his first year as a medical resident, and although he was hardly ever around, he was here this evening. The one time she'd met him, he had spoken about a pediatric patient who'd had a severe concussion after suspected child abuse. The boy had lost consciousness, and when he'd come to after nearly twenty-four hours, which was apparently considered an alarmingly long time, he hadn't recognized his parents. One of the other doctors assumed it was some sort of traumatic response to the abuse, but Hari suspected there was something else going on and recommended further tests. He'd been right; they discovered an underlying malignant brain tumor that was pressing on the brain stem. Even though Hari had been lauded as a hero that day, he'd come home pretty rattled.

Jordan had listened, fascinated. She'd been tempted to ask him some of the questions that had recently been weighing on her, but she couldn't. Age was only one of the things she didn't want to talk about with Khalid; she didn't want to talk about her experience on the soccer field, or the headaches, either. She couldn't say why, exactly, although part of it was just practical; there seemed no way to tell him about the soccer game without getting into the subject of her age. But another reason was that she was ashamed of herself for constantly thinking about it. It was only a stupid concussion—it wasn't like a brain tumor that was pressing on her brain stem! On top of which, Khalid was one of the few pockets in her life that was concussion-free. Even her college applications were practically concussion brochures. First, there was a personal statement explaining why her courses during the spring semester of junior year were taken pass-fail, as an accommodation to all the classes she'd missed; then, although she didn't know for certain, she assumed that her teacher recommendations had mentioned her absences, her overcoming of difficulties; and naturally, she'd written a personal essay on "Me and My Commotion of the Brain," even though she wished she hadn't gone there. She was so sick of this subject. It wasn't even that big a deal, yet it wove perniciously through her every thought.

She had the odd sense that Hari, with his gentle manner, could put her at ease. She could almost hear him say that it was perfectly normal to still feel peculiar, to be somehow outside herself—for it to seem like nothing was quite real—only a year out from such a trauma. And a real trauma it was, he'd say. People tended to underestimate the aftereffects. He'd quote stuff from the medical books. He'd say yes, it was a concussion, but it was more than that, too. *Look at the definition, Jordan*, she imagined him saying. *There was violence involved! Concussion, from the Latin* concutere, *"to shake violently."* For all anyone knew, there might have been structural damage to her brain; her molecules might have rearranged themselves in some completely freaky way that no one could even explain, causing her to become some other person. (A person who was suddenly bold enough to flirt with an age-inappropriate guy at a party and then continue to throw herself at him, for example.) People tended to dismiss this like it was no big deal, but the brain was a complicated organ. Maybe Hari would share with her some intriguing medical mysteries, comforting in their strangeness, about people who had had organ transplants and experienced strange personality changes. He'd tell her stories like the one she'd read in a magazine about a man who emerged from a coma and went from being a heavy-metal rock aficionado to someone who cried when he heard Céline Dion sing the theme song from *Titanic*, or about the amputee who felt an itch on his long-gone limb, or the mother who could still hear her dead baby's cries at night.

The three men were sprawled on the couch watching a baseball game on television. Khalid was wearing jeans and a T-shirt, and his hair was cutely mussed. "Hello, love," he said to Jordan, kissing her. And then he turned to Dorrie and kissed her once on each cheek. So sophisticated! (So pretentious was perhaps another explanation, and Jordan could imagine the words coming out of Dorrie's mouth with a slightly stoned laugh.)

Lewis and Hari both stood up and greeted them as well, shaking Dorrie's hand, giving Jordan kisses on the cheek. "Would you like a drink?" Lewis asked. "We've got beer . . . Heineken, I think there's some Amstel, Coke, and maybe even an open bottle of white wine in the fridge."

Jordan was hyperaware of all this, trying to imagine every detail through Dorrie's eyes. *See!* she wanted to say. Isn't this so much better than hanging out with Paul and Deegan and Mike? They're polite! And they drink something other than Budweiser! Dorrie asked for a beer, and Jordan got herself a Diet Coke, which, given her mother's moratorium on soda, actually felt more forbidden and thrilling than liquor.

"Come," Khalid said. He took Jordan's hand and led her over to the sofa. He motioned to Dorrie to sit in the nearby chair.

"I know it looks like we're a bunch of lazy bums," said Hari, "but I was in the hospital all day and your friend Khalid got back from the aquarium only about an hour ago. As for Lewis—I don't know what his excuse is. He'll tell you that he's been busy splitting atoms, but I suspect he's just been lying here all day watching Court TV or something."

"You're onto me, at last!" Lewis joked.

Jordan hoped that Dorrie was observing the way they were talking about things other than who was currently hooking up with whom, or where they were going to go to college, or who was bringing toilet paper to the beach.

They watched television for a while and passed around a bag of chips. Dorrie asked for another beer, which Lewis happily produced. Jordan was leaning into Khalid; he had his arms wrapped around her tightly, his head nestled in her hair.

After she finished the second drink, Dorrie checked the time on her cell phone. She put it back in her pocket but then pulled it out twice more in the space of about five minutes. She seemed to be getting restless. "What about this stuff you wanted Khalid to show me?" she said to Jordan. "We should probably get that over with and then hit the road." She'd had only two beers, but she'd smoked a fair amount in the car, which might or might not have explained her rudeness.

"It's early!" Jordan said. "We've only been here half an hour."

"Yeah, but it's starting to snow pretty heavily."

Jordan looked out the window; by midwestern standards this was a dusting, but given that she'd learned to drive in Maryland and had no experience in inclement weather, she knew she didn't have standing to laugh. Some people emerging from a bar across the street began making tiny snowballs from the small accumulation on a nearby windowsill.

"Khalid, I said you'd show Dorrie the pictures of your niece and nephew, and the one of Minnie."

"Minnie?" Dorrie asked.

"I just told you about Minnie in the car. Remember? His favorite lobster? Are you completely wasted?"

Dorrie let out a high-pitched laugh by way of an answer.

"The one we had for dinner last night?" asked Hari in another endearingly lame attempt at a joke. Lewis appeared to have fallen asleep.

"Come," said Khalid. He took Jordan's hand and led them toward the bedroom. Jordan had once quipped that the room looked like a page from an IKEA catalog, and he'd confirmed that in fact he had done one-stop shopping there when he first arrived in D.C. On a corkboard above a small metal desk was a collage of photographs, and Jordan pulled her friend close. She was pretty sure that Dorrie would melt, the way she had, when she saw the pictures of the kids: there, in a light blue ballerina frock, was a little girl who looked to be about three; and in a white and red soccer jersey was a feisty-looking boy about a year older, a cleat raised, a ball flying toward him. There were dozens of photographs of each of these kids, as well as some crayoned drawings of fish and other sea creatures. It wasn't as if Jordan was already planning a family, yet the fact that he liked kids was surprisingly touching.

"Aren't they the cutest?" she asked.

"They are," Dorrie agreed. "Are these your sister's kids, or your brother's?" she asked Khalid.

"My sister's."

"Your older sister or your younger?"

"I have three sisters," he replied. "They're all older."

"Is that your sister, there? She doesn't look like you!" Dorrie pointed to a picture of a young woman sitting on the stoop of a building that looked suspiciously like it could be in Barcelona, not that Jordan had any real idea what Barcelona might look like, even though she had traveled there on Google Earth to locate his girlfriend on the map for reasons she couldn't explain.

"You know, it really is coming down out there. Maybe we should go," Jordan said.

"Don't go yet," Khalid said, putting an arm around her waist, ignoring Dorrie's question.

The phone in Jordan's pocket began to ring.

"You should answer it," Dorrie said. "It's probably your mom again. It's really past your curfew now!"

Jordan could not believe this. Her friend was trying to sabotage her. She looked at the screen and hit a button to silence the call.

"You two *should* probably go anyway," Khalid said. "Dorrie's right. The roads are going to get slick."

"Wait, she hasn't seen Minnie!"

"Okay, let's see her . . . it . . . whatever it is, and then go," said Dorrie coolly. "How exciting. A lobster!"

Jordan didn't like her friend's tone or the way she was picking at her boyfriend. If *boyfriend* was the right word, which it almost certainly was not. Khalid pretended not to notice, and instead he went over to his desk and pulled a photo album from the drawer. Jordan had seen Minnie's picture before, but never this collection. On the front was a cute cartoon picture of a lobster, with wavy antennas and big googly eyes and a sweet, toothy, not very lobsterlike smile. Someone had colored it in with a red crayon. Presumably the nephew or niece, but who could say. Maybe Khalid himself had drawn this picture. What he seemed to lack in human warmth—at least with any consistency toward Jordan—seemed to be compensated for by his love of sea life. It could be a little weird, the way he sometimes talked about creatures he had known—crustaceans and mollusks and your basic boring fish—with the same level of affection that most would reserve for a family pet. Jordan wondered if she ought to be trying to extrapolate more meaning from this.

In fact, once they began to flip through the pages of the album, it wasn't really as weird as all that. It was essentially a montage of the summer he had worked at the lab on Cape Cod; and interspersed with a few photos of the lobster—in a tank, on a table with Khalid in the background, and floating along the shoreline with another lobster as if they were on a holiday—were photos of friends he had worked with, normal shots of a bunch of young people goofing around.

Dorrie didn't even bother to feign interest. Instead, she announced that she wasn't feeling well, and if they didn't leave right away, she was going to be sick. At first Jordan thought she was saying that metaphorically, like she found the saccharine lobster pictures nauseating, but in fact the minute they got outside, and fortunately just before they got inside the car, Dorrie vomited in the pristine snow, turning it a vile shade of yellow.

While she was busy being sick, Jordan sent Khalid a text.

U ok? Sorry about my friend!

They got into the car and drove in silence. They had gone only about a mile when she checked her phone. He hadn't replied. She checked again at every red light as they drove for the next thirty minutes, to no avail.

"Why do I have this feeling, like this is meant to be and yet . . . like it's not meant to be? Do you know what I mean?" she asked Dorrie.

"No," she replied.

They didn't speak again for a few more miles, until they reached Dorrie's neighborhood. Dorrie lived in one of the few remaining wooded areas in Verona; winding and hilly, the roads here were largely untraveled this late at night, and it was slippery. Jordan wished she could have a meaningful conversation with Dorrie about Khalid. She was her best friend, and even if Dorrie was completely hostile to Khalid and had just ruined her night, Jordan thought she could at least appreciate the drama, the complications.

"I know this is really lame, but I think the universe is telling me something, sometimes. But it's giving me mixed signals. On the one hand, I think it's meant to be because of my name . . . Jordan . . . you know, like I'm destined for something different somehow, and there he is, on his way to Tunisia . . ."

"You're right, that *is* pretty lame, I'm sorry to say. What are some of the other so-called signals?"

"Oh, I don't know, just small stuff, like I'll be in the middle of thinking about him and someone will send me one of those stupid chain letter e-mails about standing up for myself and not taking any crap from men. And already I'm taking a lot of crap, I guess . . . Still, what if I never meet anyone like him again? I mean, I already have this feeling like I can see the future, and even if I'm happy someday in my boring conventional life, with a big suburban kitchen or whatever it is you are supposed to aspire to, nothing is ever going to be as romantic as this."

"Oh my God, Jordan, pull over," Dorrie yelled.

Jordan slammed on the brakes, thinking that Dorrie had seen something in the road, but she was about to get sick again. She didn't get out fast enough, however, and wound up spraying vomit on the dashboard. She finally got the door open, slid out, and vomited again, then leaned against the car, taking deep breaths.

"You okay?" Jordan shouted.

"Yeah. Just give me a sec." She wiped her face with her sleeve.

"So, what I was about to say before I was so rudely interrupted," Dorrie continued, as if this disgusting vomit incident hadn't just occurred, "is that it depends how nice the kitchen is." She let out a little laugh at her own supposed joke and climbed back in.

"None of this is very funny. My dad is really going to kill me! We need to clean this up."

"Chill, will you? It's not that bad. Here . . . I've got a tissue or something . . ." She dug around in her bag. "Well, hmmm, how about . . . a tampon?" She took one out of the wrapper and began to wipe the vomit; then she threw the tampon into the snow.

"That is so gross," Jordan said. "Ewwww."

"Have you totally lost your sense of humor? I don't know, Jordan. I mean, I get that you really like him, but I think the whole thing is weird. Like the pictures of that lobster. It's twisted. What kind of guy makes photo albums anyway? That's sort of gay. And those kids. It makes no sense."

"You say something even more horrible every time you speak! What are you talking about? What makes no sense?"

"If he has a bunch of nephews and nieces, why are there only two kids on the bulletin board?"

"He never said he had other nephews and nieces. Why are you trying so hard to find some flaw? I mean, I get that he's older, but it's not like he's *that* much older. Now you're trying to suggest that he has a family or something? That's crazy!"

"I'm not trying to find some flaw—not that it would take much work, mind you. But I *am* trying to protect you. I mean, don't those people have, like, multiple wives? And anyway, even if he's not like that, he obviously has a girlfriend."

"He's from Tennessee. And I already know about the girl-friend. But if he really, truly loved her, would he be spending so much time with me?"

"Could you be any more naïve?"

"Could you be any less romantic?"

"Right, whatever," Dorrie said. Now they were in her drive-way, and she opened the door. "I'm sure you're right. He's going to ditch the girlfriend, and even if he figures out that you're seventeen, this will have a really happy ending. My mind is totally warped."

But she didn't say this with any hostility. It was hard to make Dorrie mad, especially when she was stoned. Anyway, Jordan didn't care what Dorrie thought, although of course if that was really the case, she wouldn't have dragged her along this evening.

"Let me just ask you one more thing," Dorrie said, unbuck-ling her seat belt and fishing around for her glove, which had fallen to the floor. "How come it's been so easy for you to pull off this lie? Doesn't he want to see where you live? Doesn't he ask about your schoolwork? Hasn't he noticed that you don't have a Facebook page at UMD?"

At least she had a good answer to this last question. "He doesn't do Facebook. He thinks it's a waste of time. Which it is."

Jordan knew that Dorrie had a point about this, too, and it was one that she'd been trying hard to not consider for some time. Khalid seemed to have so little interest in what was going on in her day-to-day life that she was able to pull off this rather enormous lie with no real effort. Didn't he want to see the pretend off-campus apartment? He'd never even asked her where it was. Didn't he wonder why she didn't have a UMD sticker on her car, or why she didn't seem to have more work (although she'd be hard-pressed to believe college students could have significantly more work than Verona High School students)? Still, she supposed that even the best relationships were full of imperfections. Certainly she got the impression that if her parents didn't go out of their way to at least *pretend* everything was fine, they would have already stabbed each other with kitchen knives.

"Okay, take the age thing off the table," Jordan said. "And also forget about the girlfriend and whatever crazy thing you were driving at with the niece and nephew. If you forget about that stuff, what did you think?"

Dorrie shrugged her shoulders. "He's cute, I guess."

"Cute? *You guess?* Is that all you can say? He's gorgeous."

"Yeah, I suppose," Dorie agreed, smiling.

"Well, he is. He's like . . . out of a movie or something."

"So he's really good-looking, but think about it—never mind the other 'issues,'" Dorrie said, making quotation marks in the air with red woolen fingers. "He's leaving in June. So what's the point?"

"God, Dorrie, that's so defeatist. I mean, June is a long way away, and if you look at life that way, what's the point of anything right now? I mean, why don't you and Paul just stop seeing each other, then? Why don't we just stop hanging out, since we'll be going our separate ways."

"Well, we don't know for sure about that. I mean, probably I'll go to Princeton, but I might decide on Columbia instead, and you'll go to NYU, so maybe we can hang out!"

Jordan had not previously considered this scenario and quickly concluded that she found it extremely unappealing. If she did decide to go to college, one thing she knew for sure was that she didn't want to hang out with anyone from home.

"Well, the point is that we have a history—you and me, and me and Paul. And you and Paul, too, for that matter."

"Don't remind me," Jordan said. "Sorry. That was mean."

Dorrie let it go. "Anyway, we've all been hanging out for years . . . well, maybe not that long with you, but with everyone else . . . and even if we're going to grow apart, which I guess we will, we still need to see this through. That's what senior year is about. It's kind of a yearlong celebration before we go our separate ways."

"Yeah, more like a yearlong drinking binge."

"Oh, come on. The drinking hasn't even begun. Anyway, the real celebration will be at Beach Week. It's going to be so amazing. I'd say I wish we could fast-forward, but I also want to enjoy every minute of the rest of this year. I mean, I don't even mind getting up for school in the morning. I can't believe that the best years of our lives are about to come to an end."

"These are the best years of our lives? I hope not! I have to admit I'm kind of burned out on high school. I'm ready to be finished. I don't even especially want to go to Beach Week. I figure maybe I'll go, and maybe I won't."

"Don't start in on that again. We're going bathing suit shopping this weekend, and you're coming."

"It's kind of hard to think about bathing suits when it's snowing out. Do they even have bathing suits in the stores yet?"

"You're so cute, Jordan! Maybe not in *Nebraska*, but here they do. It's April! Plus, you can always buy bathing suits, any time of year. People go on holidays and stuff? You know?"

Jordan didn't reply. She was really sick of all the hick implications of being from the Midwest. People in Nebraska took vacations, too. She watched her friend climb out of the car.

Dorrie held up her hands in a playful, gleeful way, batting at the snow. She opened her mouth wide, to catch a flake. She was always so happy, Jordan thought. Of course it was true that she was also frequently under the influence, which could be related.

Jordan waved goodbye, and Dorrie waved back and blew a kiss, smiling hugely. Before pulling out of the driveway, Jordan checked her phone again. Three text messages from her mother, zero from Khalid. She was pretty sure this was a bad sign. Then again, she reminded herself, it was after 2:00 a.m. Maybe he was just asleep.

6

●　●　●　●　●

Idling at the traffic light, waiting to make a left turn onto the busy main road, Leah opened her window and imagined she'd just driven into some vortex where worlds collide. For a brief moment she mistook the sound of cars off in the distance, whooshing around the Beltway, for the churning of the sea. She thought of ears pressed to shells, oceans rumbling inside, of a Mediterranean seaside with lounge chairs and striped umbrellas. A man across the street was even circling his arms in the air, as if he were doing the breaststroke. Her husband's voice brought her back to reality. That was Charles waving crazily, trying to get her attention. He had just emerged from a bus.

"Leah! Wait up!" he shouted. She pulled to the side of the road and watched him wade through the snarl of vehicles. It was 7:00 p.m.; rush hour should be winding down, but here on Verona Boulevard it looked like a movie set for the sort of traffic jam that might signal the apocalypse.

"Where's your car?" Leah asked as he climbed into the passenger seat. She entertained the strange thought that although she'd been living with this man for nearly twenty years and had seen him in countless random situations—hunched over a drafting table, designing urban streetscapes; on any number of tennis courts, racquet poised mid-serve; and once she had even spied him pushing a vacuum cleaner—she had never actually seen him alight from a bus. Before answering, he put his computer bag on the floor of the Subaru and reached for the seat belt. "Wait," she warned. "I'm not actually going home. But I can turn around and drop you off, if you want." This seemed to her unnecessary—they were only a couple of blocks from the house. It was a pleasant evening, and he could walk.

"Jordan took my car this morning, remember? I took the Metro today. But I'm feeling a bit peaked, so I caught the bus home. I didn't really feel like walking a mile from the station, and I couldn't find a cab. So where are we going?" he asked jovially. She assumed the "we" was his attempt at a joke.

"We're going to a Beach Week meeting!" she said, trying to match his fake chipper tone.

"Hilarious."

"No, seriously. There's a meeting at the Linds' house. But don't worry, I don't expect you to go. I left you a voice mail. There's some cold chicken in the refrigerator, and a couple of salads in Tupperware containers in the middle drawer of the fridge—"

"Sorry, I had a bunch of meetings this afternoon, and I haven't had a chance to catch up with my messages. But what's the deal? Are you sneaking off to these meetings now? You weren't going to even mention it to me?"

"That's not it at all, Charles." She had pulled back into traffic and was in line again, waiting to make the left turn.

"Then what is it?" He sounded hurt, which was oddly touching. But it was also confusing: Did he *want* to go to a Beach Week meeting all of a sudden?

"I didn't want to have another fight about this. Obviously this isn't our best subject, and anyway, since I was only going for the hell of it, I figured why get you all upset again."

"But what's going on? Have you had any more discussions about this with Jordan? Is there something you're not telling me?"

"No, not at all. I mean really, it's completely pathetic, but since I don't have anything better to do, I figured why not go to the meeting? On the off chance that Jordan does go to Beach Week, why not be fully informed? That's all. I'm not saying she'll go, or won't go, or anything at all . . ." Leah couldn't believe they were having this conversation again, particularly since she'd been slinking off to the meeting precisely to avoid this exchange. Why was it that other people were able to live deep in lies—conducting years-long affairs or assuming new identities as spies—whereas she got caught instantly in whatever it was she was doing, even something as innocuous as going solo to a meeting? It was as if there were some cosmic security camera pointed right at her, ready to snap her picture walking off from the pharmacy with the wrong change.

Charles seemed suspicious, which was itself a little sweet; she'd come to suppose that he didn't particularly care what she was up to in her spare time, as long as her activities didn't appear on the credit card bill. "It seems like you're hiding something, or trying to cut me out of the loop . . ."

"No, Charles, truly I'm just going to a Beach Week meeting, and I didn't mention it only because I'm as exhausted by this subject as you are. I didn't bring it up, because I didn't want to have a fight about it again. And yet here we are anyway—"

"Well, we're not having a fight about Beach Week, I might point out. Now we're having a fight about you not telling me about the meeting."

"Oh, the irony," she said. "Does that mean you want to come?"

"*Want* is not the exact word I'd use, but as long as I'm already in the car . . ."

Leah had not previously heard of the Bacchus Maneuver. She leafed through the packet of materials Janet Glover had distributed to the few parents who had already arrived, and among them was this disturbing primer on alcohol poisoning.

"Friendly drinking games and celebrations can and sometimes do kill people," she was warned in a weird Gothic typeface that seemed designed to convey terror. By way of further visual aid was a poorly drawn man with hair so wiry it looked like it had been photoshopped from the end of a broom. He lay prone, his abdominal muscles bulged, his hands stretched above his head as though he were about to do a sit-up or a crunch. But nothing quite so salubrious was going on, because on the next page the man was rolled onto his side in the eponymous maneuver that was meant to prevent him from choking on his vomit. Leah felt a pang of shame, but she wasn't sure if her embarrassment had to do with the indelicacy of the act being depicted or with this twisted invocation of the Roman god. Wearily, she looked at her husband.

It was nearly 8:15. The meeting at the Linds' house was

meant to have begun forty-five minutes earlier, and Janet Glover had only just arrived, as had Martin Krazinski, looking natty in pastel again, this time in the form of a light blue shirt and yellow tie. Apparently there had been a bad accident along the main thoroughfare connecting north and south Verona, which had delayed this small contingent and presumably explained the absence of the rest of the group. Leah and Charles must have gotten tangled with the rerouted traffic, which explained their own slow, frustrating journey.

Once they arrived at the Linds', they'd been greeted at the door by a maid who informed them that neither of the hosts was going to be able to attend; one of them had a work emergency and the other a personal crisis. She didn't elaborate on what the latter might involve. The maid led them through a long hallway, the walls of which were adorned with an eclectic mirror collection that bounced the light around in blinding fragments, creating a disorienting entrance that seemed possibly deliberate in intent. Although it was not her primary motivation for attending, Leah had been curious to see the Linds' home, which had been recently featured in *Architectural Digest* with a six-page spread that compared it favorably to the Mediterranean villa upon which it was modeled, where the Linds had evidently spent their honeymoon. No one was sure what the Linds actually did to have amassed so much money. Something to do with soup, was the most detailed answer Leah had yet to hear.

The Linds' cockatoo seemed to be staring at Leah, its white feathers puffed imperiously as it balanced on its perch; she found the bird unnerving. Charles's gaze was fixed somewhere beyond the gleaming swimming pool outside the picture window. Perhaps he was focused on the ninth hole of the lush golf course adjacent to the Lind estate. Tiger Woods had once played here, and Leah couldn't help but wonder if this might have had something to do with Charles's otherwise inexplicable decision to accompany her this evening when she'd given him a clean pass.

The girls were also meant to attend this meeting, and Leah could hear them in the next room, talking and laughing against the backdrop of one of those cooking, or dieting, or fashion-designing reality shows. Jordan was not among them, or so Leah surmised from the absence of her voice and also from the fact that Charles's car wasn't parked out front. Leah sent her a text message reminding her of the meeting and of her earlier promise to appear.

At least Leah had had the good sense, this time, not to have offered to host. She decided not to avail herself of the opportunity to chill some expensive wine and set out platters of sushi and homemade baby quiche in an effort to erase doubts about the Adler family's solvency, demonstrating that they still occupied a house in which electricity flowed and that their cars had not been repossessed. Yes, they had bounced a check for the security deposit on that second Beach Week house. So what? Capitalism was in crisis. Banks were collapsing left and right. There was no shame in bouncing a check—it was practically in vogue. It made them one of the people, if not necessarily one of the people from Verona.

The request for that new check had caught her off guard, particularly as it had come in the midst of preparing for a family dinner involving labor-intensive shredded beef tacos, a meal her teenage daughter would forget to attend because she was preoccupied with a boyfriend named Khalid with whom she planned to run off to Tunisia to see some fish museum. Leah had simply grabbed the wrong checkbook all those weeks earlier. It wasn't that there were insufficient funds, but rather, the bank account back in Omaha had been closed for two years. These things happened! She had sent over another check, confirmed that it cleared the bank, and avoided troubling Charles with the matter. She still felt a little embarrassed about the incident, nonetheless. She was also uncertain about how to deal with the Moores, who had yet to pay her back for that first security deposit. She planned to remind them again this evening.

Leah had by now read the Bacchus Maneuver brochure three times and had moved on to the highlights of the "Twelfth-Grade Parent Peer Meeting: Surviving Beach Week" pamphlet when, at last, a few more members of the group arrived.

"Jesus, what a nightmare," said a father Leah couldn't immediately place. "That's the worst accident I've ever seen up close."

"What happened?" Leah asked.

Another unfamiliar mother stumbled through the door and shook her head, looking like she'd just come off a battlefield.

"It was horrific!" she said. "I could really use a drink." Her eyes scanned the room. "Are there any—"

"No," Leah said, parched herself, as well as a little smug about her own, superior hostessing skills.

Leah felt bad that she couldn't positively identify all the members of this small group, and she wondered if this reflected poorly on her memory retention or if at least a couple of these people hadn't shown up at the last meeting. It hardly mattered, as they were really just one amorphous Greek chorus of worry and contention, nine sets of bickering parents with whom she'd soon be done. She supposed this was not a particularly nice thought, but Beach Week was not bringing out the best in her.

"Right near the entrance to the Beltway, there's a car that's overturned, and two more cars slammed into it," said the mystery woman. "They closed the road, and there are a bunch of ambulances, a helicopter, news cameras . . ."

Now Millie and Arthur Moore walked through the door. "Did you see that body?" Millie asked. "It was like, on the complete other side of the road . . ."

Leah supposed it would be tacky to pounce on them for the check right away.

"I know! I saw that. But did you see . . . the leg?"

This question was met with a buzzy excitement. Evidently a few people had seen . . . the leg.

All this talk made Leah more concerned about Jordan. Where was she? That their daughter might have been somehow involved in this roadside carnage was too awful to even privately contemplate. She looked at Charles, wondering if he had the same thought, but he seemed to be engaged in animated conversation with Martin Krazinski about college basketball.

Leah checked her cell phone anxiously; still no reply from her daughter. She tapped another text with some difficulty. She was not very good with these tiny keys, and the whole methodology of this was foreign to her.

Where r u?

"Let's get started," Janet said. She waited a minute until everyone settled down. "I'm assuming the others are on their way. I don't know if we lost anyone to the other meeting, though."

"What other meeting?" asked Charles.

"The Alternative to Beach Week meeting," Janet replied. But she said this in a sort of dismissive way, not as though she was seriously suggesting there might be any crossover between these two sets of parents.

"There's an alternative?" he asked. Leah was a little embarrassed by the seriousness with which he posed the question, as if there were only two choices in this matter and you had to register as either pro or con. In truth she had shielded Charles from this knowledge. She didn't want him to understand that the opposition to Beach Week was so fierce that an actual splinter group had formed and had recently held its own anti–Beach Week meeting in the school auditorium. The anti–Beach Week manifesto apparently advocated that the children (as they were quaintly called) do something socially useful for the seven days in question, such as volunteer in inner-city schools or clean the towpath along the C&O canal or work in animal shelters. Someone had even proposed that the children spend the time learning to knit. A seven-day Mediterranean cruise with stops in Athens and Crete was also being organized by one of the history teachers as an educational option, although it was hard to imagine that was likely to produce less parental anxiety when it came to controlling teen behavior. As anyone who had ever watched *20/20* knew, bad things happened on Mediterranean holidays: children disappeared from their beds at night, people drowned, stray hookups occurred, and eventually, unwed mothers gave birth, abandoning their young on bathroom floors. It was as bad as Beach Week, and even more expensive.

Leah had heard from Janet that disparaging things were said at the anti–Beach Week meeting about the permissiveness and irresponsibility of the pro–Beach Week parents. She had been surprised to learn that there was this much divisiveness among a bunch of parents who were essentially like-minded on most major political and social issues. Although there were a handful of Republicans, mostly drawn from the small but elite Catholic community, you'd be hard-pressed to find anyone in Verona who could field dress a moose. Hybrid cars proliferated in public parking lots, plastic bags were on the verge of being outlawed by the city council, and smoking had recently been banned inside the city limits. Yet when it came to the subject of raising young adults, it was easy to find levels of discord and vitriol unrivaled even in the last presidential election.

Another reason why Leah had not mentioned the existence of the splinter group to Charles was that she did not want to have him point out that if you looked closely at the values of these other parents, the ones who were *not* sending their kids to Beach Week, they were more closely in sync with those of Charles and Leah Adler, and that in normal circumstances they might more naturally align, even if, in truth, the philosophical differences were so slight, in the great scheme of things, it was like splitting one of his already thinning hairs.

"Okay. Well, it's getting late," Janet said, "so regardless of the few who are missing, I think we should get started. Does anyone want to summon the girls?"

Leah volunteered and went into the next room to invite them in. Not for the first time in recent weeks she braced against a complicated wave of emotion that was grief, joy, pride, and envy as she took in the sight of the young women, Jordan conspicuously not among them. At this point Leah was beginning to bore even herself with her observations of these adorably clad teenagers, variously perfumed and bedecked with hoops and jangling bracelets, palms invariably clutching tiny electronic gadgets that beeped and vibrated and spontaneously burst into song. Oh, to be eighteen again. She would wear a miniskirt every day and communicate only in SMS!

The girls came into the living room and settled on the floor at the feet of the adults, who were mostly seated on pink silk furnishings. Four men had reassembled in a corner of the room and were looking at some golf trophies on the Linds' mantel. Charles was laughing and smiling, and she saw him slap Martin Krazinski on the back. Leah was unsure what to make of this.

"So . . . let's recap here," Janet said. "We have a lot to jam into this one meeting, since we've had to reschedule this darn thing so many times and now it's late. We have a lot of ground to cover. One, we want to review with the girls certain rules involving safety at the beach. We also want to talk about logistics—who is driving, who is chaperoning, who is bringing what in the way of supplies . . ."

"We took care of that already," said Dorrie.

"Oh, great. Excellent. I think, also, Alice wanted to say a few words . . ."

Leah hadn't noticed her arrive. She was standing in the corner, leaning against a Corinthian column that looked like the backdrop for a Victoria's Secret commercial. Leah's earlier speculation that Charles's willingness to attend this meeting had to do with the six degrees of separation from Tiger Woods was suddenly superseded by the wild card that was Alice Long. Although Leah refused to dignify this with too much thought, she had found her husband several times in the last few weeks asleep in front of the basement television in the middle of the night, and it had been tuned to TNT. Maybe he'd been watching *Law and Order* reruns, but maybe he'd been watching *The Winged Wife*, which she couldn't help but notice had been on a couple of hours earlier. It was a question of how long he'd been lying there prone on the couch in his T-shirt and boxers, two empty beer bottles and a contraband can of Pringles beside him on the floor. She wasn't about to start creeping downstairs to spy on her husband sneaking junk food into the house, but she could see how swiftly a person might descend into some emotionally messy place that involved stalking one's spouse as he watched television in his own home.

"Also, there are still a few matters we need to discuss about the house itself," Janet continued. "The Realtor called to say there's some problem with the upstairs plumbing, but it's being taken care of as we speak, so not to worry. And there was another unrelated issue with the owner, which—well some of you might be concerned, but you shouldn't be, really. I'll get to that in a second."

Charles stared at Leah and raised his eyebrows, which made it look as though his eyes were bulging; it was not his most attractive pose. Still, he looked less angry than amused, and she supposed this bonding over sports talk in the corner might have had a mellowing effect.

"Also," Janet continued, "I believe that Faye Andrews has brought her addendum for us to all sign. You know, the one that spells out our individual responsibility should anything unfortunate come to pass. Which of course it will not."

"Actually," said Faye, clearing her throat, "I'm afraid I've blown it. Should I confess that I completely forgot about the addendum? I've been unusually jammed up at work these last few weeks. I'm extremely sorry, but no worries, I'll do it this week and . . . how about if I just e-mail it to everyone. Then you can sign it and send it back to me. I mean I suppose it would be better to have one document with everyone's signatures, but—"

"Can't you draft an addendum explaining that the ten individually signed documents essentially stand as one binding agreement?" asked Arthur Moore. "That's what we did when we bought our house and Millie was out of town. I think she was in Miami for an Estate and Gift Tax Conference. We had to fax in her signature . . . didn't we, honey? And the lawyers had to draft something saying this was still binding even if it was all piecemeal."

"Yes, we can probably do something to that effect," Faye said.

"Okay, perfect. Thanks," said Janet. "Now, moving forward, I believe that Courtney Greene has volunteered to speak on behalf of the girls. Yes, Courtney?"

Courtney Greene smiled sweetly and stood up. She'd been seated on the floor, and when she rose and stretched the kinks out of her legs, one of her flip-flops flew off her foot and landed on Arthur Moore's lap. He picked it up and dangled it in front of him playfully before tossing it back to her. Something about this struck Leah as slightly inappropriate, but maybe she was just a little uptight, her antenna too finely tuned to the darker aspects of life.

"Okay," said Courtney, slipping the flip-flop back on her foot, looking a little unsettled. She reached into her back pocket and unfolded a piece of paper and began to read from the pledge the girls had signed a few days earlier. Leah was beginning to panic, unable to concentrate on what Courtney was saying. Where *was* Jordan? Had she struggled through these hellish couple of years only to get into a car crash on her way to north Verona for this stupid Beach Week meeting, which would weigh on Leah guiltily for the rest of her days? No, no—it was much more likely she'd just forgotten. Probably she was with Khalid again. Thank God for Khalid—she was holed up, probably having unprotected sex with a man who might well bear an innate hatred for her people, and her absence had nothing at all to do with the overturned vehicles and . . . the leg.

Surely that's all that was going on, although what did Leah really know about the lives of her husband and daughter anymore? Everyone seemed to float about all night, like balloons untethered. With bittersweet regret she remembered that she'd once been the anchor of this nocturnal theater, rocking in a chair, a baby at her breast. And there'd been years of nights when Charles would nudge her awake as he wrapped her in his arms for warmth, or just for comfort; now she couldn't recall the last time that had happened. These days she could sleep twelve hours straight if she so desired; she could snore or sweat or scream mid-nightmare, and it was unlikely anyone would notice.

She wondered what would become of them once Jordan left home, whether they could find a way to reconnect. Like everything else going on in their lives, this, too felt pathetically clichéd, but really, was there some original way forward? That this was normal midlife stuff didn't make it any less painful. People grew apart, and she supposed that people might grow apart even more than she and Charles had if you threw in a move, a concussion, money problems, and a mother-in-law who was day by day becoming increasingly batty. They'd been fielding stressful calls from the nursing home about her behavior these last few weeks. Having just watched Jordan apply to college, Florence had weirdly gotten it into her head that she was in high school herself and it was time to take the SAT. Twice she'd summoned the nurses, raving that she was late for the test and she couldn't find her number 2 pencils. Leah and Charles had had to take her from the nursing home and have her stay in their guest room until the doctors successfully adjusted her medication. They'd talked to experts about this in an effort to understand her obsession. Florence hadn't gone to college herself, and the doctors' best guess was that this was her way of manifesting unrealized dreams. Either that or she was simply looping back, trying to lock into a happier moment in her life. Maybe this wasn't so strange. Leah supposed that her mind, too, wandered idly to random nesting places. Lately she found herself flashing back unexpectedly to the first apartment she and Charles had rented when he was in graduate school and she had just begun student teaching. It was a time of relative insignificance in the Leah/Charles narrative, just an interim period post-college and pre-career when they'd lived in a shabby apartment in a shabby part of town, so broke that they paid their rent out of cash they'd set aside in the sock drawer each month. But they'd had big plans, and she'd been as much of a dreamer as Charles back then. Maybe this seemed romantic now simply because it was pre-disillusionment. Twenty years later they had a money market account, a mortgage, a child, and not only were they still broke, they'd also accumulated a whole lot of debt.

On top of all this was a looming empty nest. In all fairness, Leah knew she'd have to put her degeneration into a mildly depressed housewife on the list of things contributing to choppy midlife conditions; her unhappiness had become so pronounced it had taken on a life of its own, like an angry little pet she kept in her pocket that sometimes peeked out and bit Charles on the wrist.

Still, he'd changed, too, although it was hard for her to map his metamorphosis from so close up. She was tempted at times to actually sit down at his drafting table, pick up one of his fancy mechanical pencils, and plot his transformation from a shaggy, happy guy with a lot of goofy big ideas to this somber person in a suit and tie who wore a mask of worry and concern. The smile on his face as he'd joked in the corner just now with Martin Krazinski was the lightest she'd seen him in months.

SUSAN COLL

Then again, it was entirely possible they had just hit one of those proverbial rough patches that Charles was always waxing eloquent about. She was frequently overthinking things with regard to Jordan, too. On a couple of recent occasions when Leah had worked herself into a middle-of-the-night frenzy, sure that her daughter was still out on slick roads or even off with this new, mysterious boyfriend, she'd gone into Jordan's room and found her asleep, snuggled in bed with a stuffed animal. But now it was after 8:00 p.m. and Leah was beginning to feel justified in her concern, especially in light of this horrific accident that everyone was still thrumming about. She leaned over and whispered into Charles's ear.

Charles flipped open his cell phone and handed it to Leah, showing her a text message:

At library. B there soon. xo.

Leah absorbed this slowly, confusingly. So Jordan had chosen to convey this information to her father, and not to her mother, who had sent her two queries. Fair enough. She had read about this sort of thing, it was normal development stuff, girls shunning their mothers, preferring their fathers— probably just some sort of textbook reverse oedipal thing. She should be grateful that she was experiencing this slight for the first time. Or was she? Who knew? Taking personal rejection out of the equation, there was still the absurd assertion itself. At the library? In the last semester of senior year when she was already into college? *Please!* This sounded like a lie, although she couldn't imagine what Jordan might actually be up to that would necessitate a lie, given that they were already aware of the existence of Khalid.

Courtney read from the list of things the Beach Week girls had promised to do, which included having a buddy system, not having parties, not allowing boys to spend the night, not drinking or otherwise using controlled substances, taking digital pictures of the rental house when they first arrived, checking out the town ordinances in Chelsea Beach, knowing the local emergency numbers, using sunscreen, and watching for the warning flags and swimming conditions posted on beaches near lifeguard stands.

There was a burst of applause when Courtney finished reading, as if she'd just performed at a piano recital. This seemed to Leah a bit unrealistic. She was not alone in this thought.

"This is all fine and well in principle," said Alice Long, "but I don't believe it for a minute."

"No, really," said a sweet-looking girl whom Leah had not previously seen. She joked that they had pricked their fingers and smeared some blood onto the document as a symbol of their sincerity.

Alice laughed skeptically. It pained Leah to find herself in agreement with this woman. She would have personally felt more comfortable if the document had said something about always using condoms, or included the promise of no "binge drinking" or keeping the drinking under control, having a designated driver—anything to acknowledge that bad things were likely to happen, but the girls were at least on top of the situation. She couldn't believe that *she*, Leah Adler (a potential closet Alternative to Beach Week splinter group member), was entertaining these thoughts.

"We're serious," said the girl, whom someone had just referred to as Rene. "We all met yesterday at Starbucks and sat for more than an hour and hammered this out." She looked incredibly nice, and Leah wondered why Jordan didn't hang out more with this girl.

"We understand what a privilege this is, and we take it really seriously," Rene said. "We just want to go to the beach and have a good time and be together with our best girlfriends and have one last wonderful bonding experience before everyone goes separate ways. We're going to bring board games and have a big blowout game of Monopoly!"

A sound of something like an angry puff issued from the fabulously red lips that belonged to Alice Long. (Although Leah was trying to stop thinking like this, she couldn't help but recall the article she had recently read about lipstick and lead poisoning.)

"Maybe we should take a quick poll of the girls," Janet suggested, trying to be diplomatic. "Let's caucus, make sure everyone is in agreement about proper Beach Week behavior. Is everyone here?"

"Jordan isn't here," Dorrie volunteered.

This was more than a little humiliating. Leah wasn't just the writer of bad checks, she was the mother of an AWOL child. Evidently the *only* AWOL child.

"Does anyone know where she is?" Janet asked. "Was she planning to come?"

Leah was on the verge of explaining that her daughter was, however improbably, at the library, but Dorrie spoke up first. "I just had a text from her a few minutes ago. She's on her way."

"Yes, that's right," said Leah, bluffing. "She'll be here any second." Did she just hear Dorrie mutter something under her breath? Did she say something about her daughter and Khalid? Dorrie was a few feet away and Leah couldn't be sure, but it almost sounded as if Dorrie had said she was out *stalking* Khalid. Surely Leah had just misheard.

"Okay, look, this isn't our last meeting anyway," said Janet. "We'll have another conversation about this before the girls go—a real heart-to-heart about the consequences of misbehavior, which I think can't be overemphasized, and getting the girls to have signed this document is a good, meaningful start. There's also a meeting next week at the school with a couple of representatives from the Chelsea Beach Police Department that you should consider attending with your daughters. But for now, we have one more thing that we really ought to discuss before we call it a night . . .

"There's a little something that's come up concerning the house. I don't think it's a hugely big deal or anything, but as long as I'm the informal coordinator of this, I feel obliged to provide full disclosure. As some of you know, the house was owned by Clara Miller—the woman who wrote *Peeper*? And . . . this is really silly and even embarrassing and probably, Lord knows, politically incorrect to even talk about, since all the charges were dropped . . ."

Now Charles gave Leah a look that said *what the hell*, and Leah shrugged her shoulders as if it were no big deal, whatever it was, even though she was thinking the same thing.

"Well, see, we thought it was *her* house. Which it was. Not that it should matter, but since Craig Lind has a friend who knows her sister, we felt like there was at least this personal connection. But the place now belongs to her husband. And he had a little, um, incident that some of you might have read about in the papers—"

"Oh my God," shrieked Amy Estrada's mother. "Didn't he do something really creepy, like—oh, I wish I could remember. Did he rape someone?"

"No," Janet said. "He didn't rape anyone. It's not clear that he ever did anything at all—the only thing we know for sure is that he had some sort of accident. His wife wrote a book about a Peeping Tom, and now everyone assumes it's him—the poor guy. I'd say he should get himself a lawyer, except that it's fiction, so I guess she can get away with it."

"I read the book, too," said Millie Moore. "And I saw her on the *Today* show. She went out of her way to say it was fiction."

"That's true. I read the book and also saw her on YouTube," said Courtney Greene, "and she said it was fiction. She said about ten times that that Jim guy was not really her husband."

"You read that *book*?" said her mother. It wasn't clear from her inflection whether she was surprised that her daughter had read *a* book or just this particular book.

Martin Krazinski cut in before Courtney could reply. "Of course she said it was fiction. They packaged it that way for a reason, and I'm sure her lawyers told her to say that. I'll bet they went through the whole book changing every detail that could possibly get her sued. I know. I handle a bit of libel law, even though my specialty is bankruptcy."

"Bankruptcy? Good for you—you must be billing a lot of hours just now," Mr. Davidson said.

"Amazing. I billed eighty hours just this week!"

"Okay, let's stay focused," said Janet. "The thing to keep in mind is that the lessor won't even be on the premises. Plus, whatever charges were filed, and I'm not at all clear what those were, they were dropped, and that's all that matters in the eyes of the law. We should cut him some slack. I mean, just listen to *us*! We're a group of well-informed, highly educated people, and here we are, having this awful, gossipy conversation.

Besides, we have no legal grounds upon which to tear up the lease, so we'd lose our deposit, and it's too late to find another house."

"That reminds me," said Millie Moore. "Did we ever get our deposit back on the first house?"

What nerve! Leah thought. Maybe she should point out right now, in front of everyone, that Millie Moore had never paid her back. It was tempting.

"No, but the original Realtor assured me he'd take care of returning the deposit this week," said Janet. "Look, it's getting late. I had hoped to go through these handouts together, to read some of this aloud in front of the girls, but in the interest of moving this along, why don't you be sure to read the Parent Peer Meeting tips with your daughters. Pay particular attention to the advice as it pertains to renting a house. Our girls are inexperienced in this area and need to be reminded of things like taking out the trash or knowing where to locate the fire extinguishers. You should note that three groups of Verona High School students were evicted last year for not obeying some of the specifications in the lease. One group had too many kids in the house, another group brought a dog, I think another had some sort of illegal bonfire in the backyard. There was also an incident in which a few of the kids wound up in jail because they had alcohol in the house—"

"This just gets better and better," said Alice Long, interrupting. "Just to recap: we are sending our daughters, largely unchaperoned, unless you want to call a parent planted in a house seven miles away a chaperone, which of course I don't, but you know that already . . . to a beach house owned by some sort of pervert, to engage in activities that may land them in jail, and here they are comically pledging to behave like saints—"

"Saints in bikinis!" one of the girls—Leah couldn't see which one—blurted out, eliciting giggles.

Alice ignored this. "Honestly, am I the only one here who thinks there is something wrong with this picture?"

Her daughter, Cherie, sat expressionless, and Leah wondered if she went into some sort of protective mental deep freeze when her mother transformed into her fierce, superhero persona.

Leah thought there was something wrong with this picture, and she suspected that probably everyone else in the room did, too, but as usual, Alice's tone was so ugly, her accusations so offensive that she had the unintended effect of causing everyone to embrace the opposite position, to raise their hands and say yes, we think it's just fine to send our daughters to the beach to stay in the house of a possible Peeping Tom who was, at least, determined by group consensus not to be a rapist.

Janet waited a beat to see if anyone wanted to follow up with Alice, but the room was silent. "So let's see. The girls leave in just a few weeks. I say let's have one more meeting right before they go. On, say, June 1."

"I can't make it then. It's our anniversary, and we'll be in Venice," said Amy Estrada's father.

"Yeah, problem on our end—I've got a colonoscopy that day," said Courtney Greene's mother.

"Okay," said Janet, still cheerful despite this injection of too much personal information. "I'll send out an e-mail and we'll figure this out. "Oh, wait, that reminds me. There was one other thing. Let me just run through this chaperone list again. We've had a couple of changes. Monday, Tuesday, and Wednesday we have Millie Moore and Julia Lind. Thursday and Friday we have Laura Cooper and Alice Long. It turns out that the first two nights, Saturday and Sunday, Martin Krazinski needs to be at the house, right, Martin? So we don't need whoever was going to chaperone. But what we do need is backup, and probably a dad would be best, just so . . . well you know. In case Martin is there, but in case he's not . . ." She seemed to be struggling to convey the idea that it would be best to avoid the appearance of any male/female impropriety in the chaperoning arrangements.

Krazinski cut in to explain. "It's possible that I might have to cancel at the last minute or leave suddenly. I may have to pop over to Europe to take a deposition, but I won't know until I get a call from my client."

"Right," Janet continued, "so it would be good if we could get a dad involved . . ."

Leah could not believe this. She had signed up for those first two nights, and although it was completely ridiculous, she felt as if she might start to cry. She had gone bathing suit shopping already, and had taken the radical step of buying a two-piece.

In the midst of this, Jordan had quietly slipped into the room and inserted herself on the floor between two Courtneys. She seemed a little subdued. Leah wondered if she'd been crying. It looked like her mascara had run, and Leah wasn't sure which was more upsetting—that her daughter had begun to wear makeup or that something was wrong.

"Great timing, Jordan," said Rene loudly. "The meeting is just ending!"

"Don't worry, sweetie," Janet said. "Dorrie can fill you in. Oh, great . . . Arthur Moore is volunteering. Excellent. Okay, it's really late. I'll send out another e-mail soon with updates. Hey, everyone, don't forget your handouts. Be sure you've got both the minutes from the Parent Peer Meeting *and* the Bacchus Maneuver brochures!"

Alice Long held her papers aloft and waved them ominously, like the town crier warning of plague. "Now we're handing out primers on alcohol poisoning? Truly, this is the most irresponsible roomful of parents I've ever seen!"

Leah stared at this woman, at her own daughter, and at the entire group, confused. Was this parenting at its worst or at its best? Had her parents sat around agonizing like this about her own high school antics? No, almost certainly not. Maybe the stakes were higher these days, the dangers more extreme. Or maybe the parents were just crazier. Either way, she felt just about at her limit with this Beach Week enterprise. She entertained the delinquent fantasy of one-upping Alice Long on the drama front, setting fire to the Bacchus Maneuver brochures and the "Twelfth-Grade Parent Peer Meeting: Surviving Beach Week" pamphlets, then stepping back and basking in the heat of a massive, cathartic Beach Week conflagration.

7

• • • • •

This stripped-down life had its pleasures, but it was the prospect of seeing Oliver that kept Noah going, and he bragged to every customer who stopped by the taffy stand that week that his son was coming to visit. A couple of them politely asked to see his picture, which Noah eagerly produced. He had a virtual scrapbook going on in his wallet, as well as a couple of photo albums that he kept in the cabinet in the back office. He'd also downloaded an Oliver slide show onto the computer at work, which served as a screen saver, but Maury, his boss, switched it back to pictures of candy.

The customers always said nice things: that Oliver was cute, or that he had a sweet face, which he did, with that shaggy strawberry hair and all those freckles he'd inherited from Clara's side of the family. Or they'd say that Noah was a lucky dad. One woman started crying and said that Oliver looked like her son, who'd been killed in Iraq, and Noah wasn't sure what he was supposed to say or do; he thought maybe he ought to reach for her hand or hug her, but that seemed awkward with the wooden counter between them, so he just stood there until she found some tissues in her bag and blew her nose and walked away.

A couple of people remarked that Oliver looked a bit like his dad, which was true. They had the same mouth and eyes, the same lanky build, although you couldn't really tell from these pictures, which were mostly head shots—those formal, stilted-looking school portraits they took every year in the school cafeteria. Clara must have splurged and purchased the deluxe package this time, because she'd sent him a couple of eight-by-tens and five-by-sevens along with three sheets of wallet-size. Noah wasn't sure what he was supposed to do with these, but he figured it was better to put them in frames than to just shove them in drawers, and they were all on display in the living room of his house.

The weekend finally arrived, and Oliver was coming at noon for a picnic. This was Clara's idea, of course. Personally, Noah thought picnics were generally pretty stupid things. His basic philosophy on the subject was, if you wanted to eat, just go into the kitchen and eat. And if you were stuck outdoors for some reason and you were hungry, just pull the sandwich out of the backpack and chew. He didn't see the point of spreading a cloth on the ground and setting it up all nice like you were dining in a fine restaurant, when really all you were going to do by setting food on the ground was attract a bunch of ants.

But the first event of this day involved a visit with Mitch Mingus, who was coming by that morning to take some pictures. The people who were renting the house had asked for photos, and Mitch had even had a few more inquiries, so he'd decided to post the house on the company's website to see what other business they might drum up. Jill had come over first to help Noah tidy up. She was a bit of a taskmaster, and per her instructions, Noah had been shoving some dirty place mats into the mahogany buffet when he noticed the tablecloth. It was yellow, the same exact shade of yellow as the dress Mrs. Bergstrom had been changing out of, and it took him right back to two years earlier, when he lay on a stretcher, staring at the inside of what once was his leg but had been turned into a mangle of smashed bone and exposed muscle and other anatomical stuff a person was never meant to see. The fall had landed him on an open pair of garden shears.

He remembered that he hadn't been entertaining very profound thoughts, even though for all he knew, it might have been the end, given that in addition to his leg, blood was oozing from his head. Instead of thinking about death or God or the money he'd been setting aside for Oliver's tuition someday, he'd been considering what he'd seen at the Bergstrom's just before he fell, and what he planned to record in his notebook:

1. The quilt in the master bedroom had geometric patterns that Noah personally found anxiety-producing, and he wondered if this contributed to what appeared to be insomnia on the part of both Professor and Mrs. Bergstrom.
2. Mrs. Bergstrom spent a lot of time on her computer.

There'd been something else he'd meant to record, some observation having to do with the professor's two different cell phones and Noah's concern about whether they shared the same charger, but he couldn't focus; the pain had landed him in a place he hadn't previously known existed, some netherworld that transcended language and thought, where everything was shrouded in a distinctive shade of mustard yellow. A doctor later told him he'd been hallucinating, but Noah wasn't convinced: the color still appeared at random interludes, a harbinger of what, he wasn't quite sure.

Like here he was, two years later, staring at a tablecloth that happened to be the same exact color as pain. And seriously, what were the odds of this? Probably he could come up with the answer if he worked at it, if he sat down with a piece of paper and a pencil and a calculator, but maybe not, because one thing he didn't know was whether there was an infinite number of colors in the world, how much you could add a bit of white to yellow and keep changing the tint. Also, there was the question of whether there was any quality control in the naming of colors: was it permissible to have two yellows that were exactly the same but with different names, like, say, lemon and limon? He had recently tried to come up with a formula to determine this, to no avail. Then he'd found a graphing program on the computer at work and tried to plot the yellow with predetermined gradients. Also inconclusive.

"Noah, are you okay?" Jill asked.

He knew she was there to be helpful, but it felt a little too familiar and not in a great way. For one thing, she told him that he should probably put some of the pictures of Oliver away, at least for the purposes of turning the place into a rental. She also told him that he was supposed to take the sheets of wallet-size and cut them up, literally put them in his wallet or hand them out to friends, not put all twelve pictures into one eight-by-twelve frame. But he liked it this way—so many Olivers! On top of that, she wouldn't stop going on about the damn rug. But what was the point of getting a new rug if these Beach Week kids were going to spill beer on it, and probably worse?

"Yeah, I'm fine," he said. "Just wondering, do you think this would make a good picnic blanket?" he asked, holding up the yellow tablecloth.

"Definitely. It's perfect," she said.

"I don't know. It seems too nice."

"Not so nice anymore," she said, coming closer and pointing out a series of stains near the center of the cloth. "They look a little like the Hawaiian Islands, don't you think?"

He didn't know what she was talking about. It looked like one big, amorphous stain to him.

"Red wine," she said. Then she put the cloth to her nose and sniffed. "Mouton Rothschild, 1945."

"What?"

"That's a joke, Noah. Yes, the cloth is fine. Perfect for a picnic."

"Yeah, I get it. Obviously it's a joke. It's just not very funny. I'm not a moron, you know."

People seemed to speak down to him lately, and he wondered if this was what happened when you worked a minimum-wage job. He could imagine his own father inserting quotation marks around the words *nontraditional profession* in describing his son's current state of employment, although it wasn't like Miller senior had made it to the top echelons of the professional world.

Of course it was possible that Noah was making false assumptions about Jill. It was his experience that you sometimes drew the wrong conclusions about people when you met them backwards, like when you studied them through the window before first saying hello. A person presumably had her different selves, and it could get confusing if you encountered her the wrong way first, like if you saw her yelling at one of her kids or walking around in the morning with her hair askew before she'd run a brush through it or put on some makeup.

Also, it could all just be in his head: Noah remembered one neurologist's suggestion that he was "presenting occasional flashes of paranoia," and although he didn't really believe this was true, he forced himself to consider the possibility sometimes.

At his last appointment more than a year earlier, the neurologist had spoken as if Noah weren't even in the room. "This is a difficult business, a brain injury of this sort," the doctor had said to Noah's soon-to-be-ex-wife while he dangled his legs from the examining table. There had been a poster on the wall of a cow jumping over a moon, which he supposed was meant to be soothing, or maybe it had just been sitting in the doctor's basement at home and he'd decided to bring it to work and hang it over the plastic pull-apart model of a brain that was sitting on the counter. The brain hadn't been put back together quite right, and the top of the skull looked like it might be on backward.

"Noah, do you remember climbing that tree? Do you recall what you were thinking?"

Of course he did. He was trying to prevent a murder and write up a report. He didn't say this, however. Some things were better kept to oneself, and he got the feeling that all the people he'd seen a few minutes earlier sitting in the waiting room reading their expired newsweeklies understood this, particularly the young girl who'd been clutching her folder full of brain scans. He'd seen her here twice, and he'd been here only two times. What were the odds of *this*, what with all the patients in the practice and the number of available appointments on any given day?

"I'm going to be honest with you," the doctor had said. "We can pretend that we know all the answers, and some doctors will lead you to believe that they do, but in truth even the most sophisticated imaging doesn't always pick up tears in the brain. And then, in this case, it seems safe to assume there were some problems before the incident, some undiagnosed pre-existing conditions. I think whatever was already underlying his actions will make it even harder to predict how this will ultimately manifest. It's more like a pu-pu platter—you can get any of the following combinations: paranoia, short-term memory loss, confusion, headaches, irritability, fatigue, sometimes even violence and rage—the list goes on and on. And then, of course, each one of those will have variations. It's never exactly the same. It depends on who's in the kitchen that night, if you follow."

Noah didn't really follow. This was one of the best neurologists in the region? Couldn't he at least find a better metaphor? It did make Noah pine for a pu-pu platter, though—he hadn't had one since he was a kid, and he wondered if Chinese restaurants even served those anymore.

"Holy Mother of God!" Jill shouted. She was standing in the corner with a piece of the rug pulled back and a look of horror on her face, as if she had just discovered a dead body. Or technically he should say *another* dead body, since she was the one who had found his former mother-in-law decomposing on the couch. He walked over to the corner where Jill was standing, and he had to admit the sight was pretty vile, with all these white wormlike things wriggling on the underside.

"What are those?"

"I'm guessing moth larvae? I don't know, I've never seen anything quite this gross," Jill said.

The existence of moth larvae in the world, never mind in his living room, was news to him. Unfortunately, this discovery just gave Jill license to go on again about the need to replace the carpeting, a line of conversation that was quickly getting old.

"Let's get back to reality here—you'll want to get an exterminator in before you put the new carpet down. I'd suggest you avoid wool this time."

It took a lot of self-restraint to not snap at her. It wasn't as if *he* had chosen wool the first time around or was in any way responsible for the horrid state of this wall-to-wall carpet. He was little more than a squatter in this place, albeit one who had inherited not just an apparent infestation of bugs but all the personal mementos of two dead people who had barely even tolerated his presence during his short summer visits back when he was family. The joke was on them, as now he was the keeper of everything in their drawers, from the fancy table-cloths to the place mats with their ketchup stains, to the old lady's collection of stockings and industrial-looking brassieres.

"Are these things going to turn into moths, do you think, or is this some kind of science fiction larvae-only creature?" he asked.

"I have no idea. I mean, I guess moths. But I really don't know if this is some normal cyclical thing going on here or if it's a new situation."

Whatever the explanation, he supposed this meant she had just scored a point in the ongoing argument about the rug. Nevertheless, they tamped the carpet back down when the doorbell rang, coconspirators.

Mitch Mingus didn't look too good. He was winded, even though his car was parked in the driveway, so he obviously hadn't walked very far. At first it seemed like his speech was slurred, too, but then Noah realized it was just that he was wrapping his words around a thick wad of gum. He had in one hand a ridiculous orange flag with a smiling unicorn that he said he was going to mount on the front of the house before he took his pictures, to make things look more cheerful. If Noah didn't object, he was going to put some flowers in the pots out front as well.

"That'll take care of the outside," he said, "but you've absolutely got to clean up in here."

"That's what we're doing right now," Noah said.

Mitch stuck his nose in the air like a retriever. "There's a bad smell in here. Are you aware of that?"

His face looked a little lopsided, and Noah was just noticing that the jowl on the right side was sort of drooping, as if he had some condition.

"I need to take a look around," Mitch said.

"I'm still in the middle of straightening up," Noah said, doing a quick mental inventory of the state of things upstairs. He couldn't picture it exactly, but he knew it wasn't good.

Mitch looked at Jill imploringly, which was kind of insulting.

"Anyway, one thing I don't get is, if it's just a bunch of kids staying here, what does it matter how the place looks? They're coming for the beach, not the house."

"That's not entirely true, Noah," Jill said. "When people are on vacation, they want a nice place to come home to. I mean, even if it's a bunch of kids, they at least want to be able to lie on the couch and watch television without worrying about moths."

Or dead bodies, Noah thought. Never mind the fact that there was no television reception, as he'd never bothered to call the cable company.

"Moths?" Mitch asked.

"Do you think we ought to charge a little more?" Noah asked. "I was talking to Maury, my boss at work, and he'd heard some Beach Week rentals were going for a few hundred more a week than this one. Like, what if you were going to rent out Jill's place, next door?"

"You mean that new house, over there?"

"Yeah," Noah said, nodding toward The Bank.

"Are you thinking of renting that out?"

It was Jill's year-round home, and it wasn't like she needed the cash, but she shrugged her shoulders, probably to be polite.

"Brand-new house, swimming pool . . . I'd say we could ask over six grand for that."

"Whoa. Hard not to take that personally. You're basically saying this house is one-fourth as habitable. Or is it one-fifth? Can you tell me those numbers again? Do you have a calculator?"

Mitch shook his head no, but Noah didn't believe him. What Realtor worth his salt would be walking around without a calculator? "I think it's one-fifth," Mitch confirmed.

But Noah wasn't sure, and this was the most troubling thing of all. He couldn't do the most basic math anymore, on top of which he was losing faith in this man, and in this entire venture.

"Would you mind if I snapped a few pictures of your house?" Mitch asked Jill.

"What for? I'm not looking to rent."

"Just 'cause it's a beauty. Just for my own purposes," he said. "I'm thinking of building a new home myself, and I love what you've done, the way it's sort of Victorian but with those modern flourishes. Very unusual."

"Thanks," Jill said, beaming, as if Mitch had just told her she had a nice smile.

Mitch walked out on the porch and stared at The Bank.

"Remind me when this was built," he said to Jill.

"We broke ground on it about seven years ago. It took about eighteen months to complete."

"And who did your blowfish? It's fabulous."

"Do you like it? We had it commissioned specially by an artist on Nantucket . . ."

Noah couldn't believe this. "Don't you want to take your pictures of my place?" he asked Mitch. What was the point of all this cleaning up if he was already finished? And it seemed he was.

"Nah, don't worry about it," said Mitch. "We've already got the leases anyway."

It never seemed to end, this stuff going on around him that made no sense. Noah went back into the living room, folded up his yellow cloth, and waited for Oliver to arrive.

When he'd asked his son on the phone the previous day what he wanted to do during their three-hour visit, Oliver said he wanted to have a picnic. Noah had trouble believing this was true, but now here they were on the beach, a rather enormous basket in tow, and it appeared that they were, indeed, about to have a picnic. They spread the tablecloth on the ground with some difficulty as the wind was whipping hard, and Noah felt a wave of panic with all that yellow rippling up off the ground beneath him like it was a living thing. He tried to steady himself by locking into Oliver, but even his son was rippling, the way he was growing so fast, a couple of inches taller than the last time Noah had seen him, and his hair wavier and longer than in the pictures.

"How about we go to the boardwalk?" Noah tried. This picnic suddenly seemed like a very bad idea, and he could feel his heart begin to race. "There's mini golf, bumper cars, video games, and then I can take you to the place where I work, show you how they make the taffy . . ."

Oliver looked over in the direction of his babysitter, who was planted on a bench with a book. Mrs. Zulfikarpasic was a grim-faced Bosnian woman of indeterminate age who now lived with Clara, helping with the kids. Clara apparently didn't want to leave Oliver with his father unsupervised, but she didn't want to come herself, so she sent the sitter to sit. They called her Auntie, which was kind of a relief to Noah, since he had trouble with the name even though he understood it wasn't really that complicated. Maybe it was just the way it looked on the page, the drastic letter Z followed by all those consonants, that seemed intimidating.

Auntie didn't look up from her book, so Oliver had to come up with an answer on his own. "We did that last time," he said.

"I guess maybe we did. But here we are at the beach. We should do something . . . beachy. Like maybe let's go for a swim. I can borrow some boogie boards from my neighbor's kids."

"Mom said the water's too rough today to swim. Plus she said it's still too cold."

Noah supposed this was true. The water didn't really warm up until June, from what he'd heard. Also, it seemed like there might be a storm on the way.

"Why are we just sitting here when we can go up to the boardwalk? They've got good food there. Fish-and-chips, Slurpees, pizza . . ."

"Mom says we should have a picnic, and that if you asked, I should say it would be a waste to not eat all this good food. She said that everyone loves a picnic, and she wished she could come, too, but she can't because she's got to do some shopping at the outlets."

His kid was reading from a script. "So she's actually here, at the beach?"

"Well, not all the way here at the beach. We dropped her off at the stores up the road, near where you took me to the bumper cars last time. Mom said no bumper cars today. She wanted us to have a picnic, and maybe take a walk or fly a kite or do stuff like that. But she thought we should stay here, and she didn't want Auntie to feel left out, like last time when we lost her on the boardwalk."

Noah wondered if there was something wrong with his son. Did he genuinely not want to do anything fun? Clara was going to make the poor kid crazy. She'd not only orchestrated the entire visit down to what they swallowed, but she'd tagged along to keep an eye on the woman who was keeping an eye on the kid. Not that Noah blamed her for that last part; he liked to keep an eye on things himself. On top of which, Auntie gave him the creeps, and maybe Clara felt the same way about her. There was something vaguely unsettling about the way she sat there silently, pretending to read a fat book about the Federal Reserve. She had brought the same book with her on the last three visits, and he found it hard to believe she was really that engaged. Sometimes he asked her what page she was on, to try to throw her off, to see if she was really reading or holding the book in front of her as a ruse, but she always just lifted her eyes and stared at Noah without ever answering the question.

They began to unload the basket. A bottle of juice with some plastic cups, cut-up fruit, a bag of chips, sandwiches wrapped in foil. There was more, too—a second layer, another compartment beneath the first. This was quite the picnic basket. Really it was more of a PICNIC BASKET, what with all its secret corners, its various nooks and crannies. If you caught it from a certain angle, it looked a little bit like a boat. A boat on a sea of yellow, Clara might say, making it sound more interesting than it really was. He willed himself to stop thinking about the yellow. This was part of a pattern of behavior the doctor said he was supposed to be trying to break, although in truth he wasn't trying very hard, since it was strangely comforting to drift inside this familiar place. The accident at least gave him some purpose, although he got that *accident* was a euphemism, as it wasn't like it had just happened out of the blue.

A fierce gust of wind sent Oliver's baseball cap, as well as some of the paper napkins, airborne. It wasn't only that it was too windy for a picnic, it seemed like it might start to rain. Was it too early for hurricane season? Noah hadn't been here long enough to learn the rhythms of the Atlantic.

Oliver ran after his cap, which brought Auntie to her feet. Clara had probably told her the apocryphal tale about how once, many years ago, Noah had left Oliver on the changing table when he'd gone to find a diaper, and the baby had managed to wriggle off. Clara had gone on and on about how stupid Noah was, that he should have realized there'd be diapers right near the changing table, on the shelf directly beneath in fact. That there was no harm done seemed to be beside the point.

Once Oliver returned, Noah began to rummage again through the enormous basket, this time looking for more napkins. It had special slots for the cutlery and separate compartments for all the other picnic accoutrements like a corkscrew and wineglasses.

"Pretty nice basket."

"Yeah, it was a birthday present for Mom."

"Nice of her to let you borrow it for the day, eh?"

Oliver nodded.

"Was it from him?"

Yes again, but this time he looked apprehensive. Noah was hoping he'd slip and say something, maybe give him a little glimpse of what life was like with the guy—he couldn't remember his name, but the man who was his wife's new husband. Okay, maybe he could remember and just didn't want to.

"So let's see what's what here," Noah said.

"I think there's a plastic container for me. And a juice box."

"Yes, sir . . . here you go. What is this stuff, anyway?"

"It's some noodles, from dinner last night."

"She's feeding you leftovers?"

"It's really good. Do you want to taste?"

"What, are you a vegan now?"

"A what?"

"You need meat! Protein! You need to grow! What did she pack for me? Some real food, I hope."

"I think there's a sandwich. She was trying to remember if you liked turkey or roast beef."

"Your mom can't remember that I don't eat roast beef?"

"I don't know. Maybe that's not what she said."

Noah pulled out a sandwich and began to unwrap the foil. It was roast beef. "Goddamn it!" he yelled, loud enough that Auntie looked up. "She made me fucking roast beef. And mayo. Who puts mayo on roast beef?"

"I don't know, Dad," Oliver said softly.

"I prefer mustard. Your mother knows that."

Noah didn't know what he was doing here, picking a fight about meat. In reality, he didn't have any particular aversion to roast beef. Maybe it was just all the yellow racing through him, making him anxious.

Oliver snared some noodles with his plastic fork and held it suspended midair as he stared wistfully toward the ocean, where there were a couple of teenage kids in wet suits fooling around on surfboards.

"Want to go out there?" Noah asked, knowing how angry Clara would be if he took Oliver for a swim.

Oliver shook his head, no.

"I don't really want to have a picnic anymore, Dad."

"Fine with me. Want to go up to the boardwalk?"

"Not really."

"Want some taffy? I've got a box back at the house."

"Braces," he explained.

"Braces? You're only nine!"

"Almost ten, Dad." Oliver opened his mouth, and sure enough, there were a couple of silver brackets in the back.

"When did you get those?"

"Just this week. This is just to get started, to make room for the other teeth that will come in. I won't get the full braces for another year."

"You poor kid, the stuff your mom makes you do."

"No, it's good. I want to have straight teeth."

"Yeah, but that seems like kind of a waste. Aren't those your baby teeth anyway?"

"No, Dad. I lost those a long time ago."

"Oh. You should have told me that. I would have told the tooth fairy! Your mom doesn't keep me very well informed. But fine, whatever. You don't have to eat any taffy. How about we go up to the shop—we could just go look. I can show you some tricks of the trade. I've even got some games on the computer up there, in the back room."

No again, which Noah found kind of hard to fathom. He thought that if he was still a kid, he'd be pretty excited to have a dad who worked with candy. It was certainly more interesting than what his own dad had done, selling car insurance. He tried to remember if Oliver had expressed more enthusiasm for visiting him at the accounting firm back in Rockville, but he supposed that since he'd been only about seven the one time he visited, there was no way to really compare the experiences.

"*Anything* you want to do?" Noah was getting irritated. They had so little time together, and now, for no discernible reason, Oliver was acting funny, looking over at Auntie instead of just answering the questions himself.

The kids with wet suits began to walk toward them, and he was pretty sure that one of them was Jill's son.

"Hey, Ben!" he shouted, but the kid didn't seem to hear. He lit a cigarette, which struck Noah as amusing somehow, a wet guy in a wet suit, smoking. It made him crave a cigarette himself—maybe the nicotine would calm his nerves. He walked over to see if he could bum a smoke. It was, in fact, Ben, and he was with two other boys and three girls.

"Over there, on the picnic blanket, that's my son, Oliver," he said.

"Hey, Ollie," said Ben. He had to yell to be heard over the sound of the surf.

"Oliver," Noah corrected. He considered introducing Ben to Auntie, but she was glaring at them, not looking particularly like she was in a mingling kind of mood. "Introduce me to your friends," Noah said.

"This is Rusty . . . and Teddy." The girls were standing apart, closer to the ocean.

"And?"

"Hey, Juliet, come over here and say hi."

"Did you say Harriet?"

"No, I said Juliet."

"Are you sure?"

"Of course I'm sure."

Ben had a strange look on his face, however, and Noah wondered if that meant he was hiding something. All this time he'd been trying to figure what Clara was talking about, with this Harriet business, and he wondered if this might be a clue.

The girl who claimed to not be Harriet came closer, while the other two hung back.

"Hey," she said.

"Hey, yourself. Where are you from?" Noah asked. She was very pretty, with dark hair and green eyes. Slight and not too tall. He couldn't tell much more about her, like how she might appear in normal circumstances, when she wasn't dressed like a seal. It worried him a bit that he was thinking about this, even though he wasn't contemplating anything vaguely lewd and he never really had, but now that he had this whole perv thing hanging over him, he was afraid of his own thoughts. What he really wanted to know wasn't pervy at all; he just wondered if this girl was from Verona, because this would really mean things were coming together in some pretty remarkable way. Verona, Harriet, Juliet, the perv thing.

"I don't live too far from here," she said, which when he thought about it could have meant just about anything, like from down the road or from the state of New Jersey.

"You from Verona?"

"What's Verona?" she asked.

He supposed that was a *no*. "You like to surf?"

A nod that said *yes*. This girl was not a great conversationalist.

"Been surfing long?"

More nodding. Noah thought about pointing out to her that she wasn't really being particularly informative with her answers; this, too, could have meant just about anything, like she'd been surfing for a year or surfing her whole life.

"Must be pretty cold out there," he tried.

"Yup, sure is."

"This thing must keep you pretty warm, though," he said, pointing toward the wet suit.

"Yeah."

Noah hadn't noticed until he looked behind him that Oliver had left his perch on the picnic blanket and had sidled over on the bench next to his pretend aunt.

"Hey, Oliver, come over here and talk to Harriet."

Oliver shouted from the bench, "No thanks!"

Noah wondered why his own son behaved so strangely, what kind of poison his mother had put in his head.

"Do you like taffy?" Noah asked the girl.

She hesitated before saying yes.

"Come by Joseph's Famous sometime. You know, up on the boardwalk near the arcade. I'll give you some free samples. Just don't tell anyone, 'cause I don't want everyone coming by and chatting me up, looking for handouts, if you know what I mean." He waited for a reply, but none was forthcoming.

"I'll bet you like . . . vanilla."

He couldn't get any more of a read on her level of enthusiasm for vanilla taffy than he could guess her middle name. Although that was not entirely true, since everyone liked vanilla taffy.

"Sure," Harriet said, and she flashed a little smile, so maybe it was the case that he was wrong, that things were really okay.

"Do you think you could teach me and my son how to surf?"

"I'm not sure I could really teach you, but maybe you could ask Ben? Anyway, it's pretty cold out there. I don't think you'd want to go out without a wet suit."

"Let me just borrow your board for a minute?" He needed to feel the water, had the sense it would be clarifying, somehow.

She didn't look happy about this, but she handed him the board.

"Come with me over to the shoreline. Just a few feet."

"I've really got to go and catch up with my friends," she said, seeming to rethink this entire arrangement. "I kind of need my board back? Maybe we can do this another time?"

He was only kidding around, teasing her, when he took her board and ran into the surf. He wanted to see what she'd do, wondered if she'd follow. The water was colder than he'd imagined, and he could feel a frigid sting, like novocaine screaming up his spine.

"Hey, Harriet!" he yelled playfully, but when he turned around, he saw her running toward Ben and the other kids, who were climbing up the bluff that led to Jill's house. Headed in the other direction were Oliver and Auntie, walking toward the parking lot. She was lugging the heavy picnic basket, and Oliver had the yellow tablecloth trailing behind him, dragging along the sand. Noah yelled to them to stop, but they kept on walking and didn't look back.

8

• • • • •

Now Jordan had something new to add to her Verona legacy, which wasn't lining up very well when she thought about it. Not only was she the kid from Omaha who'd had a concussion on the soccer field, but she feared she might also be remembered as the moron with the bad judgment to have fooled around with Paul Schramm—an indiscretion it seemed everyone at school was not just aware of, but versed in each mortifying detail. (A stuck zipper, condom confusion, coming to her senses at the critical moment.) As of this afternoon, she could add this to her résumé of shame: Jordan Adler, the girl who had a mini-meltdown during a school-sponsored field trip to the Kennedy Center.

The only bright spot here was that the auditorium had been dark, and from what she could tell, half the kids in her row had been asleep; Deegan Krazinski had been snoring so loudly that their teacher, Ms. Russo, had passed a message via tapped shoulders and muffled whispers along two rows of seats, instructing someone to shake him on the shoulder to wake him up.

Although *Madame Butterfly* didn't have much to do with their English curriculum, Ms. Russo had a friend who worked for the Washington Opera, and she agreed to set aside a block of tickets for a matinee of whatever was being performed each spring, so that Ms. Russo could bring her class. This outing was not generally beloved—the word *opera* produced much groaning, as well as the occasional unoriginal pantomime that involved sticking a finger down the throat—but Ms. Russo offered extra credit to anyone able to stay awake and focus on the story line enough to write a one-page mock review. Even though it was spring and most everyone's college fate had already been decided, the words *extra credit* had the same effect on this crowd as throwing raw meat into a pack of hyenas.

Jordan wasn't feeling well. A little nauseous and dizzy, she was sweating all of a sudden, even though just a few minutes earlier she'd been so cold in the air-conditioned auditorium that she'd pulled out the cardigan her mother had pressed on her as she'd left home that morning. "You can't be too careful in summer around here," Leah said. "There's one climate going on outside, and then you step into a building and you're in the North Pole." Jordan had rolled her eyes at this hyperbole, but she'd allowed her mother to stuff the sweater into her bag all the same.

She took the sweater off again and studied the *Playbill*. She'd never understood why her parents spent a small fortune on opera when you could watch the same thing on television, or at least on a DVD. Sometimes her dad would buy opera tickets for her mother on her birthday and she'd act all thrilled and surprised, or vice versa. Jordan didn't get the appeal; she could imagine making the effort to go hear an orchestra play, but why would you want to listen to something you couldn't even understand? In the car CD player there were always recordings of people singing in foreign languages, and sometimes her mother even sang along, pretending to speak Italian or German, although fortunately for them all, she made no attempt to hit the high notes.

But when the curtain lifted, Jordan was mesmerized by Madame Butterfly's gorgeous silk robes. She heard something magical in the arias, too. In a bizarre coincidence, this turned out to be the saga of Jordan and Khalid writ large; she could tell what was going on without even reading the subtitles. (Okay, so she'd just read the entire synopsis in the *Playbill*, and that helped.) It was the oldest story in the world. Two people fell in love, fate pulled them apart, and things got a little complicated from there and never got much better. Granted, if you wanted to nitpick and look more closely, the details didn't entirely align. Jordan, unlike Madame Butterfly, was not a Japanese concubine. And Khalid was not an American naval officer. Also, well, to be really honest in her analysis, to compare and contrast like it was a question on the reading comprehension portion of a standardized test, it was way more intense in the opera for the naval officer to have *married* the concubine, even if it was a sham marriage from the start, than for Khalid to have hooked up with Jordan a few times. And the naval officer came back to Japan with his new wife, which was also way worse than just having a girlfriend on her junior year abroad. And fortunately for Jordan, there was no baby involved, unlike in *Madame Butterfly*, where the young woman had a son. And in the Jordan/Khalid saga there was the detail having to do with the boyfriend finding out the girl was still in high school, and then being angry about having been lied to. Also, Jordan had to admit that even if Khalid was sort of a jerk like this Pinkerton character, at least she had a lot more freedom of choice in life than Madame Butterfly did. But still! It was a story of thwarted love, of broken hearts, of miscommunication, of longing, and she could totally relate!

She pulled out her cell phone and tapped out a text to Khalid:

U wld luv madm butterfly.

Dorrie elbowed her as she typed. Jordan ignored her. Then Dorrie whispered in her ear, "Seriously, put it away. You're gonna get in trouble."

Jordan knew she was right. Ms. Russo had lectured them extensively about this on the way here: no cell phone use in the auditorium. Not only had she said this multiple times, but she'd required them, annoyingly, to recite the rule aloud before getting off the bus, like they were in preschool or something.

By the beginning of the second act, Khalid had not replied to her text. She texted him again later, during what was evidently called the humming chorus, which seemed appropriate in that it was about waiting. Just like Butterfly, the jilted heroine who sat on the floor with her son and her maid, humming, waiting for her lover's return, Jordan was waiting, too, if only for the screen on her phone to light up blue.

She sent him another text message at the beginning of the third act:

M bfly was 15 when she met pinkerton!!!

"Put the phone away," Dorrie whispered to her. "You're obsessed. And not in a good way."

"Is there a good way to be obsessed?" she asked. She didn't like her own tone.

"You really need to be careful. Didn't you hear that Mary Friedman got suspended for sexting?"

"That's ridiculous. I'd never do that. I'm just sending a normal text. There's no law against that."

"There is right now, at the Kennedy Center."

If Khalid would reply, if he'd say anything at all, she'd put the phone away.

Now she was feeling cold again. More than cold, actually: she was shivering, and she put her sweater back on.

Jordan felt a tap on her shoulder, and when she turned around, she saw Ms. Russo motioning for her to hand over her phone. She loved Ms. Russo, and she was not one to buck authority, but there was pretty much no way she was going to relinquish her phone. She snapped it shut instead and shoved it into her back pocket. Ms. Russo scowled, but she walked away after giving Jordan a severe look that she supposed was meant to convey that she'd better quit fooling around.

Another ten minutes passed. Things were not looking good for Butterfly. She'd just discovered that her lover had another wife. The American wife was legitimate, whereas according to some obscure custom governing and supposedly excusing the behavior of venal Caucasian men as they roamed around the world in the old days, Madame Butterfly had no legal claim to their marriage.

Poor Butterfly! Jordan started crying, and while she was doing her best to be quiet, she found it necessary to blow her nose a couple of times. Then she flipped open her phone and started to compose a text explaining to Khalid that she was going to come over to the aquarium as soon as she got back from the field trip. She needed to talk to him for a minute. She had just hit send when a hand reached across her shoulder and grabbed the phone and yanked it away. Now she let out an involuntary little yelp. The next thing she knew, there were arms around her and she was being hustled out of the middle of her row, which caused a small commotion. She kept looking over her shoulder toward the stage as Ms. Russo moved her toward the exit at the back of the auditorium. She needed to know how this ended—*Madame Butterfly*, that was, and not her own opera abduction. Not well, in either case, she had to assume.

Khalid suggested that they go to a museum nearby. She deduced from the stricken look on his face when she showed up at the aquarium, and from his lack of response to her earlier texts, that he was going to say something cruel, and her best guess was that he wanted to do this in a place where she couldn't make too much of a fuss.

They began the conversation sitting on a bench in front of a Diebenkorn. Khalid spoke in hushed tones. "It's over" was the gist of what he said. There was no need to repeat it in a dozen variations, like *he* was an opera singer, going on and on and on. When he finally finished, she tried to argue with the premise.

Who cared about age? Who cared about geography? Girlfriends on their junior years abroad—okay, somewhat more problematic, perhaps. But these things were manageable! Besides, she was desperate to get away herself. She'd gone to Google Earth to find the fish museum, and even though it wasn't there, she imagined she could see the two of them, holding hands, sitting on a Tunisian rooftop staring out at some ruins. Of course even this part of the fantasy required a lot of conjecture, since she couldn't get a picture in her head of what a Tunisian rooftop might involve visually, what kind of furniture they might have, what the skyline would look like in some faraway place. She had no experience of foreign countries; she'd never even been to Canada. Was there pollution? Congestion? Sprawl? She wanted to see! She told Khalid some version of this. At first she'd been so fired up, so anxious to tell him about the opera that she'd forgotten she was feeling a little weird, and now as she was talking to him, she was having trouble following the thread of her own thought. She was even beginning to have trouble stringing sentences together coherently. Or was she? Maybe she was just having trouble hearing. Was the talking too fast or was the listening too slow or was it just that everything seemed to be winding down, like on a malfunctioning classroom projector, the images bending out of shape?

She hadn't had a headache in a few months and had almost forgotten the weird precursors of one coming on. It wasn't all bad. The headaches themselves were horrendous, of course, the pain intolerable. As best she could describe it, it was like a science fiction movie where a tentacled creature is injected in your ear and then swims to your brain and starts looping around and squeezing hard, pulverizing every bit of matter in your head. When it was finally over, sometimes after a couple of days, she would try to erase the memory. How else to go on without being paralyzed by fear of its return?

But the preheadache sensation—the doctors called it an aura—was different. Sometimes it felt magical, or maybe what she meant was mystical. She imagined that the way her head swam with colors and shapes might be sort of like the effects of the psychedelic drugs the old hippie types used to do—mushrooms and LSD and whatever else it was that made them enjoy listening to the Grateful Dead. Sometimes in the midst of this, she could think so clearly it was like she'd achieved some higher state of being. It reminded her of that soccer field moment all over again, when she was floating up above the goalpost watching everything unfold, except that in these new visions she didn't have to contend with Cherie Long.

Now that she thought about it, she was starting to feel a little weird like this right now.

A woman around the same age as her mother, who was studying the painting behind them, looked at Jordan and smiled. *Oh, young love!* her expression seemed to say. Perhaps the woman hadn't noticed that Khalid was leaning away. Jordan looked at the woman and entertained the surprising thought that it wasn't Khalid she wanted just now, but this woman, this simulacrum of her mother. Of course she knew it wasn't her mother, she wasn't even sure the woman was anyone's mother, but Jordan could tell just by looking at her that she'd know how to make her feel better. Why was she wasting her energy on this guy? She pressed on anyway, as if she were on the after-school debate team.

She floated her irrational idea that it was meant to be: Jordan and Tunisia. Jordan and Khalid. Madame Butterfly and Pinkerton. She was failing to persuade herself, by this point.

"You're talking nonsense. It was a mistake that got a little extended, that's all," Khalid said coldly. "This is getting kind of twisted. You're a sweet girl, but you need to just forget about this and go to college next year and get on with your life. And I need to get back to the aquarium."

Suddenly she could see them from above and then, a moment later, from far across the room, as if they were on display in this museum. She stared at a painting called *Girl with Plant*.

Girl with Khalid, the card might read. *Girl Mid-breakup.* She was feeling dizzy. She leaned into Khalid to brace herself, but he didn't understand, and he leaned away. *Girl in Love. Girl Adrift. Girl in Pain.*

"I don't feel well," she said.

Narcissist that he was, he thought she was talking about the breakup. Maybe she was. All she knew for sure was that she needed to lie down. What she really needed was her mother.

"It's only been two months," he said. "We've only been together a handful of times. You're behaving a bit like we're ending a ten-year marriage."

She wished he'd just shut up already. The room was spinning, which now seemed more urgent than the matter of their breakup.

What happened next, she wasn't entirely sure, but somehow she'd walked with him back to the aquarium, across the street. Had she left her backpack there? She tried to piece this together later. She had wanted to call her mother, but then she couldn't find her phone and she assumed it was in her bag, which maybe she'd left on Khalid's desk. She'd gone with him to see. The bag was there, but no phone. Then, out in the public viewing area and on her way to the elevator, she'd found herself mesmerized by the glowing tanks in the dimly lit room. Her senses were now even more out of whack. She was hot and cold and cold and hot and things were floating and descending like musical notes and suddenly this seemed the most wonderful place in the world to have a migraine, if a person had to have a migraine. She sat down on a bench and stared at some fish whose stripes made them look like they were in their pajamas, and then at the French angelfish with their big yellow eyes. They looked like cartoon characters, happy creatures from *Finding Nemo*. She felt herself nodding off.

She had no idea what time it was when Khalid shook her awake and suggested that she go home.

"Of course," she said, dazed. "I must have fallen asleep." She wanted to check the time on her phone, and now she remembered that Ms. Russo had her phone. Oy. Talk about your bad day.

"I'm just finishing up in here, and then I'm going home. I suggest you do the same. The security people are pretty ruthless when it's closing time—they want to get out of here."

"Okay," she said. "Of course. That totally makes sense." She tried hard to sound normal.

She headed toward the exit again, pausing at the glass window that separated the public area from where the employees worked inside. She looked through the window at Khalid for what she supposed might be the last time. He was doing some sort of work on sea horses; she couldn't tell if they were dead or alive. How could you determine such a thing, anyway? With a tiny sea horse stethoscope? He lined a few of the creatures up on a piece of glass and seemed to deliberately keep his head down so as not to catch her eye.

Man with sea horse.

He had magnifying goggles strapped across his forehead, and a hint of T-shirt peeked through the unbuttoned lab coat. He picked up a sea horse and turned it over, then walked to his desk and scribbled some notes on a pad. He left the room, exiting through a door that must have led to an interior hallway, and then he returned after a few minutes with a folder full of papers. This time he looked at her and mouthed the words "Go away." He politely added the word "please."

"Okay," she said. And that was her intention.

So how was it that she found herself curled on a bench at what she was eventually able to determine from the clock above the reception desk as 4:36 a.m.? Her throat was dry and scratchy, and she could barely swallow. She hadn't heard any guards passing through, rattling keys. She wondered, now with a little bitterness, if Khalid had known she was still there when he left. In his defense, she supposed she had managed to find a rather isolated corner in which to fall asleep.

It was kind of scary, being alone in the basement of a federal building with a bunch of illuminated fish. But it was also quiet and peaceful. The tanks glowed eerily, magnificently in the darkened room, and she felt like she was in the company of living, breathing, swimming works of art, as worthy as anything she'd seen hanging in that museum. She could see why people became collectors of fish, not that she would especially want to do that. She composed in her head the text she'd send to Khalid if they were still on a texting basis. And if she'd had a phone. *Fish r crazy!* She'd say. How moronic was that? Texting about fish to a marine biologist?

Anyway, it was her mother she ought to be thinking about, not Khalid. Her parents would be worried sick.

She walked over to the elevator and pressed the button. Nothing happened. She supposed they must switch them off at night for security reasons. Then she tried the door that led to the stairwell, but it was locked. She looked around for a phone and found half a dozen of them behind the locked door where she'd last glimpsed Khalid.

Where was the headache, she wondered? Normally by now the pain would have begun to descend. At the same time that she felt like crap, she was also beginning to feel weirdly like she'd dodged a bullet, like maybe for the first time in ages something sort of normal was happening to her, like she was simply getting the flu.

Now she was face-to-face with a tankful of sea anemones. A grayish one, tall and stalky, had tentacles spilling out like hair. If she had to draw a picture of the thing that sometimes clamped around her head, this was a good artist's rendering. She pressed her nose to the tank, making peace with the creature. So maybe she'd just had a sea anemone inside her head, and now it was gone, stuffed in a tank. This made complete sense and was a far better explanation than that she was going insane.

Jordan's fantasy was to slip into the house and crawl into bed without being forced to participate in one of her mother's ridiculous family meetings to discuss where she'd been. Sometimes it seemed like it would be so much easier to just be punished instead of going through this whole song and dance of having them try to analyze everything to death, to be all big-minded, to deconstruct and understand.

She knew they'd be worried, but after all the half lies she'd been telling these last few weeks without incident (although really, she preferred to think of them as partial truths), she hadn't anticipated that her parents would be standing angry vigil at the door. The look on her mother's face was nearly as alarming as her words. Her mom never swore, but in this case she used the word *hell*, as in "Where the *hell* have you been, young lady?"

The message was unambiguous: it said that after all the leeway she'd been given, the parental blind eye turned to late nights that had blurred into morning, the blithe acceptance of the long list of ridiculous excuses that never made any sense, Jordan had finally crossed the line.

She was *so* not in the mood for this! She'd actually found herself thinking tender thoughts as she approached the house after trudging a mile from the Metro. She didn't feel well enough to walk by a long shot, but she wasn't thinking clearly and had been unable to come up with some alternate plan. It was 8:00 a.m. and Jordan could see the mothers on the street heading toward the elementary-school bus stop on the corner. Dog leashes splayed colorfully from hands that juggled lunch boxes and school projects, and one mom had a baby in her arms and a steaming cup of coffee, too. Young kids with over-size bulges protruding from their backs ran; others seemed to drag, hunched from the weight of their books. Some moms were clustered on the corner, ignoring their offspring entirely, talking to one another. One was even smoking a cigarette, something Jordan realized she hadn't ever seen a Verona adult do. She kept hearing about how much things had changed, how she had so many more options than even her mother's generation—the one that had supposedly gotten liberated—yet really, where were the dads? Why wasn't there a single one at the bus stop? She remembered how much she used to like having her mom meet her at the end of school each day, even if that sometimes involved being picked up after a couple of hours in extended day care in the gym.

Only when she'd been let out of the aquarium by a startled guard did she allow herself to appreciate the trauma that being locked inside had been. Couple that with the realization, at last, that Khalid was . . . well, it wasn't just that Khalid was not her boyfriend, but that he was a total jerk . . . and add a dash of Kennedy Center mortification, and all she could think of as she walked toward her house was how comforting she found this boring suburban landscape and the idea of going home.

She'd been refusing to think of this as home for nearly two years, but now the idea of crawling into her bed and propping her stuffed animals around her seemed the most soothing thing in the world. She'd been floating in this haze of mostly pleasant, random thought, remembering their house in Omaha, how the dog would knock her down and cover her with slobbery kisses whenever she came home. She missed the cute little kids who had lived next door, too. Sam and Sydney used to wander by for breakfast so often that Leah had begun to stock their favorite foods: frozen waffles, orange juice without pulp, and strawberry Fruit Roll-Ups. Jordan wondered what had happened to them. It had been nearly two full years, and she was only just realizing that while you kept in touch with your friends and heard all the important school gossip, it was these informal relationships, the ones you took for granted, that got lost forever in a move.

All of these warm, fuzzy thoughts evaporated at the sight of her bedraggled mother on the front porch. "Where the *hell* have you been, young lady?" she asked again, as if once was not enough.

Leah was sitting on the stoop, clutching a giant mug of coffee, and her hair was pulled into a sloppy ponytail that sprouted from the center of her head like a troll's. She wore sweatpants and a faded University of Wisconsin T-shirt—an outfit that did double duty for both sleeping and the gym, so it was possible she'd been en route to her yoga class, although this seemed like wishful thinking. Jordan hadn't noticed before that her mother was going gray, and she was struck by the sudden realization that Leah was starting to get old.

"Hi, Mom," she said, trying to be nonchalant, as though it

was perfectly normal for her to have stayed out all night. Had she been entertaining the thought of flinging herself into her mother's arms a mere minute ago? Now all she wanted was to brush past her and lock herself in her room. She didn't want to talk, unless it was just to receive sympathy for a very bad day.

She opened the screen door only to find her dad, who was usually pretty calm, leaning against the wall in the foyer. He was wearing his tennis whites, but his shirt was untucked and he had on two different socks. Jordan supposed she ought not point this out. She could see the racquet and his gym bag sitting on the table in the hallway, and a glance at the grandfather clock in the living room made her realize that she'd probably caused him to miss his game. All of a sudden he looked old, too, and she wondered if this was her fault or whether it was just a particularly harsh slant of morning light.

"We've been up all night," he said flatly, which was actually scarier than if he'd yelled. "Well, your mother has been. She woke me up at three when you hadn't come home."

"We woke up half of Verona," her mother said, opening the screen door and following Jordan inside. "I tried to call Dorrie, and when she didn't answer, I called her mom, and she didn't know where you were, and she couldn't even wake Dorrie up!"

"Yeah, she can be hard to wake," Jordan agreed, thinking a calm, understated response might be better than going on the defensive. Maybe there was some easy way through this.

"And then I called Courtney Moore, and then . . ."

"You called Courtney Moore? I'm not even that friendly with her!"

"You aren't friendly with the police, either, but we called them, too," her dad said.

"Touché," Jordan said.

"Don't be sarcastic, miss," he said.

Miss? It sounded like both of her parents were reading from some guidebook: *employ the use of formal pronouns when disciplining the errant child.* This seemed entirely plausible, actually.

"I'm sorry. I didn't mean it that way. I just meant that you're right. I feel really awful. I tried to call, but I didn't have my phone. Ms. Russo has it. It's a long story . . . Wait, you called the *police?*"

"We did, but they said it was too soon to put out an alert, and you'd probably run away with your boyfriend or something."

She supposed it wouldn't help her cause to point out that in fact she *would* have run away with her boyfriend, if he'd have anything to do with her.

"I'm really really really sorry," she said. "I know that you have no reason to believe me, but . . ."

"Are you okay?" Her mother was approaching her, the heel of her palm outstretched toward her forehead. Never in her life had Jordan been so glad to be sick.

"You're burning up, sweetheart," she said. "Let me go find the thermometer." Her mother left the room and sprinted up the stairs.

"Oh, no no no no. Your mom is always making excuses for you, but you're not going to brush past this one quite so easily, miss!" her dad said.

"Seriously, enough with the *miss!*" Jordan said.

"We've been trying to give you a lot of room here, more than most parents would," he continued, ignoring her. "We get that you've been through a lot, and we're glad to see you adjusting, coping so well after the move and the concussion, and I know that you're a young adult . . ."

"I'm not technically an adult, Dad. I'm only seventeen."

How ironic that she should say this, given how hard she'd been pretending to be twenty-one. Still, she found it something of a relief to remember she was just a kid who wanted to curl up in her mother's lap right now and cry.

"Don't be so contrary. This is important. Your mother tells me you've been out late three times this week! This is not acceptable behavior."

"Look, I'm graduating in three weeks. I know you're worried, but you shouldn't be. *Everyone* is out late. All night, even. Half the senior class has stopped even going to school. Anyway, I'm not even doing anything that bad."

"Really, Jordan? I've been trying hard to ignore certain facts, but I have to say that my car smelled a little bit like marijuana last week."

Under different circumstances, she might have laughed at the way he said the word, with too much emphasis on each syllable. *Mare-a-wan-na.* She wished her mom would get back with the thermometer already. She was trying to calculate how high her temperature would have to be to get her out of this jam.

"That's insane, Dad! Now you're really getting paranoid. I've never smoked marijuana in my life, and that's the truth." Thank God he hadn't opened his glove compartment recently, was all she could think. She wondered if he'd smelled the vomit.

Leah came back with the thermometer and stuck it into Jordan's mouth. She continued to defend herself even with it sticking out of the side of her mouth. "Look, none of this is as bad as you think. I'm not doing any of the crazy things you seem to imagine. You should see what my friends are up to right now, with school almost over. Everyone's completely out of control. I'm pretty much the only sober kid in Verona!"

Her parents were both staring at her, like they were hungry for more nuggets of reassurance to spill from her lips.

"I'll be completely honest—just promise me you won't freak out. I got locked in overnight at the aquarium. It was all a big mix-up—Khalid didn't realize that I was still there when he got off work. I fell asleep on a bench, and I didn't wake up until the janitor came in this morning. Then I got up and came straight home. Now all I want to do is go to bed."

"What kind of boyfriend would forget about you?" her mom asked.

"He didn't forget about me. He didn't know I was there," she said, although she knew the real answer: *a boyfriend who is not your boyfriend. A boyfriend who is an asshole, actually.*

She could see her parents begin to relax a bit, which was a little sad, in a way, since she wasn't telling them anything particularly comforting, if you stepped back and thought about it. She supposed they were so desperate for the truth that they had some infinite capacity to process and absorb information they probably shouldn't tolerate in more normal circumstances.

"Look, go ahead and do whatever you feel you need to do. Ground me! There's no place I want to go anyway. Tell me I can't go to Beach Week. That's more than fine with me. If it will make you happy, I'll stay in my room for the rest of the school year. I'll stay there all summer . . ."

"No, sweetheart, that's not what we want at all!"

"No, not at all!" her mom echoed. "We want you to be happy! We want you to be with your friends! We want you to go to Beach Week . . ."

"Well, let's not go there so fast," her dad said.

"You don't even know how I was going to end that sentence! I was going to say . . ."

"Don't start fighting about that again!" Jordan said.

"I wasn't going to," her mom said. "Your dad cut me off before I could finish saying that . . . Oh, just forget it. I give up. Maybe that's not such a bad idea, spending some time in your room."

"Yes, you should spend some time in your room," her dad said.

Her parents exchanged a weary glance that said they were sort of clueless about what to do in this situation.

The thermometer beeped. Leah pulled it out and squinted her eyes. "Yikes—103.2. I'm getting the Advil and I'm calling the doctor right now."

Her dad put his arms around her and gave her a hug. Her mother did the same. The three of them stood in one big happy family embrace, which was sort of nice, although it was also a bit much.

9

. . . . .

Porn was the wrong instinct, although, like ordering up another round when already drunk, there was a fleeting, giddy moment when it had seemed like a good idea.

They had planned to go to a movie, but nothing in current release seemed worth the hassle of trying to park on a Saturday night in downtown Verona. They considered playing cards but couldn't find a deck. Then Charles announced a strange yen to play checkers, but it turned out that too many pieces were missing from the set. They decided to watch television, but the only thing on of even vague interest was *CSI*, and five minutes in they realized they had already seen that episode. Somehow or other, just as they were about to give up and read, the remote control made its way to the adult pay-per-view menu, and an awkward, tacit agreement was made to watch.

Selecting from the dizzying array of options with your spouse beside you was a tricky business, however; one had to be careful not to demonstrate a proclivity toward any particular . . . anything. Leah didn't want to probe too deeply her own psyche in this arena, nor did she really want to know what privately turned Charles on, whether he was partial to teenage Asian cheerleaders or German cougar nurses. Even if she laughed and said it didn't matter, this insight into her husband's wiring was likely to haunt her for the rest of her days, or at least the rest of her marriage. She was preparing to relieve him of this dilemma by blithely suggesting that they settle on the first thing featured. Charles had apparently been about to do the same, which would have brought them the unsubtle *Blow Job Sandwich*, when another selection caught Leah's eye: it was halfway down the list and was called *Beach Week*.

It had been a horrible week on top of a horrible year, and the brief moment of giggling over the shocking coincidence of the title brought a surge of warmth and some much-needed levity: Leah was reminded that she and Charles had a shared sensibility, that they found the same things amusing and ironic. On the heels of the aquarium debacle, Jordan had spent four days in bed, delirious, with what turned out to be a horrendous case of flu. She'd moped around the house for another couple of days, and this evening she'd finally gotten dressed and announced that she was going to Dorrie's. Leah and Charles had both been irrationally thrilled when Jordan had called an hour earlier to say that a bunch of their other friends had just come by, and they were going to pick up salads and watch a DVD. What more could parents want than to have their daughter healthy and hanging out with her girlfriends on a Saturday night? At least one worrisome thing in their lives, the most important one, appeared to be resolving well.

Having Jordan felled by flu had been only one of several bad features of the past week, however. Problems with Charles's mother had intensified; her behavior had become increasingly erratic, the nursing home was once again threatening eviction, and the next quarterly bill for her care had just arrived with a surprise monthly increase in fees. On top of this, Leah and Charles had spent hours in front of the computer trying to sort through loan options for Jordan's tuition next year, which only served to remind them that the balloon payment on the house back in Omaha was weeks away from its devastating pop. There was at least the prospect of good news: Charles had just learned that the transportation planning board was finally scheduled to meet next week to make a final decision on whether the Cobalt Line would get approval. While related issues remained unresolved, getting the go-ahead on the Metro would likely help the other pieces fall into place, and the deposit injected into the Adler bank account once the project broke ground would go a long way toward correcting the course of this recent bad spiral. Or not.

If *Beach Week* the movie was going to distract them, even just for an hour, it was well worth the embarrassment and the $12.99.

Charles hit SELECT with a daring flick of the thumb. They watched the first ten minutes in the semidarkness, pillows propped against the wooden headboard. Across the gulf of the queen-size bed, they held hands—a stab at solidarity meant to massage the fact that they had been snapping at each other all week and that there were at least half a dozen other, more subtle irritants in their lives beyond the ones they could readily identify. Still, here they were, trying.

An initial illicit thrill as the camera began its unsteady, amateurish pan of the seaside—sand; waves; blankets; pails and shovels; girls and boys playfully, innocently frolicking in the foamy surf—slowly reconfigured into something darker, and then profoundly disturbing. There was no story line involved:

it was just a guy with a camera trained on kids who had filed into a house where there was a party under way. The camera lingered on a very sunburned guy floating in a swimming pool, asleep on an empty keg. Inside the house, someone was passed out on the floor, and a girl was trying to rouse him by poking him repeatedly with a fork, giggling between awkwardly placed jabs. In another room, a different girl was removing her bathing suit as she was egged on by a bunch of guys. Leah and Charles stared, paralyzed. Leah felt some obligation to turn this off, but at the same time she felt a horrible responsibility to see where it was going. A voice in the background was telling the girl what to do in excruciating detail, and from there, things quickly devolved into something orgylike. Or was it more appropriately called a gang bang? What did you call it when there was one girl and, well . . . wait, now another girl appeared. Leah didn't want to do the math, but there were a lot more boys than girls. Suddenly Leah realized that this new girl looked familiar.

To say it was shocking to have possibly just recognized one of your daughter's friends in a porn video was an understatement. It was making her sick, and when she and Charles realized more or less simultaneously that this might be the sweet girl from the last Beach Week meeting, Rene Palmer, Charles grabbed the remote, shut off the television, and hopped out of bed so quickly that Leah wondered for a moment if he might have been stung by a bee. The incident was disturbing on too many levels to count, but if there was one bright spot, it was that the timing of her appearance in the movie was fortuitous, because at the precise moment that they shut the television off, they heard a car pull into the driveway.

Charles pulled himself together and stumbled toward the window. The T-shirt he wore had been involved in an unfortunate incident with a new, organic laundry detergent that had ruined an entire load the previous day, the blue now marred by erratic blotches of white that seemed to glow in the dark. Charles peeked through a corner of the curtain and announced that the sound they had just heard was indeed Jordan, arriving home in Charles's car, which was surprising given that it was only 9:00 p.m. He quickly turned the overhead lights on and propped himself back up in bed. His hand reflexively reached to the bedside table; then he peered toward the floor and began to look around for something. "Where's my . . ." The answer seemed to come to him mid-sentence.

Leah knew what he was looking for. She didn't feel great about it, but she'd won the argument about the Blackberry, and Charles was still disoriented, suffering the effects of withdrawal.

He went over to the desk and retrieved his laptop, which he brought into bed. Leah pulled her bathrobe tight, opened the bedroom door, grabbed a book, and settled in, beside him.

"Hi, honey," she called to Jordan as they heard the front door open.

"Hey," Jordan said from the foyer. It was a normal-sounding *hey*. Not much to be gleaned from this particular utterance of the three-letter word. Was she unhappy? Still depressed about Khalid? Still a bit worn down by flu? Fortunately, she hadn't complained of any headaches recently, so perhaps they were finally over at least that one hurdle. To have her home this early when she'd announced she was staying out was troubling in a counterintuitive way, however, even though, technically, she was grounded. This had seemed, parentally, the right thing to do in the wake of all the recent furtive behavior that had come to a head with the aquarium episode. Even if she was sick and wasn't going anywhere anyway, she was not allowed to leave the house, and Leah and Charles had felt proud of their ability to be such strict disciplinarians, at least in theory. In reality she was allowed to present appeals upon which they would rule on a case-by-case basis. Privately they both agreed it was preferable to have her out rather than dragging around the house, even if it made them look like wimps.

"Come upstairs and say hello," Leah yelled.

"I will in a sec. Let me just get a snack."

Charles waited for his computer to fire up, then checked the latest headlines and baseball scores before logging into his e-mail.

"There's a message here from your Beach Week friend reminding us that the addendum needs to be signed and returned by Monday," he said. "Thank God this isn't our problem anymore. Now that Jordan isn't going, we'd better be sure to get the deposit back. She found someone to cover for her, right?"

"We're working on it," Leah mumbled. Had they officially decided Jordan wasn't going? Given that Jordan was grounded, presumably the matter was resolved on a technicality. "There's some girl who's interested, but I don't think it's a done deal."

"Did we ever get the addendum?" Charles asked.

"I don't know. It doesn't matter anymore."

"Never mind. Here it is. She must have sent it earlier this evening. Not a whole lot of turnaround time."

"What do you care? Just hit delete. You just said yourself that Jordan isn't going. Anyway, even if she was going, it's not that big of a deal—it's only a one-page thing most likely," she said.

Instead of hitting delete, Charles hit print, and Leah could hear the wireless printer in the adjacent room start to churn out pages.

"These goddamned *lawyers*," he said. "She sits on this for four months and then she needs it ASAP?"

Leah wondered why he was getting all worked up about this. Perhaps it had to do with the connection between Beach Week, the source of major household tension, and *Beach Week*, the movie.

Charles got out of bed and went to get the pages from the printer.

"Do we have a stapler?" he called.

"In the second drawer of the desk, on the left."

"This thing is eight pages long."

After a couple of minutes she heard the punch of a staple, and Charles returned with the document in hand. He got back into bed and began to read. "Beach Week Shared Liability Agreement," he said aloud, unhappily. They heard Jordan moving up the stairs, and they went quiet, waiting for her to enter.

"Hey," she said again, standing at the doorway. She looked tired and pale, which was of course to be expected after half the week in bed.

"Are you okay, honey? Did you find a snack?" Leah asked.

"Yeah, I'm fine. I'm not really hungry."

"Are you sure? I can make you something."

"There's nothing down there."

"I'll make you some pancakes!"

"You only have that whole wheat kind," Jordan replied. "I tried it—it's kind of gross."

"You're going to make pancakes at night?" Charles asked.

"Why not?"

"That's ridiculous. Isn't there something else to eat, like cookies or something? Can't you buy some normal food?" he said to Leah.

Had he really just said this? She supposed it wasn't *that* horrible a thing to have said, and it was arguably even rather mild given other things he might have said, but she was feeling a little pent up, and this enraged her. "I'm sorry, but are you incapable of finding your way to the grocery store?" This was a mean thing to say no matter what her tone of voice, so it was admittedly overkill for her to have nearly shouted.

"Jordan?" Charles called. Their daughter had already turned and was walking toward her bedroom. "Come back for a minute. Do you want to come sit with us? We can watch TV. Maybe there's something on you might like. One of your cooking shows or something?"

"I don't want to listen to you guys fight."

"Honey, we're not fighting. Really. We're both just a little tired."

"I'm fine, Mom. I'm going to bed. Maybe we can have pancakes for breakfast," she offered. "We can make them together. We can bond." There seemed the slight possibility that this might have been offered with sincerity.

"Why are you home so early? Is everything okay?"

"It's fine, Mom! I just didn't want to hang out anymore. They were talking about Beach Week again anyway, and since I'm grounded, I assume I'm not going, so there was no point. They were starting to argue about who was sleeping in which bed, if you can believe it."

"Was Rene there?"

Charles gave Leah a sharp elbow, and they exchanged a look that said it was hard to believe they had managed to conceive this child—that they had, at one point in their relationship, not only had sex without a little pay-per-view enhancement, but had found a compatible sperm and egg.

"Why?"

"Just curious."

"What the *F*, Mom? You are being seriously weird! I'm going to sleep!" They heard the door to her room close.

Charles turned his attention back to the Beach Week Shared Liability Agreement. "Do you believe this goddamned thing?"

"Seriously, why are you dwelling on this?"

"I don't know, I guess I find it . . . enlightening? At this point it's like an anthropological study or something, some social experiment: the behavior of suburban parents as they prepare to sacrifice their young in the peculiar ritual known as 'Beach Week.' Admit it: you're obsessed with it, too, the way you were hounding Jordan about Rene."

"That's about something else entirely. And that hardly qualified as *hounding.*"

He was right, though. She was sort of obsessed with this subject, and she couldn't say why.

What she did know was that she felt precariously close to the brink. Between the scarring glimpse of porn, the moods of their inscrutable daughter, the endless marital squabbling, and this cascading pile of very real money problems, she had the sudden, overwhelming desire to grab the car keys and go . . . somewhere. She wasn't sure where. Maybe she'd run away, or maybe she'd only drive around the block a few times, but either way, she'd be making a statement that there was a limit to what she could tolerate. How was it that a person finally decided to act? She wondered what the long-term emotional consequences might be if you had an epiphany so powerful that it grabbed you by the collar of the ugly bathrobe you were wearing and screamed in your ear that this was it—right now! This was the moment you should change your life! Time to get up and go. And then, the next thing you knew, the moment had passed, the epiphany was walking out the door, and you were leaning over your husband's shoulder, reading a Beach Week Shared Liability Agreement.

"This is astonishing," Charles said.

"Well, it looks like a lot of this is perhaps just a rehash of the actual terms of the lease, so maybe she's just being overly cautious. Like this is her way of having us—well not *us* anymore, thank goodness—sort of virtually sign the original?" Leah offered.

"No, actually . . . I mean . . . *what?* Okay, for instance here, just start at the very beginning," he said, pointing to the first page:

SHARED LIABILITY AGREEMENT

This SHARED LIABILITY AGREEMENT (the "**agreement**,") is entered into by and among the individuals whose names appear on the signature page of above-referenced **agreement** (each, a "**parent**" and collectively, the "**parents**.")

"Are we already in deep, or what?" Charles asked.

"So there's a lot of legalese. She's a lawyer."

He ignored this and continued to read.

Recitals

A. The **parents** are the **parents** of ten lovely teenage girls (the "**girls**,") who are renting a house located at 4200 Ocean Breeze Lane, Chelsea Beach, Delaware (the "**beach house**"), pursuant to a lease dated January 29 (the "**lease**") with Mingus Realty, as agent for Noah Miller (the "**landlord**").

B. Although only two sets of the **parents** have executed the **lease**, the **parents** have agreed that all should be held equally liable pro rata for any loss, damage, or injury arising under the terms of the **lease** or resulting from the **girls'** occupancy or use of the **beach house** except to the extent that the loss is established to be the fault or responsibility of one or more of the **girls** ("**a naughty girl**," as defined in section 8, below) all as more **fully** set forth below.

C. To memorialize their **agreement,** the **parents** have entered into this **agreement**.

"Why is 'fully' in bold type?" Leah asked.

"I think it's a typo," Charles said. His entire body was so tense that Leah wondered if he might be in danger of a stroke.

"Charles, relax! Really, you're getting yourself all worked up over nothing. It was a mistake on my part to have started this."

Leah expected some acknowledgment of this radical confession, but he seemed too absorbed by this material to admit that he might have just scored a critical point in this slow-burning feud.

"A *naughty girl*? Does she really think it wise to set this up in such a way as to pit one group of girls against another? The original point of this was supposed to be that if something bad happens, we're all equally responsible."

"Yes, you're right. But think about it . . . if this Rene girl, for example . . ." She couldn't think of the right way to end that sentence, so she let it drift into a different thought. "What exactly does she mean by a *naughty girl*, anyway?"

"Well, I'm glad you asked," Charles said. "Let's leap ahead here to page . . . four, after we've of course covered Obligation to Share Lease Payments; Obligation to Contribute or Reimburse; Covered Losses; Pro Rata Share; Attorneys' Fees; Further Assurances; Severability; Notices; Governing Law . . ."

"Is the governing law Maryland or Delaware?" Leah asked.

"Maryland," he said, looking at her suspiciously, as if she'd crossed over to the dark side with this question.

"Successors and Assigns . . . Counterparts."

"What does that mean, counterparts?"

"That's not the point, Leah! I have no idea what that means . . . but here, look at this:"

Naughty Girls

For the purposes of this **agreement**, a **girl** shall be deemed a **naughty girl** if she is found by a court or an arbitrator to be partially or totally responsible for an event or omission that causes a loss, damage, or injury covered by this **agreement** or if she or her **parents** acknowledge such responsibility in writing. In the event that more than one **girl** is found or acknowledged to be a **naughty girl** for a specific loss, damage, or injury, then the **parents** of all of the **naughty girls** shall share equally in the contribution obligations of the **parents** of **naughty girls** for that loss, unless the court or arbitrator finds, or the **parents** of **naughty girls** agree, on a different allocation of responsibility, in which case the **parents** of the **naughty girl** shall be obligated in proportion to that allocation.

"Would you like to continue? Would you like to know the legal definition of a parent, perhaps?"

"No, Charles. Let's stop."

It seemed he couldn't stop. " 'In the event of twins or triplets, each girl shall count separately' . . . Are there any twins or triplets in our group?"

"Not actually in our group, but that Krazinski guy—by the way, who is he? Is he someone famous?"

"No, he's just another lawyer," Charles said.

"Doesn't he look like that guy on the back of buses? The guy who looks like the Clinton foreign policy adviser?"

"Which buses?"

"Never mind."

"I don't recall him being in the Clinton administration."

"Seriously, drop it."

"He has twins?"

"Yes, but not in the group—a girl and a boy, so the boy is presumably staying elsewhere."

Charles returned to the document: " 'If all or any portion of any provision of this agreement is held to be invalid, illegal, or unenforceable in any respect, then the parties shall reconstitute this agreement to—' "

"Well she *is* a senior partner at Weiss and Schraub. I mean, I'm sure it's all legitimate."

"You can see why she's so successful at what she does. She's a total type A, take-no-prisoners Washington type. I mean here, she acts as though she's doing us all a big favor, signing the lease, offering to write us this easy little addendum pro bono, and then she produces this ridiculous, and frankly offensive, document."

"It's not that offensive, Charles. She's just trying to inject a little humor into this. Besides, just for the sake of argument— since Jordan isn't even going to go to Beach Week—think about it. What if some girl, say Rene—"

"Would you stop with Rene, already?"

"Sorry . . . if one of the girls managed to get the rest of them all in trouble and the house happened to catch on fire or a door got kicked down or a garbage disposal got jammed or someone fell off the roof and broke her leg, should they really *all* be held responsible?"

Leah thought back to that initial meeting, when someone had mentioned the possibility of some worst-case God-forbid-it-should-ever-in-a-million-years-come-to-pass kind of scenario in which a kid was killed or maimed for the rest of his or her life and it was the fault of one stupid, drunken, *naughty girl*. Didn't a clause like this in the contract *benefit* them as the parents of a girl presumably unlikely to behave badly—at least in the ways spelled out in this contract?

As far as Charles was concerned, this was obviously not the point. The point was that the Beach Week Shared Liability Agreement highlighted the pure insanity of Beach Week itself. Now Charles was out of bed, looking for the phone. "I'm going to give this woman a piece of my mind," he said.

"Honey, cool off. Seriously. Come back to bed and just sleep on it. You're the one who's always telling me to let something that upsets me settle in before acting. On top of which, may I just repeat, this is no longer our problem?"

Again he appeared to be reaching for his Blackberry, and she could see the recollection of current circumstance manifest in a scowl as he began to pace the room, looking for his new, emasculated cell phone. He checked his trouser pockets and the bedside table; he got on his knees and looked under the bed, to no avail, and then renewed his rant.

"The tone, the language, the arrogance, the eight pages of single-spaced legal bullshit. The condescension. Do we really need to define *parents* as a 'male and female unit who are the responsible guardians for an individual girl?' I mean, if we are going to all this trouble to account for the possibility of twins and triplets, why not consider . . . lesbian parents as well? Or two gay men? Or what about a single parent . . ."

Charles's phone began to ring from the pocket of his suit jacket, which was hanging on the doorknob of the closet. He attempted to answer it, but was still unfamiliar with the mechanics of the keypad, and he put it on speakerphone by mistake.

It was Arthur Moore, Courtney's dad. He was saying that there was a scheduling conflict on his end, and now there was the need for another male chaperone. It would be great fun, and there was a brand-new-sixty-five-inch plasma TV at the Krazinski beach house, also DIRECTV with a major-league baseball package, and a swimming pool and Jacuzzi, a Ping-Pong table . . .

Leah stared at Charles, her eyes widening as her husband continued to listen. The thing to do was to tell Arthur Moore that Jordan was no longer going to Beach Week, so there was no way he could chaperone, but for some reason Charles didn't seem to be relating this information.

"What are the dates?" Charles asked instead. "I have to just double-check at work . . . I'm in the middle of a big project, but it's on hold right now, so it's probably not an issue, and I usually teach on Mondays, but the semester's over, although I have a bunch of papers to grade, but . . ."

Leah made a throat-clearing noise.

"And I need to check with my wife, of course . . . Sure, I'll call you back tomorrow . . ."

"What in the world, Charles? What are you thinking? You can't chaperone if Jordan isn't going," she said.

"Well, let's talk to her. It seems like in her current frame of mind, it might be good for her to go. Look how pale she is. She could really use some sun. And where's the harm if I'm right there. What could go wrong?"

Charles couldn't bring himself to look at Leah, but the beach was beckoning, and he could really use a break.

10

. . . . .

Back when they were still married—but right before they weren't anymore—Noah heard Clara concede to the neurologist that it might have begun innocently, at least in the context of the warped way in which Noah tended to view the world. *It*, she always said. And the other thing she always did was talk about him as if he weren't sitting right there. But Noah wasn't stupid. He heard her loud and clear, and he understood that the implication was that *it* wasn't innocent in the end.

The neurologist had asked him what it was he thought he'd been doing, and then Dr. Pu-Pu Platter had hesitated for a moment, like he was searching for the right words, before he settled on these: "What was going through your mind when you were *looking at people*?"

Noah hated the way he'd put this, as if it were a chronic problem rather than something specific to the mystery of Bergstrom family life. He was trying to prevent a murder, try-ing to understand why Mrs. Bergstrom had told someone on the phone that someone was trying to kill her. How many times did he need to explain this?

"I wanted to understand," he'd said after thinking about it for a minute. "I was doing it for Clara." Clara was always complaining that he was a moron when it came to reading other people's expressions, but even so, he was pretty sure his wife's blank stare meant this was not a satisfying answer.

Maybe it wasn't the whole truth, but that didn't make it a lie. In the background of everything he did was the simple desire to make Clara happy. Yes, he'd been trying to save Mrs. Bergstrom in her yellow dress (which was how she was now permanently etched in his mind—the buttons undone, one arm out of the sleeve), but he'd also hoped to determine if she spent as much time locked in the bathroom, sobbing, as his wife did. Admittedly this involved a bit of a white lie, because for one thing he couldn't actually see inside the master bathroom of his neighbor's house, even when he climbed out onto the limb that arched closest to her house.

He'd come to love the Bergstroms and had become familiar with their schedules. They opened their front door every weekday at 7:15 sharp, and the four of them filed out looking so happy, kissing each other, shouting "I love you," dashing in and out with forgotten school lunches, briefcases, car keys, cell phones, Mr. B. and the boy getting in the car, Mrs. B. waiting on the corner with the daughter for the school bus, then walking back and getting in another car, their movements purposeful and interconnected, a morning ballet. You would never know from a distance that at least one member of the Bergstrom family was in mortal danger.

Clara insisted that his timing was off, that he had this backward. She claimed that she hadn't begun her crying until he'd begun his peeping. He'd never hit Clara, and he never would, but when she spoke that awful word, *peeping*, he had to admit that he might have lost his temper. Dr. Platter had scolded them both and reminded them that he was not a marriage counselor, just a neurologist trying to achieve a clinical understanding of Noah's condition, and for a moment there, this had united them in anger. But only for a moment.

It had begun to feel as though Mitch Mingus was a regular fixture in Noah's life, some stock sitcom character who was always coming around to harass him week after week after week.

Mitch seemed in a bad mood when he showed up at Joseph's that afternoon. "We need to talk," he said. He put both hands on the counter and leaned in. Drops of his perspiration pooled on the countertop.

"Real estate market must be even slower than they're saying in the papers, given all the time you've got to hang around and harass me. But maybe you're just looking for some candy."

"A real comedian, you are. I'll take a piece or two of whatever you're offering, but you know that's not why I'm here."

"I know. Sorry. I'm gonna take care of this tonight . . ." A group of kids on skateboards clamored by, and a baby started screaming from the smoothie stand next door, and it was too hot to have another one of these conversations about the fact that he hadn't signed the leases.

"What's holding you up?" said Mitch, unwrapping a long stick of peppermint taffy. "I'm not sure I understand. We've done all the paperwork and collected the deposits, so really your signature is just a formality at this point, but you know me, I like to do things by the book, and it would really make me happy if you'd just cross these last *t*'s."

Noah didn't really know Mitch, didn't know he liked to do things by the book, but he didn't want to make him even more upset by pointing this out, because Mitch didn't look so well with all that sweating he was doing. "Come back this time tomorrow, and I swear, I'll have it all here. I gave the leases to my neighbor just to have her look things over. I forgot to ask for them back."

"Jesus, Noah, you've been saying this for two weeks already." He wiped more sweat from his forehead with his sleeve. Noah pushed another piece of taffy across the counter.

He wasn't telling a complete lie. He *had* given Jill the documents, although he didn't know whether she had looked them over. This he could say, however: she had moved them from the kitchen table to her office and then she had moved them again, back downstairs, and he knew this because he had seen her do it. He knew something else about Jill, too. Something that made him think that perhaps she wasn't giving his papers the proper amount of attention—because Noah had seen *him* there, too. Mr. Blowfish, the husband. When he'd mentioned this to Jill, she seemed a little angry. She puzzled over the Blowfish name, too, until he reminded her of the icon on her roof. How people could be so forgetful about the circumstances in which they lived never failed to amaze him.

"He's the father of my children," she said. "He picks the boys up, drops them off. Fixes things. We've had our problems, but he's still my husband. Anyway, what do you know about it?"

"I've seen his car."

She seemed to consider this before replying. "Yeah. True. I suppose you would have."

Noah didn't get what she was so upset about. He was just making an observation, and a rather obvious one at that. It was hard to miss the guy's car; you could see it from a block away, and it wasn't exactly like he was making any effort to be inconspicuous in his giant Lincoln SUV.

Jill was starting to act funny. He was lately having trouble getting her attention. It seemed she'd begun to drift a few weeks ago. Maybe something happened when she and the kids had gone away to visit her mother in Wilmington over Easter. She'd been gone a couple of weeks, and when Noah had come by to welcome her home, she seemed distant. They'd made a date to go out Route 1 together, down toward Ocean City, where she said there was some giant carpet warehouse, but now she was blowing him off even though this had been her idea. Three weeks in a row she'd rescheduled, and then just yesterday she'd canceled again, claiming that Ben was sick. Noah had prearranged to get off early that day, and when he got home, he went over with some taffy to make Ben feel better, but no one answered the door, even though he could see Ben sitting on the couch with a bowl of popcorn watching TV. Noah understood that you couldn't say for sure whether someone was sick just by watching him watch television from twelve feet away, but in his layman's opinion, the boy didn't look unwell.

It was possible that Noah was just reading too much into things again. After all, he had a medically diagnosed propensity to do this, he reminded himself, with the whole paranoia thing. Maybe everything was status quo with Jill. Maybe Ben had been sick and her husband had come around to fix the toilet. They'd go figure that carpet out soon enough—there were places that could do same-day installation, he'd heard. It was possible that all that was going on was that Noah was a little jealous, since he hadn't fully appreciated at first how much he'd taken Jill for granted. Now he wondered if he might have missed his chance.

Noah turned his back to the wooden counter and was busy reorganizing the boxes on the shelves behind the register when he heard the noise. The tattooed kid with the ring through his lip who worked the occasional weekend shift was not very organized, and whenever Noah came back on duty, he had to spend at least an hour putting things where they belonged. Also, Noah had devised a pretty elaborate spreadsheet program on the lumbering old desktop in the back that they used to track inventory, and he'd set up a secondary program, broken into subcategories that recorded which customers liked which flavors, as well as their age and race: a saltwater taffy exit poll. But this kid with the tattoos (Chip was his name, which seemed a bit too all-American for him) not only refused to enter the data, he wouldn't even keep tabs, so Noah had to figure out from the absent boxes what had sold. He was restacking, doing the calculations in his head, or trying to anyway, when he heard what sounded like an animal dying. He turned and saw Mitch Mingus lying on the boardwalk just outside the video arcade, two shops north of Joseph's. He was a large man, and he was on his back, writhing. From a distance he looked like an enormous beached whale, except that he was wearing a light blue shirt.

By the time Noah reached the spot where Mitch was lying, a small crowd had formed. Mitch's face was a shade of gray that made Noah think of Silly Putty, and he seemed to be barely breathing. Noah pushed through the crowd. He wanted to give him mouth-to-mouth resuscitation, but he didn't know how to do that, and someone else was already leaning over him, pounding on his chest.

This couldn't be happening. It wasn't like he really *knew* Mitch Mingus—certainly he couldn't call him a friend—they'd never had a conversation that didn't pertain directly to the sale or rental of his house, and even then Mitch had been curt. But still, Noah had been joking around with the guy not more than five minutes earlier, and here he was, possibly about to die.

It seemed like hours passed before the ambulance arrived, but someone said that it had been exactly eight minutes, which was generally agreed to be pretty good time in rescue squad terms. One of the technicians went over to Mitch and knelt on the ground while the other tech did a little crowd control, pushing everyone away, so now they were all standing on the sidelines like they were watching a show. Noah had seen crowds like this form to watch kids break-dance on the board-walk or to hear the guy who drummed a pretty good rhythm on an upside-down trash can, but he didn't realize that watching someone lying on the ground was considered entertainment.

Things were mostly still for a while, except for some gulls swooping in, scooping in their beaks the french fries someone had dropped during the commotion. That the rescue squad guy was crouched on the ground for this long didn't seem encouraging, although Noah wasn't sure what was meant to happen. It wasn't like Mitch was going to pick himself up off the ground and start shaking hands and thanking everyone, even in the best of circumstances. After a while they got Mitch on a stretcher and placed him in the back of the van. There was no way to tell from a distance whether Mitch Mingus was dead or alive, but Noah hoped the fact that he could glimpse a bit of his face was at least a good sign, in the sense that they hadn't thrown a sheet over him and pronounced him gone.

Noah thought about how strange it was the way these things crept up on you, strong emotions, fierce attachments you didn't even know you had. He felt this way about the Bergstrom family, too, and hoped everyone was getting on all right and that no harm had come to Mrs. B.

PART TWO

Beach Week

11

• • • • •

Inauspicious *adj.* **1.** not auspicious; boding ill; ill-omened; unfavorable. **2.** crossing the city limits into Chelsea Beach and being pulled over by a policeman who looks not much older than the teenagers in the car ahead whom one is meant to be chaperoning. **3.** having the vehicle one is driving, a 1998 Subaru Wagon, towed because the out-of-state registration expired a month earlier. **4.** being crammed into the backseat of one's own Honda Accord with five giggling teenage girls, then deposited ignominiously at the empty Krazinski beach house.
—**Syn.** Unpropitious, ill-timed, unpromising; the utterance of the following sentence by one's wife: *"If you go to Beach Week, Charles Adler, don't bother coming back."*

Though he was giddy, strung out, and exhausted, so many things about the Krazinski beach house made Charles irrationally happy that, were he asked to describe his initial impressions, he wouldn't know where to begin. He supposed an obvious place would be the television. It had been advertised as big, but the reality was truly mind-blowing: sixty-five inches of LCD HDTV, with full 1080p resolution and three HDMI inputs for high-quality single-cable connections to HD components. He didn't know what most of that meant— although he liked his gadgetry, he wasn't an especially high-tech guy—but the television appeared to be new, and the accompanying literature and instruction manuals were spread on the coffee table along with three bewildering-looking remote controls. In addition, although Charles had been made aware of the existence of a major-league baseball package, he hadn't anticipated that Krazinski would also subscribe to the NASCAR, cricket, rugby, and four international football channels. Charles hadn't even known such things existed, that the world contained such luxuries.

Never mind the breathtaking ocean view or the heated swimming pool and adjacent heart-shaped Jacuzzi with its froth of steaming bubbles: there was a Bose surround-sound stereo system with speakers in every room, even in the shower, and ones outdoors disguised as rocks. Perhaps most astonishing in its aesthetic blend of tacky and retro cool were the vibrating, cup holder–equipped, twin leather recliners with tray tables that pulled up out of the arm rests. They reminded him of those decadent business-class pods he sometimes glimpsed on airplanes as he made his way back to coach.

What Charles would put first on his list, however, was even more pedestrian, and that was ice. Ice! He hadn't realized the extent to which he missed having an automatic ice maker until he pressed a glass to the side of the Krazinski refrigerator and, instead of hearing the familiar existential churning sound that reminded him the contraption was broken (eternally and beyond repair, according to the plumber), out dropped small rectangular miracles, perfectly formed cubes of frozen water. Charles filled a glass to the brim, and just for good measure, he switched the setting to "crushed," and filled another. He set them both on the counter and took a step back to admire this tableau.

Exhausted after being up most of the previous night fighting with Leah, and then this hellacious day of traffic and being towed, he'd vowed to evacuate his brain, to avoid contemplation of any sort. Yet ice sent him straight back into self-pitying mode: here he was at age forty-five and he had no ice maker, never mind a beach house, and his biggest indulgence had been to go for leather seats in his Honda Accord—a luxury he enjoyed only when his daughter let him have the car. He was drowning in bills, his mortgage a disaster and his marriage stuck. He'd said this last bit to Leah that very morning in self-defense as she hurled an accusation at him—he could no longer remember exactly what—and she'd paraphrased some quote from the Iris Murdoch novel she was reading for her book group: "One doesn't have to get anywhere in a marriage, Charles. It's not a public conveyance."

That was just one of several astonishing things she'd said that morning as he waited in the kitchen for Jordan to come downstairs with her bag.

Leah had punctuated her remarks with a wooden spoon, causing puffs of brownish flour to float in the air like storm clouds each time she made a point. Once, mid-sentence, she paused to answer the phone and reconfigure Beach Week driving arrangements with Janet Glover while stirring muffin batter, occasionally turning in the direction of Charles to glare.

Charles wondered how his wife's head didn't explode with

contradiction: she was forbidding Jordan to go to Beach Week, yet she was baking multigrain, trans fat–free whole soy flour muffins for her daughter to take with her so she didn't eat too much junk. She was telling Charles that if he went, she never wanted to see him again, and then she asked him what time she should make a dinner reservation for them following Jordan's graduation next week. Leah's parents were flying in from Des Moines, and they planned to invite Charles's mother, too, assuming that by then her medication would be recalibrated sufficiently. The doctors were working on this.

Charles studied Leah from across the room as if she were some curious problem on the take-home exam he had given to his students just last week: Create from these disparate design elements a model of sleek form and function; think outside the box. Who was this woman, and why was she wearing such a pretty summer dress beneath her grungy blue apron? Was she planning some expedition so early in the morning? Was the dress new? Did she have some secret plan to abandon him as soon as he absconded to the beach with their daughter? He supposed it was possible that she frequently wore pretty summer dresses, that she might have even worn this particular one before and he simply hadn't noticed. And her hair: had she done something new? It looked different somehow. When had these soft streaks of gray appeared, blending subtly, attractively really, into her natural brown? And those gold hoops in her ears . . . they looked familiar. Could it be he had given them to her for some important event . . . speaking of which, didn't they have an anniversary looming?

Leah hung up the phone and picked up the conversation where she'd left off. "This is the height of betrayal, Charles," she said. "In the context of everything we've been through, this qualifies as treason."

He had stopped trying to defend himself. He entertained the image of himself sitting on the tennis court, in the line of fire of one of those automatic ball machines. That's what Leah's continuing string of invectives felt like to him.

Treason. The word had now worked its way into the muffins, which were dry and rough and flavored with treachery. He washed one down with some acidic, freshly squeezed juice and watched Leah pull a muffin tin from the oven; it clanged noisily onto the kitchen counter. He took another bite, and some crumbs fell onto the floor. He bent to pick them up but not in time to avoid being scolded.

"Could you please eat that at the table?" she snapped. "You're making a complete mess, and we have ants all of a sudden." She started to say something about not wanting to use ant spray, because . . . He tuned out, recalling why it was that he no longer spent much time contemplating his wife with affection.

Treason? Betrayal? This seemed a little rich. If anything, he was loyal to a fault. There were plenty of worse ways to betray his wife, and in fact he sometimes wondered if he was the only man in the world who hadn't given in to *that* particular form of treachery. Nevertheless, it was true, he was about to become his own version of a middle-aged cliché, going off the reservation, climbing out on a limb, acting on a lark, telling, demanding really, that his daughter pack a bag and go. He'd have time to think this through later, but what he knew right now was that he had reached some sort of breaking point, and volunteering to chaperone was at least a semi-legitimate way to go rogue.

"Jordan isn't well enough to go to the beach," Leah said again.

"We both know she's better. The beach will do her good."

"She's still grounded, Charles."

"I know."

They'd had this conversation already, more than once.

"If you take both cars," she tried instead, "I'll have no way to get to the dentist this afternoon."

About this, he did feel bad—she had an appointment to begin work on a new crown. Another thing they couldn't really afford.

Again he tried to clear his head, but he found that in the absence of deliberate thought, like weeds in an empty flower bed, beer jingles rushed in to fill the void: *"If you've got the time, we've got the beer . . ." "Here's to good friends, tonight is kinda special . . ."* This reminded him that it wasn't ice that had brought him to the refrigerator; it was beer. If ever a day demanded a beer (or two or three or even four), it was this one. He found a bottle opener and popped the top off a Heineken, which he sucked down in three straight gulps.

It was extremely hot in the house, and he was beginning to perspire: he looked around for a thermostat but couldn't find one. He took off his shirt, opened another beer, and flipped on the television, which was even more complicated than it looked, as it required coordinating the three remotes, which between them were tricked out with enough small, glowing buttons to launch a nuclear device. He watched the Orioles for a few minutes, but the game was pretty dull, as they were being routed twelve to two in the bottom of the eighth. He checked in with a couple of other games, then found a station that, incredibly, broadcast eight games simultaneously: "TEX4/ NYY 1; BOS 2/DET 0; LAA 5/TOR 0; CHC 2/ATL 0; MIL 3/ FLA 0; SF/WASH RAIN; KC 0/TB 4; COL 0/HOU 0."

Beyond his wildest dreams, this was! He could sit here all day. Except that less than an hour later he was already bored. Now that he was free to watch as much sports programming as he wanted, with no one to chide him, to remind him of more productive things he might be doing, to suggest, joy-crushingly, that his obsession with televised sports was his way of sublimating . . . sublimating what, exactly, she never did say . . . well, without anyone to mock him, his favorite pastime was weirdly losing its appeal.

He switched to the local news: "Hordes of teenagers flood Chelsea Beach for 'senior week'; 100 extra police recruited for the month of June; local bars asked to be on the lookout for fake IDs; a mother of six rushed to the hospital after being stung by a poison jellyfish; weather sunny and clear, high today of 87 . . ." At least this qualified as news you could use. He flipped over to CNN, half hoping for some sort of catastrophe that would put in perspective his own petty concerns, but the world seemed disarmingly peaceful.

He returned to the kitchen and began to rummage through Krazinski's pantry, hoping to find some food. A brief perusal of the cabinets turned up enough liquor to host a block party, but not a single thing to eat, apart from a few condiments. He opened another beer and reminded himself that this was great, this was exactly what he needed, there was no better place to be. This was the sort of mini-break he'd privately longed for these last few years, the only glitch being that he was very hungry. He hadn't eaten a thing since that godforsaken muffin, and his stomach let out a little rumble of hunger and despair.

There was a note on the counter from Martin Krazinski that he hadn't previously noticed, telling him to make himself at home. "Had to take a deposition," it read, "will be back soon." Soon? Charles wondered what that meant, since he had no idea when the note had been written. It was possible to suppose it was intended as a generic explanation of his whereabouts, that Martin Krazinski took depositions frequently and this was a sort of placeholder, like "in the garden" or "out to lunch." Nevertheless, the greeting emboldened Charles to be more aggressive in his search for food, although closer examination of the cupboards didn't yield anything more interesting than tea bags and instant coffee, sugar, some packets of soy sauce, and a variety of mixers. How could there be no food in the house? he wondered. Of course, the house was used only seasonally, so presumably no one spent much time here preparing inedible muffins or chewy beef tacos. He was reminded that there didn't appear to be a Mrs. Krazinski in the picture, and he supposed this might be a useful glimpse of what his own pantry would look like when he no longer had a wife. He wondered, hypothetically, how long a person could survive on beer and Bloody Mary mix, although the question was actually a little more complicated than that, since a second look inside the refrigerator turned up the existence of ketchup, mustard, mayonnaise, and a brand-new, unopened jar of relish, which could theoretically sustain a person for days.

Much more encouraging was the pizza delivery menu he only just noticed, affixed by a magnet to the refrigerator door. With great seriousness he studied the long list of toppings, finally settling on half pepperoni, half sausage. It occurred to him that this was actually his usual selection, and he wondered if, like the hamsters under stress he'd recently read about who were unable to change behavioral patterns, he was destined to repeat this pizza order for the rest of his life. This was not the right moment for self-analysis, however.

He looked for a phone, which proved as elusive as the thermostat; there was evidently no landline in the house. His own phone had run out of batteries about an hour earlier, and he'd left his charger in his suitcase, in the car.

Talk about your bad day. He had, at first, been cheered by the sight of all those Chelsea Beach police officers lined up in black and yellow vests, bright like bumblebees. He saw some thirty troops—in cruisers, on motorcycles, and on bicycles, too, and he thought briefly that all this parental angst, his own included, had been for naught. Who could possibly get in trouble with this many police around? One of them was even waving to him, welcoming him to town. Or so he thought.

It took Charles a moment or two to figure out what was going on as the police kid—he looked to be about fifteen, although of course that was impossible—fired up his motorcycle and began to follow the Subaru. The way the cop was weaving in and out of lanes, coming up beside him, made Charles wonder if the guy was drunk. It finally occurred to him that he should stop.

Apparently they were on the lookout for any infraction, no matter how small, these overbearing, trigger-happy, asshole police, and Charles was a sitting duck. He'd been hectoring Leah for months, but she'd never bothered to register her car in the state of Maryland. Now the Nebraska tags had expired, and he was in violation of the law. He was asked to wait on the side of the road for the tow truck to arrive. Jordan and her friends were at least kind enough to pull over and wait with him, and then to give him a ride.

Sitting on the hood of his car for an hour, Charles had had plenty of time to absorb his grim surroundings. He'd never been to the Eastern Shore before and could only hope it had more to offer than this dreadful stretch of traffic-choked sprawl. Where was the beach? The last few miles had been one big box store after another, until they crossed the city limits into Chelsea Beach, and then things surprisingly just got worse. If there was anything more depressing than strip mall after strip mall, it would be a dead strip mall. Or more specifically, a dead outlet mall. The place appeared stalled mid-renovation, or possibly mid-teardown—he couldn't tell which. Cranes, bulldozers, Dumpsters, and Porta Pottis, like slain rusting beasts, sat idle.

He thought sadly of Downtown, the fate of which would be decided any day. If the Metro didn't get approved, he'd move on, there would be other projects, this wouldn't mark the end of his career, yet he'd hung so much on this. He'd uprooted his family and put everything in jeopardy by agreeing to take the bulk of his compensation on the back end. These plans were just lines on the page, but in his mind he'd seen something more. Downtown, to him, was a living thing, an installation with movable parts. He could see dogs off leash, frolicking in parks; families walking from their apartments with colorful rafts and brightly striped towels to the pool for their afternoon swims (he could even smell the chlorine); men and women in their business suits walking from their homes to the subway without getting into cars. He imagined that scrapping these plans must be like putting a novel away, never having it see the light of day. Although who could say, maybe it was possible that all of those characters went on to have rich, fulfilling lives, even in the backs of drawers. And his imagined Downtown residents might still thrive, even if they lived only on a drawing board.

Because he'd had ample time to soak up his surroundings, too much time as it happened, Charles knew that the nearest commercial district was not within walking distance of the quiet, gated community where the Krazinski house was situated. He was apparently about seven miles from where the kids were staying. He didn't know for sure, because he hadn't seen their beach house yet, because he didn't have a car. And because he didn't have a car, he couldn't use his cell phone, which was sitting on the coffee table, lifeless beside the winking remotes. Surely there was some logical solution to the pizza-ordering dilemma if he just thought about it long enough.

He filled another glass with ice just because he could, and opened another beer to help him think. It was extremely hot, and he took off his trousers, then sat back down in the other leather recliner to see which one was more comfortable. He supposed he could walk next door and ask to use a phone to order his pizza, but this would require more effort than he could muster just now, plus he'd have to put his pants back on, and he had only just taken them off.

Once more he approached the refrigerator and stuck his head inside, pausing for a moment to absorb the delicious cold air. He retrieved the jar of relish and found, in the drawer, a spoon. He sat back down in the first recliner—they were essentially the same, he concluded—and turned the vibrator on.

He closed his eyes and imagined vibrating his way to some other life in a business-class pod. This was not the most auspicious start to Beach Week, but he was exhausted and, truth be told, not at all unhappy to be alone.

12

• • • • •

Jordan steered the car into the driveway at 4200 Ocean Breeze Lane, and for a brief moment she wondered if they were at the wrong house. The same silly unicorn flag she'd seen in the photograph when she'd gone to the Mingus Realty website that morning to download directions still waved from the front porch, and the same ceramic pots framed the walkway, even if the flowers were long dead, but something was clearly wrong, and it wasn't just that this place was a complete dump. Adding to her confusion was the presence of Paul Schramm and Mike Seltzer, who lay spread-eagled on the lawn, and behind them, on the front porch, slumped in a chair that looked like it belonged indoors, was Deegan Krazinski, who had a beer in one hand, a cigarette in the other, Rollerblades on his feet, and Rene Palmer sitting in his lap. Two other guys whom Jordan couldn't identify from the vantage point of the driveway lay on the porch, and Marta Krazinski was propped against an oversize cooler on wheels, with about a dozen empty beer cans beside it.

"Sorry we took so long, you guys," Jordan said as they got out of the car and dragged their luggage toward the house. Dandelions sprouted through cracks in the pavement, and Jordan banged her toe hard as she stumbled on a piece of broken cobblestone. She bent over to inspect, but there was nothing visible other than a chip on the bright pink nail polish she'd applied that morning to pass the time as her parents fought in the kitchen.

"Did you get our messages?"

"Yeah," said Rene, "but even so, what happened? We've been locked out for, like, three hours already!"

Jordan's group had stopped at the realty office to get the key, which had been left in Dorrie's name. Although they had set off from Verona that morning in a convoy of three, Jordan had lost Marta's car at the first light, when much to the amusement of her passengers, she refused to run the yellow. From there, they continued to lose more ground. Not only did Jordan obey the speed limit, but she slowed down even more once she came to understand both the quantity and variety of illegal substances she was apparently transporting. Although she was feeling fine physically, the intensity with which the flu had hit had been disorienting, and between that and her gratitude that she'd been able to avoid another migraine, she had this sense that her body was a vessel to be cherished and protected, and she was comporting herself accordingly. They'd been further stalled, of course, by the embarrassing debacle with her father and the police, after which they had to detour to drop him at the Krazinskis'. What the hell was going on with her parents? How could her mother, who was always so on top of things, have failed to organize the paperwork for the car?

While this explained why their housemates were locked out, it didn't account for the presence of all these boys or the amount of crap on the lawn.

"What's going on here? It looks like a refugee camp," said Dorrie.

"Yeah. As the house manager, I feel like this is unacceptable," said Amy. She seemed a little too psyched about this role and had created on poster board three different charts meant to track household chores and monitor supplies, and she'd also brought a box full of cookbooks. The girls were all indulging her, but it was clear that a few of them, like Cherie and Dorrie, were beginning to wonder if Amy had some fundamental misunderstanding of what the week was going to involve.

Strewn across the lawn were suitcases, surfboards, an Xbox and Guitar Hero accessories including a plastic drum set, some real guitars in their cases, amplifiers, beach towels, lounge chairs, a baseball bat, a volleyball net, and an enormous inflatable dinosaur that some boy Jordan had never seen before was trying to inflate by mouth.

There was a commotion, suddenly, next door. A sweet-looking Labrador retriever ran from the front door toward one of the bags of groceries someone had left sitting on the lawn; the dog clamped a box of Cheerios in its jaw and ran back toward its home. A pretty woman around the same age as Jordan's mother came chasing after it, laughing and apologizing.

"I'm so sorry!" she said. "I'll bring you another box, I promise!"

"No worries," said Dorrie.

"You kids let me know if you need anything," she said before going back inside. "My name's Jill. Just knock on the door if you want me."

Jordan realized that there must have been some mix-up: Jill's house looked suspiciously like the one she'd seen in the photo. It was new and gleaming and enormous. It looked a bit like a bank. *This* house had paint coming off in strips the size of banana peels and frankly looked kind of decrepit. Someone should really point out the error to Mingus Realty, she thought. She hadn't even stepped inside, but already she was reminded of the essay on Dickens she'd just written for her English exam, invoking Miss Havisham. At least there was an ocean right behind it, as advertised.

"What are you guys doing here?" Cherie asked nervously. "And where are the others? Where are the Courtneys?" Although Cherie had clearly come prepared to party—she'd already chopped and snorted one of her father's OxyContins in the car, then washed it down with a swig of vodka from one of twelve bottles of Evian she'd poured out and refilled with Grey Goose—she nevertheless seemed determined to adhere to their pledge in her own loopy way, which included, however absurdly, a vow to not allow boys in the house.

"A bunch of people already went down to the beach. And to answer your other question, we're moving in with you," said Mike.

"Hilarious," said Jordan, assuming this was a joke. She was pretty sure the follow-up would involve an explanation that they, too, were just waiting for someone to arrive with their key.

"We've been evicted," said Deegan, sounding almost cheerful about this.

"How could you have been evicted already?" Cherie asked. "You've been here all of . . . what, an hour?"

"Well, we got here a few hours ago actually, but we didn't even get in the door," Deegan said. "This is a total ruse, man.

You wouldn't believe what just happened to us. We were totally entrapped. The cops are standing guard like snipers, just waiting to pounce."

"Snipers tend to shoot, not pounce," said Dorrie. She, too, seemed more annoyed than Jordan might have supposed, given that she'd already announced in the car that she was claiming the master bedroom for herself and Paul.

"Yeah," said Cherie. "This is not exactly the most serendipitous beginning."

"Okay, cool it with the Shakespeare, Princeton girls. The point is that this is fucked up," said Deegan.

Deegan had overreached on his applications and was generally pretty bitter about the fact that he was on his way to some remote satellite campus of Penn State. Both Cherie and Dorrie were into Princeton, and his own twin sister was on her way to Stanford, which had rather comically been Deegan's second choice, after Yale.

"We were unpacking the car," he explained, "and this really nice guy shows up from nowhere, asks if he can help. So we're talking to him, he asks where we're from, what we're doing, totally eggs us on. Says he goes to some private school in Delaware. So we're just bullshitting, and as soon as we start unloading the beer, he pulls out his ID, a bunch of other cops come out of nowhere, he calls the Realtor, and that's it. We're evicted. On top of which, there's some sort of fine involved."

"I don't even think that's legal," said Zack, fishing a beer out of the cooler and popping the top. "I'm gonna ask my dad about whether we should talk to a lawyer."

"So you think you can stay *here*?" Cherie just about shrieked.

"Yeah. I mean I don't want to be a downer or anything," Jordan said, "but if you guys already got in trouble, do you think you might try to be a little more discreet? Look at this place—it's like you're having a tailgate party on our lawn!"

"Jordan, you are *totally* a downer," said Paul. "That could be your middle name! Jordan Downer Adler."

"You're a real comedian, Paul," she said. Just about every interaction she had with him lately left her so enraged that she could imagine getting to the point where she snapped, did something crazy, like throw something at him. She considered the half-eaten apple in her left hand and envisioned the unimpressive velocity with which she'd hurl the projectile, the spot on his chest where it would make its lame, light contact, the hilarity that would ensue among her friends. That there would be a communal understanding of the history contained in this lobbed piece of fruit was ultimately what enabled her to maintain her composure.

"There's no way," said Cherie. "You *cannot* stay here. My mom's gonna flip out!"

"Your mom isn't even here. When is she coming?"

"Not until Wednesday. But she said I shouldn't count on that. She might come earlier and pay a surprise visit."

"Well, one day at a time and all that," said Deegan. "Who's chaperoning now?"

"Jordan's dad," said Mindy.

Deegan pulled a bong from his backpack, and Jordan wondered if this timing was coincidental or spoke to the lack of fear inspired by proximity to her dad. Even Deegan, who hardly knew her dad, could sense that he wasn't very formidable. Although her dad wasn't oblivious or even all that lax, Jordan knew it was easy to take advantage of him and even manipulate him on the extremely regrettable occasions when it was necessary; he seemed to want to overlook the obvious and believe in his daughter's better self.

"Actually, Deegan," Marta said, "Dad called me this morning and said it's possible he'll get here later tonight, but he wasn't sure if he'd wrap up the deposition today or tomorrow."

Deegan put a lighter up to the bowl.

"Seriously!" said Mindy. "Could you at least wait until we get inside the house!"

"Did Jordan's dad say when he's dropping by?" asked Mike, now standing near the door with his bags.

"Well, I wouldn't worry about it right now," said Mindy, "since he doesn't even have a car." She went over to the door and turned the key, and everyone began to pile in.

Dorrie raced up the stairs, Rene so close behind her it looked like they might crash into one another and wind up on the wrong side of the banister. Jordan could hear a catfight erupt in the continuing debate over possession of the master bedroom. Deegan set the bong on the coffee table, then glided over to the television and began to rig up the Xbox. "This set is about a million years old," he complained.

"Jesus fucking Christ, open the window!" Cherie shrieked. "There's a bad smell in here."

"Yeah, open all the windows," Jordan agreed. "It smells like . . ." She wasn't sure what it smelled like, but whatever it was, it was extremely foul.

"What's up with all these moths?" asked Mindy. She was standing in a corner of the living room, surrounded by a cloud of tiny white flying creatures. "It's like something out of a Stephen King novel. *The Moths* . . ."

"Ewwwww . . ." said Cherie. "Actually there *is* some story like that . . . have you heard of the Mothman? It's like, a real thing—somewhere in Ohio or West Virginia, a bunch of people saw this flying creature that was half moth, half man. He made a bridge collapse, killed a bunch of people. They made a movie out of it."

"How many pills have you swallowed?" Mike asked.

"No, really. I mean it's a real thing. *The Mothman Prophecies* . . . or something like that? Google it!"

"Maybe the place is haunted," said Deegan. He didn't seem particularly fazed by this possibility.

"That reminds me," said Cherie. "I promised my mom we'd take pictures, just in case they won't give us the security deposit back or something. Why don't you do that, Jordan," she said, tossing the digital camera in her direction. "I need to find the bathroom . . . I'm not feeling so well all of a sudden."

Jordan stood in the living room, camera in hand. The open windows seemed unlikely to do much in terms of airing the place out, given the heat and the wall of humidity outside. Probably the thing to do was just take these pictures and then get out of there, go down to the beach and inhale some clean air, maybe take a swim and cool off.

She supposed she might be the only kid in the entire history of Beach Week to be here under protest, not to mention while grounded. Previously she'd never doubted her centrality in her parents' concerns, but at this point it was hard not to feel like a pawn in their messed-up marriage. Things weren't looking too promising on the Mom and Dad living-happily-ever-after front. There'd been so much change in the last few years that it was dizzying, and she got the feeling lately that the metamorphosis was actually just beginning, that there was the real chance her parents were going to split up once she left. Once she left for where . . . that was a different question, another blind spot in her vision of the future. She wanted to go to NYU, and the money seemed to be slowly coming together, but she wasn't so sure that she wanted to go right away. Now that she'd forced herself to turn her Google Earth wanderings in a different direction, India seemed to be beckoning, and she had with her in her backpack a book about gap year.

She supposed she could have protested the Beach Week mandate: "Let's go! Let's get out of the house! Let's live our lives!" her dad had said, or really ordered, which had sounded highly suspicious. Was he talking about himself or about Jordan? She didn't particularly want to have a conversation about this, even though she wondered if she bore some responsibility for telling her parents to quit behaving like they were back in middle school.

Stay home, go to Beach Week, go to college, defer . . . it hardly mattered. She'd hit some wall of inertia in the wake of the Khalid breakup. Intellectually she could put it all in place quite easily. It was a fling that had come to an end. A spring fling, a complete cliché. As clichéd as her parents splitting up in the wake of an empty nest. Here she'd even gone out of her way to do something different, to find a boyfriend who wasn't some dumb high school jock, who was more mature, who seemed vaguely exotic. Nevertheless, it had fallen apart like every other boring end-of-high-school relationship. And her parents . . . well, who knew what went on between them privately, but she had always had some image of them as being somehow unique, as actually liking each other, as even being *friends.*

Processing all of this emotionally was another matter, however, and she felt like she was walking around with something heavy pressing on her chest. She could sit in her room with this thing weighing on her or pack it up and haul it to the beach. For reasons she wasn't all that eager to explore, this seemed to be what her father wanted her to do, and even more confusing was that when push came to shove, when her mother was telling her to stay and her father was telling her to go, she found herself taking his side, however inexplicably.

This house at the beach was truly astonishing in its weirdness. At least the funky smell was dissipating. Jordan couldn't tell if the fresh air had washed it out, or if, more logically, it had simply sweetened as it mingled with the pot. Ground zero of what remained of the odor seemed to be the grungy couch, but this evidently didn't concern the boys, who were already congregated on and around it; it took them all of ten minutes to completely sink into a game of Guitar Hero, with four of them jamming to an annoying Aerosmith song. *"That dude looks like a lady . . ."* Paul Schramm wailed into the microphone, swiveling his hips grotesquely. "Dude, dude, dude, dude . . ."

The moths in the corner were pretty freaky, the way they stayed in one area, circling like vultures homing in on a carcass. She took a picture of them. The carpet was both hideous and horribly stained, and she wasn't even the sort of person who tended to notice such things. She took a picture of this, too. There were photographs of an adorable little boy all over the place, also very weird; everywhere you looked, he was peeking out of a frame, sometimes in entire sheets of two-by-threes. Jordan thought she saw something—a shadow, maybe, at the window, but when she turned, it seemed to disappear.

She turned back toward the living room and took a picture of the pictures of the boy.

"Did anyone get the liquor out of the car? There's also

some tequila in the trunk," yelled Cherie from the bathroom. "It's probably not good for it to sit in the hot car. It could be flammable for all we know!"

"Yeah, I've got it up here," someone, maybe Amy, replied from upstairs. Jordan couldn't identify all of the voices without the faces attached.

"Lime? Anyone have lime?" That could have been Rene, but Jordan wasn't completely sure.

"There's some in the cooler," Deegan called. "What's going on, are you guys having a party upstairs? Did you hear that Ruth Corbett stole some IV bags and lines from her dad's office?" he continued without missing a beat of the song.

"Why? What for?"

"So they can drink intravenously, get drunk faster."

"No way," said Marta, who'd come downstairs to get the lime.

"Way."

"I don't believe that. That sounds apocryphal."

"There you go again with your big fucking vocabulary words."

"Deegan, have you always been such a moron?"

"Word."

"Word."

Jordan had to confess that half the time she didn't know what anyone was talking about. Various words, like *word*, seemed to become part of the lexicon for a while, and just as quickly they were gone, usually at about the time Jordan caught on to the fact of their existence. Then there was a secondary, ironic use of a word once it had gone out of fashion, which she suspected might now be going on . . . kind of like saying something was *groovy*.

Jordan took a picture of the boys playing Guitar Hero.

"Jordan, be a sweetheart, get me another beer, will you?" Mike asked. He turned and mugged for the camera, and she was reminded that he was pretty cute. For some reason this made her want to check her cell phone for any sign of Khalid, but she forced herself to reach into her pocket and turn it off.

She went to the front porch and fished a bottle of Budweiser out of the cooler. There was a guy still sitting out there, breathing into the plastic dinosaur, which was now bigger than he was and still half limp.

"We totally promised we wouldn't have a party in this house," Cherie protested as word was being spread via text message and Facebook. "Seriously, am I the only one who paid attention at that meeting? Does anyone else remember the pledge we signed? My mom is going to kill me!"

Paul grabbed her cell phone and took a picture of her slumped in a chair. It was only 7:00 p.m. and already she appeared to be wasted.

"Don't you dare hit send," she said.

"Or what?" he said, hitting, or pretending to hit, send.

Cherie popped up out of the chair and began to fake pummel him; he grabbed her, and they wound up on the floor, wrestling for possession of the phone. Paul flipped her onto her back and lay on top of her, pinning the arm that now held the phone to the floor. Cherie had changed into a bathing suit, over which she wore a flimsy, sheer sarong that had come undone in the tussling. Jordan was glad that Dorrie was upstairs; she'd go completely nuts if she saw Cherie and Paul flirting like this. Jordan thought this seemed likely to turn into random hookup number one, except that she knew she wasn't privy to half of what might be going on upstairs. She also wondered if she was turning into her mother, since she couldn't stop thinking about how unhygienic it was, the two of them rolling around on the gross carpet.

"Okay, who wants to go with me to the grocery store?" asked Amy implausibly. She bounded down the stairs with what looked like a grocery list in hand. On the drive over, she'd gone on at length about the dinner she planned to make for them that night as she'd thumbed through a book called *Awesome Recipes from the Sea*. Occasionally she'd blurt something out like, "It would never have occurred to me to put bacon in seafood paella!"

"Actually," said Deegan, surprising everyone, "I'll go with you. I think we should have a barbecue. I noticed a grill out back . . ."

"But I was thinking lobsters," said Amy.

"We'll do both. Surf and turf! Can you give me your car keys, Marta?" He skated over to his sister, who was in the kitchen making a pitcher of something involving "Evian" and blue Kool-Aid. She reached into her pocket and tossed him the keys. "Are you sure you should drive? I'm not keeping track, but it seems you've been doing your share of consumption over there. Not to mention that I don't think you can drive with Rollerblades on."

"Just watch me," he said, and rolled toward the door. "Besides, I forgot to bring any other shoes, so I don't have much choice."

"Wait, I think we need more 'Evian,'" Marta said.

"I don't have an ID," Deegan said. "Amy, do you have one?"

She shook her head no.

"Dorrie has one," Marta volunteered.

"Seriously, do you think I can use Dorrie's ID?" Amy asked.

The answer was too obvious to warrant a reply. Dorrie had blond hair and blue eyes, and Amy was dark-haired, with brown eyes.

"You should take Jordan's," Deegan said.

Jordan and Amy stared at each other awkwardly, neither one of them wanting to comment on the extent of their similarities, or really the absence thereof. But they both had shoulder-length hair, which was likely to suffice. Jordan rummaged through her bag and found the ID.

She walked out to the front porch with Amy and Deegan and watched them drive away. Outside, the guy was still blowing up the dinosaur, which was now about ten feet tall and still inflating.

13

. . . . .

Noah got that his level of despair was disproportionate to the facts of the relationship. The facts being that there was, essentially, no relationship with Mitch Mingus, apart from a few professional and frankly chilly interactions having to do with the summer rental of his beachfront property. Yet he mourned Mitch's death as deeply as he might a member of his own family. He felt he owed this to Mitch, because so far as he could tell, although Mitch had had the occasional visitor at the hospital, no one had kept vigil at his bedside, and it seemed someone should have. At the very least, Noah thought, there ought to be someone offering to bring him water, and Noah had kept a cold pitcher beside Mitch's bed even though he didn't appear to be all that thirsty, given that he was in a coma. Mitch had spent two days like this, hooked up to machines, not eating or drinking anything, before his sister came in with her husband and their kids. She looked just like her brother but with breasts, which wasn't an especially desirable addition to the Mitch physique. They gathered around Mitch's bed for an hour or so, and then she went out into the hallway and signed some papers, and shortly thereafter they wheeled Mitch out of the room with a sheet pulled up over his head.

By the time Noah stumbled out of the hospital, he'd completely lost track of time. He'd slept on the chair in Mitch's room the previous night, then gone straight to Joseph's for his shift. He felt a little disoriented, and at times like this he found it helped to try to work things out in his notebook.

1. Mrs. Bergstrom had been wearing a yellow dress.
2. The daily average number of sales for assorted taffy sticks so far, this first week of June, was 42.
3. Oliver was no longer allowed to visit—at least not for a while, until Clara cooled off about the fact that Noah had talked to some girl about learning to surf while Oliver was sitting on the yellow tablecloth.
4. Yellow.
5. Mitch was dead, and it was possibly Noah's fault. He shouldn't have given him the taffy. He should have cleaned up his house a little more and aggravated him a little less.
6. Jill hadn't wanted to come to the hospital to visit Mitch. She said she didn't actually know him that well. She told Noah that Mitch was not really his responsibility.
7. It was June 5. It was the first day of Beach Week.
8. Someone was trying to kill Mrs. Bergstrom, and although he might be the only one in the world who could do anything to prevent this, he'd been banished from Verona.

Because there was no common denominator, the math proved impossible:

$$\frac{\text{Yellow dress}}{\text{42 boxes}} + \frac{\text{No Oliver}}{\text{Yellow}} + \frac{\text{Dead Realtor}}{\text{Jill negativity}} + \frac{\text{June 5}}{\text{Murder}}$$

It was like trying to merge languages with different alphabets.

He could see them through the window at his house, the Beach Week kids. They were everywhere he looked, playing some game hooked up to the television, filling the kitchen cabinets with food, laughing. A boy and a girl tussled on the floor like puppies. He couldn't remember the last time he'd played around like that or even touched someone so casually, or intimately, although perhaps that wasn't true. Just a few weeks earlier he'd been able to hug his son, to ruffle up his curly hair.

Had he ever been as young as these kids? Had he ever been that light? There was no such thing as Beach Week where he came from. He wondered if it was a generational thing, or if there was perhaps the presumption that if you grew up in southern Florida, life was Beach Week all the time. His childhood had actually been kind of the opposite of Beach Week, even if the sun was always shining. His mother had run off when he was seven, and then she died of cancer (punishment for leaving, his father quipped, although this seemed not quite right to Noah, even as a kid). Never mind Beach Week, he couldn't remember anyone even baking him a birthday cake or making a fuss about his high school graduation, even though he'd won himself a scholarship to MIT. Then he'd married Clara, and he was the one who hadn't wanted a proper wedding and had insisted on visiting a judge during his lunch hour.

Maybe this had been a mistake. Maybe a person *needed* to fuss, or everything just blurred into one long, flat line, like the pathway that led from one end of Palm View Vistas to the other, where he'd watched the old people recreate, pacing back and forth in what passed as fun.

Was there something to be gleaned by watching these kids? he wondered. Their rituals seemed to him curious: One of the kids was walking around with a digital camera, photographing his things. He supposed this was a compliment until she took a picture of the picture of Oliver, which struck him as a creepy thing to do. Then she looked in the cupboard and took out an old box of taffy. He wanted to yell to her to stop—it was stale, and she should throw that box away and come down to the boardwalk and he'd give her a fresh batch. As he moved closer to the window, prepared to tap on it to stop her before she put a piece in her mouth, he recognized her—it was almost too strange to be true, but it was that girl from Dr. Pu-Pu's office, there, in his house. Harriet? Or was Harriet someone else? That girl from the beach, perhaps? He was having a little trouble remembering. Nevertheless, it was still pretty weird, and he wouldn't even know how to begin working out the odds on this one; he didn't even know what questions to ask or what words to record in his notebook.

14

• • • • •

Charles opened his eyes and saw above him a small, nattily dressed man. He smelled of Scotch, peppermint, and lime-scented shaving cream.

He assumed he was dreaming, but the man persisted in calling his name. "Adler?" he said in his hard-to-place accent. "Are you okay, mate?"

Charles felt like he'd been put under. The only other time in his life he'd been this logy and thick was when he emerged from anesthesia after having his wisdom teeth pulled during graduate school. He took stock of the empty beer bottles in the cup holders and on the floor beside the chair, and he realized that what was going on was pretty mundane: he was drunk. Extremely drunk. He thought it safe to say that he hadn't had this much to drink since college and that, on second thought, this could well be a lifetime record.

"Krazinski?" he asked. He'd meant to say *Krazinski*. Perhaps he had.

He'd been in a deep sleep, dreaming about . . . what *had* he been dreaming about? He was quickly losing track of the narrative, but he could remember something do with that shopping mall across from the pizzeria. And in his dream there had been an ocean in the shopping mall. And his house, in the ocean. No need for Dr. Freud on that one. With the balloon payment due on the mortgage, the house was officially underwater. But it had actually been a happy dream. There'd been lots of amusements in the mall: a mini golf course, a batting cage, a Ferris wheel painted and polished and spinning gaily, and . . . had it gotten stuck? Were the nuts and bolts falling out of the thing, crashing rhythmically to the ground? It was coming back to him in trippy fragments, and he realized that it had blurred into the sound of someone banging on the door.

Krazinski's tie was green with little swirls of white, like the ugly linoleum on the Adler kitchen floor. Charles thought of the smell of lime that hung on this man and wondered if it had to do with all this green. Maybe he was completely losing his mind, veering into such random free association territory it might qualify as some psychotic split. He began to say something but felt a wave of nausea accompanied by the nagging sense that he was meant to be doing something, that there was someplace he was meant to be other than in a vibrating leather recliner, the back-and-forth motion of which was making him seasick. The semester was over, and he'd told his colleagues at Mirage Development that he wouldn't be in for a couple of days. Leah, having implied that he ought not return, surely wasn't counting on him for dinner—or breakfast, depending on what time it was right now. And Jordan . . . yes, that was it! He was meant to be chaperoning. But he *was* chaperoning. Well, he was here at the beach, anyway, in the capacity of chaperone. No one had spelled out, explicitly, what it was a chaperone was meant to do.

Nevertheless, he felt horribly irresponsible. What had he done, essentially dragging his daughter here? He'd been privately mocking Leah these last few months for trying so hard to negotiate this confusing, conflicted Beach Week ritual, thinking that if he simply refused to engage, he couldn't be implicated in this communal parenting atrocity. He'd supposed that the answer was to just opt out. But he'd been wrong, he now realized in a panic. If you chose to raise your child in this community, you had to embrace your surroundings, play by the rules, and accept the consequences. It was like . . . well, what was it like? With his head still awash in beer, it was hard to come up with the right analogy, although something to do with drinking too much and being hung over seemed about right. It was possible that he was about to be sick.

"Are you okay, man?" Krazinski said. He leaned in close, and Charles could smell the addition of garlic on his peppermint-Scotch breath. "You don't look so good, my friend. I'm really sorry I'm late. We were delayed out of Zurich, and then I missed my connection in Munich."

Zurich. Charles had never been to Zurich. Or Munich. And at this rate, he never would. The closest he was likely to come to any luxury travel was right here, in this make-believe business-class reclining chair. The least he could do was present himself with some dignity to this man who'd just flown halfway around the world to greet him. He resolved to stand up straight and wipe away the green pickle relish that was mashed into his chest hair, to put on his trousers and shake the hand of his host.

When Charles swiveled his legs to stand up, however, he

heard an ominous creaking sound in his upper back, just below the neck, which was followed by a searing stab of pain. He screamed involuntarily. He had a colleague at work who'd been out for three months after slipping a disk, the result of . . . taking a nap on the couch. This seemed just about right as a precursor to a Charles Adler–style slide into official middle age. Instead of some romantic tale about colliding with a small aircraft while hang gliding in Peru or tipping his sailboat in choppy waters off the Cape of Good Hope, Charles would wind up in traction after falling asleep in a reclining chair.

He managed to stand up and roll his head in circles while pressing his hand to the back of his neck. This didn't do much to ease the pain, but it at least assured him that he hadn't lost mobility. He combed his fingers through his hair, a drop in the bucket of presenting well.

"Jesus, man, you're quite a sight. And I must say, you scared the hell out of me. I didn't think anyone was here . . . There was no answer when I knocked, and there's no car out front. Are you sure you're okay?" He looked at Charles with concern.

"Yeah, yeah, I'm fine. Well, *fine*'s not quite the right word— Jesus, I think I threw my back out. And I had a bit of a bad day yesterday. Or earlier today, I guess . . . I've kind of lost track of time. My car, or really my wife's car, got . . . towed. And my phone charger was in the car, so I couldn't order a pizza." He understood even as he spoke that this might seem a non sequitur to someone who had just walked through the door, unaware of how large the unattainable pizza loomed in his narrative of Beach Week thus far.

Charles remembered that Leah had thought this Krazinski fellow might be someone famous, and he had dismissed this idea with some condescension. But now he wondered—between this beach house and the Zurich-through-Munich globe-trotting—whether Leah might have been right.

"Can I ask you a question?"

"Can I ask you a question first?" Krazinski replied. "Is there some reason you haven't turned the air-conditioning on?"

"I couldn't find the thermostat," Charles said.

Krazinski turned around and flipped on the switch, which was in plain sight, just behind the recliner. "Ask away, man," he said after adjusting the temperature.

"Were you in the Clinton administration?"

"I'm in bankruptcy," he said.

"Can I ask you another question, then?" asked Charles. He was aware, as he spoke, that he should not speak. Words were just sort of bouncing around in his stomach, then bubbling up through his esophagus and dribbling out of his mouth like a belch.

"Fire away," Krazinski said.

But Charles could no longer remember what he'd meant to ask, even though he sensed that his query would have been profound. He was feeling morose all of a sudden, his self-pity list compounding. On top of his life's other shortcomings, he was never going to take a deposition, or even be deposed, although he supposed the latter was not something to aspire to. Still, what would it be like to sit at a table and answer questions of critical importance, to have a table full of lawyers hanging on your every word, to have them record your utterances on their yellow legal pads?

Depose me, he considered saying to Martin Krazinski.

"The kids okay?" Krazinski asked.

"I wish I knew. Without a car or a phone . . ."

"I'm sure they're fine. You know, I'm just here to appease

my wife . . . my ex-wife, rather. She tends to worry a little too much. But these kids, I mean, let the kids be kids. They're about to go off to college anyway, they need to learn how to be independent. For God's sake, they need to learn how to hold their liquor!"

He loosened his tie and walked over to the refrigerator. "What's up with all this water?" he asked.

"Oh," said Charles. "I was just doing some stuff with ice . . . Ice stuff."

"Ice stuff?" Krazinski said. "What, like a drinking game?"

"A drinking game?"

Charles couldn't think of any time in his life when he'd felt like more of a schmuck. The last thing he was going to do was tell Krazinski that his domestic life had fallen into such dysfunction and disrepair that he was actually coveting another man's ice maker.

Krazinski chattered on obliviously. "I've never played it myself, but there's some game called ice-cube curling. You know, based on the Olympic winter sport. We can't play it just now, though—it requires preparation. You need to freeze the cubes in a certain way so that there's something sticking out of the top, to grip. Unlike beer pong, which doesn't require any advance work. Well, apart from buying red cups and a Ping-Pong ball. And beer."

"Beer pong?" said Charles. "Now, there's something else I'd like to do someday. What I mean is that I like games. Sports. I mean, I like beer *and* I like Ping-Pong, so it sounds like a good combo."

"You've never played?"

Charles shook his head, no.

"You haven't played it with your kids?"

"Kid," Charles corrected. "And no, I haven't. I can't quite

imagine my wife . . ." He tried to imagine himself suggesting to Leah a family game of beer pong.

"Well, let's fire up a game, then," Krazinski said, taking off his jacket and rolling up his sleeves. "I'm pretty sure we've got some cups." He opened a cupboard. Two tall stacks of plastic red cups fell down on his head. "Okay then," he said. "Meant to be, I guess. And beer we've got, if you haven't drunk it all."

"Very funny," Charles said.

"And a Ping-Pong ball, which of course we can find on the Ping-Pong table. So we're good to go."

"The cups have to be red?"

"I don't know, that's what my kids say. Why mess with tradition?"

"Yeah, why would you?" Charles agreed.

"One thing I'm going to ask you to do, mate, is put your pants on."

Mortified, Charles found his trousers bunched on the floor between the reclining chairs and pulled them on. He then followed Krazinski into an enormous recreation room at the back of the house that he'd somehow missed on his self-guided tour. There was also a pool table, a dartboard, and one of those soccer games with the little men who rotated on poles. Not the cheap plastic version Charles had had as a kid, but the expensive kind you'd find in a pub. Charles felt like he'd just won the lottery. Or rather, someone else had won the lottery and he had been invited over to see.

Krazinski handed him ten cups, and per his instructions, Charles set them up on his side of the table in triangle formation. Krazinski did the same on the other side. Charles felt a little woozy and wobbly on his feet; he had an intense desire to lie down on the floor for a few minutes, just for a quick nap.

He wondered aloud what time it was and whether they ought to check on the kids.

"It's early," said Krazinski. "It's not even midnight yet. I'll tell you what, we'll play a game or two; then we'll call over there and make sure everyone's okay."

"Maybe we should just call over now, first . . ."

"I'll tell you what, you win this game, we drive over. I win, we call."

This seemed not quite right to Charles. For one thing, he thought he'd just proposed calling, not driving, so where was his incentive to win? But also, it would make the game more amusing if there was something real at stake—money, or honor, or blood. Who wanted to play just to determine the degree to which they ought to be chaperoning? But then, this was his first-ever game of beer pong, so it was probably just as well not to put too much on the line.

"You're already off to a wobbly start, mate," said Krazinski. "Fix that rack there, Adler. That is not a straight pyramid."

Fucking Krazinski and his fancy beer pong lingo. Who had studied architecture as an undergrad, eh? Who had been commissioned to design Downtown? Charles could make a straight pyramid if he wanted to. He was simply not in the mood.

15

· · · · ·

Dorrie burst into the room around midnight; she looked elec-
trified, like some madwoman from a Greek tragedy about to
eat her children, snakes coming out of her head instead of hair.
She wore a sleeveless crimson dress. Jordan had the same one
in navy blue. They had bought them together at J.Crew.

"I just saw Cherie leaving the bathroom . . . with *Paul*," she
said. She practically spit out his name, like a wad of phlegm.

Jordan felt like she, too, had been caught in flagrante
delicto, their first night at Beach Week, alone in her room with
a book: *Your Gap Year in India*. She supposed Dorrie would at
least be proud of her for having kept her cell phone off so she
wouldn't even be tempted to check whether Khalid suddenly
missed her and had randomly sent her a text (as if he would!)
and for managing, for impressive chunks of time, not to even
think about him. That said, Dorrie was clearly wasted, which
made it highly unlikely that she'd sought out Jordan to hold
her hand or take her temperature on the breakup.

"Maybe Cherie was just . . . helping Paul?" Jordan offered absurdly. "Maybe Paul was sick. Or vice versa? I mean, you shouldn't jump to conclusions."

"She is such a little bitch. I swear, I can't believe she'd do this. On top of which, of all people, I mean, we're going to college together! I'm going to have to see her every day for the rest of my life!"

Jordan thought it would be unwise to point out the exaggerated nature of this assertion. "Really, Dorrie, calm down." She put an arm around Dorrie and tried to steer her toward the bed. She smelled like she'd doused herself with overproof rum. "You don't look so good—just lie down for a minute and try to clear your head. You're drunk, and it looks like you already got too much sun, and you're probably jumping to conclusions. The thing to do is just sleep it off. We can figure this out in the morning."

Dorrie seemed to soften for a moment, and it even looked like she might follow these instructions, but just as she put her head to the pillow, there was a commotion outside the window and someone began banging on the glass pane. They were pretty high up, on the third floor of the house, which made this all the more startling.

Jordan opened the window, and outside was Mike. "Hey, sweetie," he said, "do me a favor . . . is there a plug in there?" He handed Jordan an extension cord. "They've talked me into doing a few songs, and I thought maybe I'd play from up here, but I need to plug in an amp."

"You should be careful up there!" Jordan heard herself say, channeling her mother again. She could see there were a bunch of other people up there, too, gathered on the ledge, drinking, legs dangling over the gutters. She wondered how they got there. She wondered how they'd get down. Some of the boys had dragged the dinosaur toward the back of the house so it could join the party, and Jordan could see it below, swaying in the wind. It still wasn't quite fully inflated, and two new guys were down there taking turns blowing into the tube. Now Dorrie was at it again, as if her batteries had recharged from the thirty-second rest.

"Hey, Mike, have you seen Paul?" Dorrie asked this in a way that sounded normal and nonchalant. From where Mike was standing, he probably couldn't see the insane glaze in her eyes; otherwise he might have given a more considered answer.

"I think he's out back, having a burger. I saw him a few minutes ago, hanging with Cherie." He began to tune his guitar, which was pretty loud now that the amplifier was plugged in. He sent a few twanging chords into the clear, starry night.

"That fucking bitch! I'm going to kill them both," Dorrie shrieked. She was upright again, tottering on her heels as she ran from the room, Jordan behind her, book in hand. She marveled that Dorrie was able to make it down three flights of stairs so quickly and without tripping, given her condition. Why was Dorrie mad at *Cherie*, and not at *Paul*? she wondered. She supposed this might just be one of those primal female jealousy things that had no rational explanation. Jordan followed her downstairs and out onto the back patio; this required dodging so many obstacles and maneuvering around so many people, many of them strangers, that she felt like she was in a movie chase scene.

Mike had just begun to play some reggae, his voice gritty and soulful. He was playing something familiar that Jordan couldn't quite place, but it was perfect. Against the backdrop of the music, Jordan could hear the sound of waves, and she could practically taste the sea. She looked up at Mike, and her heart felt full. There was something about him that was just so sweet it was hard to explain, but it made her think that the meaning of life might be contained in a simple thing like reggae and a cute boy with a guitar. She thought for a moment that maybe she was wrong, that she *would* miss high school, and these friends, more than she cared to consider.

That might have qualified as her only tender thought about Beach Week, however, because otherwise it seemed unlikely she'd feel too nostalgic for this evening. It wasn't like she was an angel herself, and it wasn't like she'd never told a lie, but when she looked around, what she saw going on was pretty extreme. This was the first night of Beach Week, and it looked as though there'd been some attempt to set a record, to break every single rule in one go. She did a quick mental tally: there were boys in the house; there were strangers in the house; there were alcohol and drugs in the house, not to mention two kegs and a four-foot bong. There was also very loud music emanating *from* the house, as well as a barbecue in the backyard, and she seemed to remember one of the parents issuing some last-minute edict against anything that involved lighting a match in or near the house. She didn't have to see it with her own eyes to know there was sex occurring in the house, because she kept seeing people going into rooms and closing doors, and she'd accidentally walked in on three people going at it in the bathroom, which was so startling that she'd stood there gaping for a minute before closing the door. (Jordan wouldn't be surprised if there soon might even be a YouTube memory of Beach Week, because there was Rene, leaning against a tree, flirting with some guys from Verona High School's rival lacrosse team.) And there was more: junk food and sugar cereal; people on the roof; undeniable drinking and driving, given the number of cars lined up on the street; and, judging by the pink faces of a few of her friends, some lax application of sunscreen.

Jordan and Dorrie ran into Mindy and Amy out back. "We were looking for you guys," Mindy said. She was wearing a white seersucker dress with a matching headband, a bad choice of outfit, as she'd already dribbled a bit of blue Evian Kool-Aid down the front. Amy had made a more sensible choice with a preppy plaid dress, and they both had plastic cups in hand. Dorrie grabbed Mindy's drink and washed it down in a few quick gulps.

"Okay, yeah, help yourself," Mindy said.

"Where is she?" Dorrie said.

"Where's who?"

"You know who."

Mindy shrugged her shoulders. "Seriously. Who are you looking for? What's going on?"

Jordan knew there was no way this was going to end well, and she made a lame attempt to distract Dorrie or at least redirect the conversation.

"Amy, what happened to your dinner party?" she asked. She realized that she hadn't managed to deflect the pain so much as spread it, however, as now it looked like Amy might start to cry.

"I'm so bummed . . . it took us, like, an hour to find the lobsters, and then we get back here and there's no pot! I mean, all I saw were these little saucepans. I suppose one of them might have been big enough to make rice in, but, like, there wasn't even one you could use to boil spaghetti! Don't these people ever cook? Plus, this isn't at all what I had in mind. I thought we could set the table, pour some wine, and have a civilized meal. Instead . . . I mean this is totally out of control. Did you even see what's going on in the kitchen? Someone stuck a rotisserie chicken in the garbage disposal and it's completely broken, and now the drain is jammed and there's chicken and bits of bone all over the place. It looks like it's going to overflow."

"Yeah, also the bathroom door, the one downstairs, got kicked in. Someone was passed out inside for, like, an hour," said Mindy. "Finally Dan and Morgan broke it down. Some girl had gotten sick in there. It was kind of gross."

"Is she okay?" asked Jordan.

"Is who okay?"

"The girl."

"What girl?"

"The one who got sick in the bathroom."

"Oh," Mindy said, shrugging. "I guess so. I mean, I don't even know who she was, but she's gone, so I guess she's okay."

"Hey you guys, eat up!" yelled Deegan. He was manning the barbecue and was stripped down to shorts and Rollerblades. He had on a backward baseball cap, and a spatula, which he was waving like a baton, extended from his hand. Jordan wondered if maybe he'd switched from dope to Ritalin, because he was pretty intent on his mission, and he had about fifty well-done hamburgers lined up on the picnic table. It seemed like someone should probably tell him to hold off on the grilling for a while.

"So where are the lobsters?" Jordan asked. She was curious, but also still hoping to steer Dorrie off topic, because she could, in fact, see Cherie and Paul sitting on chairs just on the other side of the barbecue grill, facing the ocean. She was putting herself up for sacrifice here, hoping Dorrie would start harassing her about Khalid and lobsters, would say something snarky about "going all Khalid on us again."

Amy burst into tears. She pointed at Deegan, and it took

Jordan a second to understand what it was that Amy wanted her to see. He had what looked like a leash extending from his left hand, and the other end of it was attached, somehow or other, to a lobster. "Look what he did!" Amy said. "He thought it was really hilarious. What an asshole. He's been dragging the poor thing around for an hour."

"So what? That's worse than boiling the thing alive, then chopping it up in paella?" Mindy asked. "Besides, what, did you only get one lobster?"

"Yes, of course that's worse. It's one thing to eat a lobster and another thing to torture it for no reason."

"Is it? I mean that one is at least alive!"

"Why are you defending this?"

"Okay, let's not have an argument about animal rights," Jordan said. "Are those the other lobsters over there?"

She saw a plastic tub at the edge of the patio, close to the bluff where tall tumbleweed grew at the edge of the sand. She took a few steps closer and could see them: large, bluish otherworldly things. The rubber bands had come off the claws of a few of them, and it looked like a fight was under way. A couple of boys were egging them on. "Have a drink!" someone shouted, pouring a beer on one of the creatures. It scrambled back in confusion.

"Hey, look, it's the Mothman," Amy said, pointing toward the bushes. Jordan must have just missed whatever it was she was referring to, because all she could see was a shadow, but it sent a shiver down her back nonetheless, and when she felt something brush against her leg, she just about let out a scream. When she looked down, what she saw was the neighbor's black Lab.

"Hi, you sweet thing," she said, bending down to brush its coat with her hand. "What are you doing at this crazy party?"

As if in answer to the question, the dog got up on its hind legs and grabbed a hamburger off the table. "Boy, you are one hungry dog," Jordan said. But she figured, why not? Given the behavior of everyone else on the premises, why shouldn't the dog indulge?

By now Dorrie had spotted Cherie and was staring right at her. She swallowed the blue drink and poured herself another from the pitcher on the table without shifting her eyes.

"Seriously, Dorrie, I think you should ease up. You've had way too much already, and you're starting to freak me out."

"Don't worry about me," Dorrie said. "I've never felt better." She set off in the direction of Cherie and Paul, who, at the same moment, began walking toward the picnic table. More coincidental than the timing, however, was that Cherie was also wearing the same dress as Jordan and Dorrie, and hers was crimson, too.

"You fucking bitch!" Dorrie screamed. "I thought you were my friend! You said you wouldn't wear that dress tonight!" Jordan wondered for a minute if maybe Dorrie had forgotten she was mad about Paul and was now, instead, just angry about the dress.

Whatever the catalyst, Dorrie began to charge toward Cherie, the blue liquid raised in her hand like a potential missile. Cherie leaped deftly to the side to avoid collision and was within an inch of backing into Jordan, who screamed as she entertained a fully formed flashback of Cherie crashing into her on the soccer field the day of the accident. This time she was prepared, however, and when she jumped out of the way, Cherie tripped, and her own drink went flying into the barbecue grill, causing the flames to leap.

Deegan jumped back as a flame licked his arm. "Ouch! Jesus Christ, you crazy bitch!" he yelled. He banged into a side table that was holding various barbecuing implements, which in turn knocked into the grill, causing it to tip. Flames spread along the ground, igniting the edge of the picnic table. Deegan ran, or rather rolled, toward the sand. The lobster dragged behind.

The boys who'd been pouring beer on the lobsters were at least alert enough to dump the tub of water on the flames, successfully dousing the fire, in the process turning loose a bunch of writhing, scampering, smoldering lobsters.

Jordan stared in horror, trying to think what to do. The dog wandered through the crowd with a bag of hamburger buns in its mouth and paused to sniff a lobster. In the midst of all this commotion she heard a cell phone ring. Dorrie reached into her pocket and answered it. "It's for you," she said weirdly, handing the phone to Jordan. "It's your mom."

"*My* mom? Why is she calling *you*?"

"I don't know. She said something about how she can't find your dad." Jordan took the phone, but she couldn't really hear anything. She walked over to the side of the house to try to find a quiet spot, but now the line kept breaking up. She kept moving farther toward the ocean, which was now obscured behind a tall clump of brush. She lost the call and was trying to redial when she heard someone scream.

"COPS!!!!!!!!"

Five police cars pulled up to the house with sirens blaring and lights flashing, as if they were closing in on a serial killer, creating a chaotic dispersal in every direction. Someone jumped off the roof and landed on the dinosaur, which exploded with a loud pop, sending bits of purple plastic flying. After a few seconds, whoever it was picked herself off the ground and began to limp toward the ocean.

Mike continued to play. He'd switched to a Dave Matthews

song, "Pig," and was still singing. He was so in the moment, apparently he hadn't noticed the mayhem going on around him.

A fire truck pulled up, and within minutes two supersize hoses were stretched to the yard and aimed at the barbecue, although the flames were already out. Two lobsters rode a wave of gushing water across the patio. A policewoman spoke through a megaphone. "Everyone stay put," she said. "We're going to ask you to just sit down right where you are. Let's take this nice and slow. We're going to want to see some IDs."

"What the fuck did we do wrong?" one of the lacrosse players asked indignantly.

"Don't talk to the police that way," said Courtney Davidson. "We're sorry, Officer. I apologize for my friend here. He's being incredibly rude. I think I speak for all of us when I say that we're terribly sorry if we've caused some sort of disturbance. Are the neighbors complaining? We can turn the music down. Hey, Mike!" she yelled toward the roof. "Give it a rest for a few, okay?"

Mike still didn't hear.

"Nice try," said the policewoman. "Now do me a favor and just sit down right there . . . okay, not right there," she said, noticing the water and the lobsters and the smoldering picnic table. "All of you, come with me, over here, to this side of the house."

Jordan could see clusters of kids still sneaking out of the house, making mad dashes toward the beach. There must have been more than a hundred kids in the house, maybe even twice that many.

"I'd say you might have just set some kind of record," another policeman said. "For sheer stupidity. Most Beach Week kids at least wait a few days before behaving like total morons. Don't you guys have parents? Didn't anyone suggest that you at least do your partying quietly, indoors? Most of these kids from Verona, they at least have a chaperone, someone nominally responsible for keeping a lid on things . . ."

Jordan took this as her cue. She made her way deeper into the brush. She could see Deegan struggling through the sand on his blades and she began to follow him, but then she saw *him*: the Mothman. He looked like he hadn't shaved in a few days, and his clothes looked kind of grungy, but he had a gentle face and he seemed somehow familiar. He waved to her and she waved back.

16

. . . . .

Noah loved the beach at night. He'd been lying there trying to make sense of Mitch being dead, but the music had been so loud he could barely think.

If he was a writer like Clara, instead of a currently on hiatus accountant conducting a survey of consumer saltwater taffy behavior and the coincidence of yellow in this world, he'd try to put some of this into words. Like he'd write about the cold, the startling cold, really, of the sand at night, and compare it to how you couldn't even walk on it in your bare feet during the day, and he'd tie this into real estate and beachfront property, and Mitch. *A Celebration of a Life in Realty*, he'd call it, or something like that. Granted, his writing might be pretty bad given that he was essentially a numbers person, but his work would at least be generous. He wouldn't write about someone being a perv when he wasn't a perv; he wouldn't set out to ruin anyone's life. And he'd write something that paid tribute not just to Mitch, but to all the weird little creatures scurrying across the beach, like this thing with spindly long legs that was crawling on him right now. Whatever it was felt light on his skin, and he liked the way it climbed right over him like he was just a rock or something that happened to belong right here in this place.

He'd never slept on the beach before, and although he would have expected the ocean sounds to be pretty loud, it hadn't occurred to him that there would be music down here, too. It was getting on his nerves, actually. There was no way he was going to write an epic poem about Mitch and real estate, let alone fall asleep, so he figured he'd take a walk up the bluff to figure out where all this noise was coming from. Maybe while he was up there he'd swing by the house, be sure that no one needed his help in taking out the trash or anything.

He followed the sound of music, and where it led him was truly astonishing, like everything Mitch had warned him about at the outset but worse, and he wondered if this, here, was the tribute to Mitch in a backward sort of way—he'd been thinking about Mitch, and Mitch was signaling to him to climb the bluff in a kind of perverse *I told you so.*

Again Noah thought that if he could just do the math, if he could add up columns of words to describe what he was seeing and then find the square root, or put a compass to the problem and map the angles, he'd reach a conclusion that wasn't so good.

1. People on the roof
2. Girls in pretty dresses, fighting
3. Alcohol
4. Hamburgers
5. Sex

6. Pills
7. Fire!

It was almost biblical. Like the ten plagues, except he'd need to identify three more, which wouldn't be hard to do. Noah tried writing the list backward, but it didn't change anything. Then he started from number 6 and let it unspool in a different order, but no new meaning emerged. No matter how he looked at it, it wasn't good.

And those poor lobsters! He thought of that graphing program on the computer at work and tried to visualize some kind of theory of lobster outcomes, but this didn't seem helpful, and even in his head, they were crawling off the page, away from the flames.

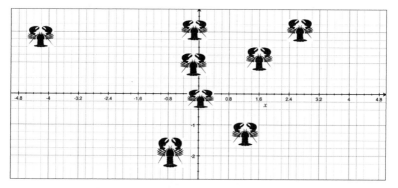

THEORY OF LOBSTER OUTCOMES

In his pocket was the phone Clara had given him, and he wondered if this was it, the reason he'd been carrying it around all this time. He called 911. He said that there was a plague on the house. He meant to tell the operator about the smiting of firstborn sons and swarms of locusts, but he was getting confused as he watched flames leap, and he said something about fire and moths instead. The operator kept asking him questions that he didn't know the answers to, so he finally just put the phone back in his pocket and felt a wave of something awful, like he'd just done something wrong.

17

• • • • •

Beer pong was beginning to seriously test the amount of alcohol a 180-pound middle-aged man could consume in one go. Charles thought he had already reached his limit, but it turned out that the human capacity to endure, or at least to absorb great quantities of beer, was more elastic than he might have supposed.

Krazinski was proving to be a devious bastard. He'd advertised himself as a casual, occasional player of the game, when the reality was that he was practically a pro. He managed to get the Ping-Pong ball into one of the cups—beer-filled bowling pins, as Charles had come to think of them—on every attempt. Each time Krazinski succeeded, Charles had to chug.

He was finding this extremely frustrating. This wasn't a game that required brute strength or a unique skill set. It didn't even involve any prowess at Ping-Pong, which made beer pong something of a misnomer, since there were no paddles involved. It was so goddamned simple, this game: all you had to do was toss the ball a short distance and get it into the cup. Charles had very good hand-eye coordination, as evidenced by his excellent tennis game, so there was no reason he should be performing quite so poorly in this endeavor, except perhaps that he was drunk, and unfortunately getting drunker. He was not enjoying this nearly as much as he thought he would, but at least it was coming to an end, as there was only one cup remaining on his side of the table, and here was Krazinski's ball, looping up in the air much higher than necessary, practically brushing the ceiling like it was a joke of a toss, then landing squarely in the cup. Charles drank it down, relieved, until he learned that it wasn't quite over yet. Now, as further punishment for his loss, he was evidently supposed to drink all of the remaining beer on the *other* side of the table, too. He could not, in good conscience, perform this requirement in his capacity as chaperone. This was what he meant to say, although something else came out of his mouth.

"You asshole!"

"Hey, friend, chill," said Krazinski. "It's just a game."

"Let's play again."

"I'm not sure that's the best idea."

"Best out of three," Charles said.

"Sure, but how about we continue that tomorrow. It's"— he paused to check his watch—"two a.m. And I just flew in from Europe, so it's really eight a.m., which means I've been up all night."

"I've been up all night myself, and I didn't even have to fly to Europe to do that!" That didn't sound quite right, although Charles wasn't sure what he'd meant to say.

"Fine. Well, you set it up. I've just got to check on something for a minute." He pulled out a Blackberry. "Just a follow-up on my—"

"Deposition," Charles jumped in. Was he feeling hostile because Martin Krazinski still had a Blackberry? Or because Krazinski didn't have a wife who had taken away his Blackberry? Or because he didn't have a wife, period? Or maybe it was something else—maybe he was feeling hostile because Martin Krazinski had important business to attend to, whereas his semester had just wound down and all he had were exams to grade and blueprints for a potentially dead Downtown and a bonus he was in dire need of, and at this rate unlikely to ever see.

Krazinski looked at him strangely. "That's right," he said defensively. "I just need to confirm that my partner received a copy of the deposition I sent earlier."

Charles began to refresh the beer pong table, which required walking over to the fridge and getting more beer. He didn't want to count or even estimate the empties. He observed his ice-cube montage, now just ordinary glasses of room-temperature water. He picked one up and sucked it down, then filled the glass with ice again and set it back on the counter.

There was quite a selection of beer; Charles spent a while considering the options. He pulled a bottle of vodka out from the back of the refrigerator and stared at the label. He wasn't much of a drinker to begin with, yet he found himself thinking . . . What about vodka pong? Maybe he'd have better luck with that? Although he supposed there was probably some reason that the game called for beer, and this might be related to the amount typically consumed. He tried to remember a bit of drinking advice from his college days. Were you supposed to drink beer before liquor? Or vice versa?

"Hey, Krazinki, is it better to drink beer before liquor or the other way around?"

"Liquor before beer, you're in the clear. Beer before liquor, never been sicker."

"Thanks. Of course." He put the bottle back on the shelf. Given that he was feeling pretty sick as it was, he didn't want to ignore this sage advice. He chose a few bottles of a local microbrew, Cracked Claw Ale, and began to pour it into the cups.

"Clean out the water cup, will you?" Krazinski asked.

This was one of the more interesting things Charles had learned about beer pong. You actually dunked the ball in a cup of water whenever it fell on the floor, in order to clean off any hair or whatnot. It was heartening to know that kids were at least practicing good hygiene as they drank themselves into oblivion. Charles dumped the water into the sink and refilled the cup.

"Don't forget the one on the other side," Krazinski said. Charles didn't like the way this guy was bossing him around. He wanted to tell Leah that she was right, that this guy was kind of an asshole. Okay, maybe Leah had never said he was an asshole, exactly, but surely she'd agree. Notwithstanding her marriage-ending ultimatum, he supposed he owed Leah a courtesy phone call, just to let her know that he'd arrived and that the kids were okay. Assuming they were okay, of course. He was also eager to share with her the news about the car registration; it wasn't often that she was the one who completely screwed up, giving him reason to gloat.

He thought of borrowing Krazinski's phone, but then, apart from it being the middle of the night, he also felt like he ought to at least check in on the kids first. Jordan was over there, after all. *Jordan, Jordan, Jordan.* What kind of a father was he, letting his little girl go off to Beach Week like this, after all he'd heard about what went on, after all she'd been through?

He'd been so sure of his position on this, too, as if it were a municipal ballot proposition that he found offensive: No to Beach Week! Of course it was better that she was at Beach Week than with this older Khalid fellow who'd let his daughter sleep alone in an aquarium, wasn't it? Or was it? He'd never even met Khalid, but that wasn't the point. As a father, he was entitled to pass judgment on any boy his daughter so much as mentioned. That was his job, his duty as a dad. As was being a responsible Beach Week chaperone.

Hadn't they made some kind of deal before the first round of beer pong? If Charles won, then . . . something. If he lost, then something . . . else. He wished he could remember what. Now here he was, quite possibly behaving even less responsibly than the kids. What if something was wrong and they'd been unable to get in touch with him, given that he didn't have a phone? What he resolved to do was this: he'd play one more game of beer pong—or really two, because this was best of three and he was determined to win, which he actually thought he could do now that he had the hang of it. Then he'd borrow Krazinski's phone or car, or maybe both (and he was willing to bet that the guy drove something fancier than a Honda Accord—not that Charles noticed, or cared about such things!), and he'd do the right thing, check in on the kids, who were probably already asleep anyway, since it was the middle of the night.

Krazinski was still scrolling and tapping at the Blackberry, and now he was actually swiveling his hips as he typed, like he was swaying to the beat, having a good time, maybe texting with his lover or something. Charles knew men like this, who were married and also actively dating, carrying on in hotel rooms, cultivating favorite restaurants, memorializing special moments and events that required the sending of jewelry and flowers. He'd always marveled at this. He had trouble enough keeping Leah happy, trying to remember her likes and dislikes, her birthdays. They'd lived together nearly twenty years and at times he still got confused about how she liked her coffee. (Was it that she once took sugar but did no longer, or that she'd recently acquired a taste for it?) What a logistical nightmare that would be! How could you manage to do all that sneaking around and not, say, leave a hotel key card in your pocket every once in a while? On top of which, affairs sounded so . . . expensive. Then he remembered that Krazinski was apparently already divorced, something Charles himself might soon be. Unfortunately, from what he understood, this sounded pretty expensive, too.

Krazinski was still typing, still swaying, and now he was even smiling. Charles felt a brief wave of empathy for Leah's annoyance with the thing. He threw the Ping-Pong ball against the wall above Krazinski's head to get his attention. "Come on, man!" he called.

"Coming sport," Krazinski said, and set the device down. "Winners get first shot, but you could use a handicap."

Charles didn't argue. He was feeling much more confident now. All he needed to do was concentrate a little harder. He took a step back and stared at the target, but once again overthrew. The ball didn't even land on the table, he had so miscalculated.

"Goddammit," he said. He hadn't meant to, but he kicked the leg of the table, and a couple of the cups tipped over.

"Come on, my friend. Let's show some good sportsmanship."

"Sorry," said Charles. "You're absolutely right." The man *was* right; he wasn't behaving with much dignity. He retrieved some paper towels and wiped up the mess. Then he went back to his side of the table.

"Try pulling your arm back a bit further, " Krazinski said. "And bend your knees. We won't count that one. You can have a do-over." He came around to the other side of the table and pulled Charles's arm back behind his head to demonstrate. Charles found it extremely irritating to have this guy, this self-important little man in his bespoke suit, with his full-service Blackberry, not just creaming him in beer pong but giving him advice. "The problem is, my friend, you're thinking baseball or something. Think light. It's a Ping-Pong ball and we're not going for distance. So not so much force this time."

The man was really screwing with his head. Charles put every bit of brainpower into this that he could and still over-shot the target. In the process, he pulled his arm back too far, causing his back to spasm again. He let out a little yelp and took another drink.

"You're really a wreck, man," said Krazinski. "I think we ought to call it quits."

"No way," said Charles.

"Really. Look, it's just the first night. We can play again tomorrow."

Charles didn't appreciate his tone. Krazinski was speaking to him as if he were a child. "Let's just finish what we've begun," he said.

The only problem with this suggestion was that Charles was feeling seriously unwell. The lack of sleep, the lack of food, too much alcohol, and now the return of this searing, burning pain. He thought he was going to be sick. He thought he should go to the bathroom. He was doing too much thinking and not enough acting, however, because now what he was thinking was that he was absolutely going to throw up. At least he had the foresight to pick up a cup of beer and vomit into that instead of onto the floor, which Krazinski ought to thank him for, considering that it seemed unlikely you could get regurgitated green pickle relish out of a white rug.

"Not to worry," Charles said. "I'll go get us a new cup."

Before Krazinski could express an opinion about this, the doorbell rang.

"Expecting anyone?"

"God, no," said Charles.

Krazinski walked down the long hallway and over to the door, and Charles could hear it click open. He heard a female voice, then another female voice. Two women. Why oh why did that make him remember the *Beach Week* movie all of a sudden? Was he really twisted? Probably not. A drunk man thinking about sex was hardly a sign of perversion. Anyway, since he'd been thrown out of the house, more or less, and was almost technically separated, he had free reign to think about anything he wanted.

He could hear the women talking to Krazinski, and he smelled perfume, which under other circumstances he supposed might have set off some pheromones, but in this case just made him feel nauseous again.

"I'm rendered speechless," said one of the female voices, but not in a sexy, suggestive way that implied the possibility of a spontaneous removal of clothing. Charles knew this tone— he even knew this voice, somehow, and it did not make for a happy association. He could hear heels click-clack their way through the entrance hall, moving toward the back room. He considered pointing out that this was something of an oxymoron . . . that since she was actually speaking, she wasn't, technically, rendered speechless, but he didn't say that because something else far more interesting occurred to him. This voice belonged to the Flying Nun.

And walking up behind her was the second voice. This one was in a uniform, and she had a gun. She said there had been some incident with the children they were meant to be chaperoning, and would they please come to the police station to collect them, as several of them were being held for underage consumption of alcohol, among other things.

"I told you!" Charles shouted. He went toward Krazinski in anger, but even drunk, he was not a violent man, and instead he punched the wall, which was pretty stupid. His hand began to throb, and then, as if his body had just been reminded that it was falling apart, his back began to spasm again. He was pretty sure he was going to be sick again, too.

He turned toward the table to reach for a cup, but the policewoman must have misunderstood and thought he was reaching for more beer. She grabbed his arm, and when he opened his mouth to explain, he threw up. All over the policewoman. Although he wasn't aware of that being against the law, he found himself a few minutes later in the back of a police cruiser.

18

. . . . .

Gephyrophobia, they called it, fear of crossing a bridge, and Leah forced herself to set aside the potentially paralyzing thoughts inspired by the four miles of arcing gray steel that loomed ahead, nearly blinding in the morning sunlight. She looked into the huge, empty void of the Chesapeake below and envisioned her rental car plunging. Briefly she considered the range of aquatic dangers and supposed there wasn't anything all that worrisome in the bay, apart from some invasive zebra mussels she'd read about in the paper as well as some striped bass with curious skin lesions. Of course this wasn't really the point, since she would likely drown first.

Get a grip, she told herself. There was no shortage of very real disasters that were already competing for prominence on her mental list of woes, and she didn't need to add to this a completely paranoid thought. Then again, those guardrails did look kind of flimsy, and by definition it wasn't phobic to be worrying about something real. Considering the collapsing infrastructure of just about everything in the country right now, bridge safety actually qualified as a legitimate concern. She wondered when the Bay Bridge had been built, when it had last been repaired, and why these questions hadn't come up in any of the Beach Week meetings. Mercifully, before she worked herself into a complete psychotic frenzy, she was on the other side.

Leah maneuvered the crappy, ancient Ford Fiesta onto what she hoped would be a quiet back road but turned out to be clogged with traffic. Had she ever seen as much traffic as she had today? Anywhere in her entire life? Maybe. But still, this was pretty bad. If she were to chronicle her journey so far, she would have to say something like this: *Traffic, traffic, traffic, traffic, traffic, traffic, traffic.*

There had been bad traffic from the moment she entered the Beltway at 6:00 a.m., the inner loop at an hour-long standstill after a tractor-trailer flip closed the outer loop at the onramp to northbound I-95 while they cleared the scene. Or something like that. She still got her inner loops and outer loops mixed up, and she didn't completely understand how movement in one direction came to impact the other. Leah thought she could live in the Washington area for the next twenty years without ever getting used to the local transportation lingo, never mind the constant gridlock.

The temperature was over 95 degrees, and the AC was broken. Only the AM worked on the radio, but at least she was able to get the news. It seemed all they were talking about on the news this morning was death. Death in Iraq, death in Afghanistan, death from a new strain of flu. Death from murder, too. Murder, murder, and more murder, as it happened. A murder epidemic on this radio station broadcasting from Wilmington, Delaware. Coincidentally, Leah was thinking about murder, too. Murder of one's husband. Was there a specific word for that? If there was, she couldn't think of it offhand. Fratricide, matricide, patricide, insecticide . . . Anyway, she wasn't really going to murder Charles, and in fact she was on a mission of mercy; she was going to bail him out of prison, arguably preventing someone else from murdering him first.

Yes, *prison*. Evidently they didn't have jails in the state of Delaware, so he'd gone straight to prime time in less than twenty-four hours at the beach. That was the first phone call she'd received from the Chelsea Beach police, at around 4:00 a.m. There'd been a second call a few minutes later— while she was online assessing her middle-of-the-night rental- car options—this one explaining that Jordan was in prison, too.

Some forty-five minutes after crossing the bridge, traf- fic eased, enabling Leah to accelerate to an exhilarating forty mph. Air began to circulate through the open windows, drying patches of her sweat. The breeze felt so good she was tempted to stick her head out the window, like a dog. She felt her equilibrium return as she turned onto an even quieter back road. Quaint farm stands appeared every few miles, and advertisements for seafood restaurants began to dot the land- scape. She tasted salt in the air and remembered how much she loved, and really longed for, the ocean.

The worst was finally over. It was important to keep one's perspective. Sometimes when bad things happened and then seemed to keep happening and happening, the details each time getting worse, it could be hard to see at that moment that it might all be part of the same one bad thing, like a wound that turns infectious. The onslaught might just be one overlong episode with a whole lot of chapters, not unlike when you moved across the country and lost your center somehow, and then your husband's job hit a wall, and your daughter, already unhappy about the move, suffered a concussion and became moody and secretive, and then money problems worsened and your marriage began to fray, and your mother-in-law's dementia intensified, and then your husband and daughter wound up in prison. Okay, maybe not. Maybe the crap really was just piling on randomly because it was hard to draw an entirely convincing line between cause and effect here. Yet it clearly was a bad idea to have just thought this through and concluded *at least it can't get any worse.*

The brown blur came at the vehicle so fast she didn't even have time to formulate the word *deer.* Leah slammed on the brakes as the beast, enormous and impressively antlered, collided with her head-on. She heard the sound of screeching tires, the car spun, the air bags deployed, and when she came to her senses, she found herself staring directly into the beautiful blinking eye of the dying creature, whose hoof poked through the jagged windshield. She stumbled out of the car, dazed but apparently unharmed.

Overhead, she saw a billboard: ARE YOU LONGING FOR SOMETHING? it asked.

"Yes, yes I am," she said aloud, and wondered if this was it—either God was speaking to her or she was finally losing it completely here on the baking asphalt of a two-lane highway on Delaware's eastern shore. She looked more closely at the billboard: it was an invitation to visit an Indian reservation some ninety miles down the road. Apparently, whatever it was she might be longing for could be resolved by a visit to the nearby church, before or after hitting the slot machines.

She used her phone to call for more practical, secular help, and the tow truck arrived some fifteen minutes later, along with some animal rescue people. Leah averted her eyes as they removed the deer, which was splayed gruesomely on the hood. They insisted that she visit the emergency room even though she had no visible injuries, and after a few minutes of arguing, she finally agreed.

For a brief moment Leah found herself actually happy to be at a prison. The taxi deposited her in front of a squat, dung-colored building that was not as intimidating as she might have imagined and which she found to be a step up from the hospital as far as cheerfulness went; there she'd seen not only a couple of bad accident victims but, nearly as disturbing, a handful of what she guessed must have been obliterated Beach Week kids. Her mood quickly recalibrated when she entered the prison and caught sight of Martin Krazinski, Janet Glover, and Arthur and Millie Moore clustered outside a small office just a few feet from the entrance. Leah drew closer and felt her pulse quicken when she saw Alice Long standing in the doorway, too. She was shouting down a policewoman who was half her size.

"No, I already told you, I'm not leaving until my attorney gets here," she said.

"I thought *that* was your attorney." The policewoman gestured toward Martin Krazinski. "Or, er . . ." She looked at Arthur Moore. Then at Millie. "Didn't you say you were attorneys?"

"We are, but we're parents, too," Krazinski said. "They're in taxes and I'm in bankruptcy. We're waiting for our *criminal* attorney. What we need to determine is whether this arrest was by the books. Did the arresting officers have cause to enter the premises? Were the kids read their rights . . . I don't want this going on Marta's record. She's going to Stanford in the fall."

"Let's see . . . we're talking underage alcohol consumption, marijuana possession, illegal prescription drugs, and that's just for starters. As for your cause to enter the premises crap, please, don't even get me started. There was a bong on the front porch. Need I say more? We could have busted them just for the noise violations alone, without even talking about your curfew violations, your minors with cigarettes, fake IDs—the list actually goes on. Yes, I'd say the arresting officers had cause to enter the premises."

"Well, that's one version of this," said Krazinski. "But there are other issues, and I'd like my attorney to look into whether they had, or needed, warrants, and whether these kids were read their rights."

"Look, I'm being honest with you here. I mean, this is bad, but it's not like anyone's going to the federal penitentiary, and there's really no need for attorneys," the police officer said. "As I keep telling you, your kids are released—all of them. Just take them and go home. Please! In a few days, or maybe a week or so, I'm not completely sure how long, a citation will arrive in the mail. At that point you can take it up with the prosecutor's office, but really, you're making too much of this. I don't mean to diminish the seriousness of what they've done, but at the same time, this kind of thing happens more often than you seem to understand. Half the time when they show up for the hearing, the judge just lets the whole thing go. They'll pay a fine, do community service, write an essay . . ."

"An essay?" asked Millie Moore brightly.

"Well, yes, that's one of the possibilities. I'm not saying that's what will happen—it varies from judge to judge, but last year a few kids were asked to write an essay, 'What I learned at Beach Week.'"

"Wait, if they write the essay, do they still have to pay the fine? And do you know how many pages the essay would have to be?" Millie seemed genuinely excited.

"I'm not sure," the police officer said, flustered. "That's not really my department. I just do the arrests and fill out the paperwork. But maybe five?"

"Single-spaced or double-spaced?"

"Seriously, this isn't my thing. I'm just telling you this so you'll relax a little bit and realize that you don't need to stay here and wait for your attorneys. You don't need attorneys. What you need is to take your children home, talk to them about this, and at least hope they've learned a lesson. So for now, go to your kids. I told you where they are."

"Where are they?" asked Leah.

Five heads swiveled in her direction, and from the steely looks on their faces, she didn't get the impression that anyone was pleased to see her.

"The next-door neighbor signed for their release," Arthur Moore said flatly. "Jill someone or other. A friend of the Peeper, who was, apparently, peeping." He said this as if it were somehow Leah's fault. She was surprised at first by his tone, but then she supposed she was guilty by association with the delinquent chaperone, even though what little knowledge she had of what might have occurred came from what she'd just overheard. She considered explaining that she had informed Charles that he was not welcome at home if he went to Beach Week, that they were estranged, but this seemed like too much information at an inappropriate time.

"They're all at her place at the moment," Arthur Moore

continued. "Well, not all of them, but a bunch of them. Anyway, they're staying there until they can find another house for the rest of the week."

"You mean—wait . . . I'm completely confused. Is Jordan with them?"

"I assume so," said Janet. "Her name was on the list of kids released. We're going to the neighbor's house right now."

"Why are they at *her* house? Instead of the rental?"

"They were evicted."

"*Evicted?* Why?"

"You didn't hear about the party?"

"What party?"

"That's what we were just talking about, when they all got arrested. There was a fire . . ."

"Someone had alcohol poisoning."

"The dog vomited all over the carpet."

"The garbage disposal got jammed and the sink backed up."

"Someone kicked a door down."

"Someone jumped off the roof and broke a couple of bones."

"I've just come from the hospital, where *my daughter had to have her stomach pumped*," said the Flying Nun, looking at Leah as though this, too, were somehow her fault. She was grateful they hadn't run into each other in the emergency room.

"They've only been here a day and they got *evicted?* Wait . . . I'm confused about something else, too. Did you say they're looking for another house? Are you saying they're going to stay the rest of the week?"

"Well, first of all, we've got to figure out if this is a legal eviction. I left my copy of the lease at home, but as soon as we sort this out, I'm driving over to the realty office, and you'd better goddamned well believe that I'm going to fight tooth and nail to get our money back," said Arthur Moore.

"I don't know, honey," said Millie. "I mean, I get that it was a little rash to evict them, but I heard there might have been some damage from the fire out back. A picnic table burned down. And the neighbor, the one who has the kids right now, she was really lovely and all, but she said her dog got horribly sick and also needed stitches after a lobster attacked it or something, and she was blaming that on the kids, and she said something about her vet bill, so I'm not completely sure how hard we want to push this."

"I heard that the fire wasn't the girls' fault. It was the boys who were barbecuing, so they should be held responsible for any damage," said Janet Glover.

"Well, who invited the boys over?" asked Millie Moore. "I mean, we shouldn't all be responsible. I'd like my security deposit back."

This still seemed not quite the right time for Leah to point out that Millie Moore had yet to pay her back. Leah wondered if she should perhaps go in for some assertiveness training after life quieted down.

"Don't we have a clause about this in the addendum?" asked Krazinski. "We should take another look at that. I heard that one of the boys involved was Dorrie's boyfriend, so maybe she ought to share some of the blame."

"How *dare* you!" said Janet. "After all that I've done to facilitate this, how dare you think you can pin this on my daughter . . ."

A cell phone rang, and Krazinski put his Blackberry to his ear. He listened and nodded as he said a few "yeses" and "uh-huhs." Then, "Good news . . . the girls can move into a house on Conch Court. Five girls from that house are going home already, alcohol and sun poisoning, evidently, so there's a few extra beds. They said we don't need to worry about the money right now since it's already paid for. We can sort it all out later."

Leah felt like she might have missed something again— either the thread of the conversation or some nuance in the events that had transpired. "Given what's happened . . . especially after all we've done to try to prevent this very thing, what with the meetings, the pledges, et cetera, it just doesn't seem right to me that we reward their evidently appalling behavior by arranging for them to stay out here the rest of the week," she said hesitantly.

"I'm with you," said Alice Long. "And I think you ought to get your husband the hell out of town." She had her hands on her hips, and her feet, in summery gold heels, were at a peculiar, wide stance. Although this looked familiar to Leah, it took her a moment to realize why: it was the position she struck on television as she was preparing to take flight, to transform into the Winged Wife.

"This is the most irresponsible group of parents I've ever seen!" Alice said. She tapped a toe to the linoleum, but there was no disturbance in the atmosphere and her feet didn't leave the ground.

19

. . . . .

Jordan had been found on the boardwalk with the perv who was not a perv, the peeper who was not a peeper. Or who maybe was a peeper but not a perv? Charles hadn't completely followed the thread of this whole peeper thing, having neither read the book nor seen Clara Miller on *Oprah* or the *Today* show. But the headline was that their daughter was fine.

She had left the party before the bust, had never been arrested in the first place. She had evidently given her fake ID to Amy Estrada, and Amy hadn't bothered to correct the mistake when she got logged into prison under the wrong name. Amy felt horrible about this, she'd explained to the police, but she was on the wait-list at Duke and didn't want to blow her chances of getting in.

The policewoman, Pat was her name, had gone to get Jordan just now, and she didn't want Charles and Leah along. Or maybe she just didn't want Charles along. He supposed he couldn't blame her entirely. He had not put his best foot forward when they'd first met, what with the vomit and all.

For lack of any better ideas, and because it was near wherever it was that Pat was going to get Jordan, she dropped Charles and Leah off at Flounder Putt Putt and told them to wait.

It had been half an hour.

They were now on the seventh hole, the point of which appeared to be to get the little ball up the narrow, looping incline of green felt with just enough thrust to bank it off the left corner, enabling it to glide through the split in the tail of the doe-eyed mermaid who was bobbing up and down like a provocative sentinel, guarding passage to the cup. She was splendid in her tackiness, with oversize breasts, garish red hair, and dents all over her shiny façade, the result of many a poorly aimed ball. Charles found her somewhat distracting.

Leah was ahead by two points. This annoyed him more than it should have. It was just a friendly game of miniature golf, intended only to pass the time until Pat returned with their daughter. He supposed he was just wound up. These had been the most harrowing twenty-four hours of his life, which was saying quite a lot, given that the second most harrowing had involved Jordan unconscious, undergoing brain scans. He wondered if Leah would ever forgive him. Never mind that Jordan's disappearance was not his fault, nor was it clear to him how a better, more sober chaperone might have prevented this from happening unless he'd been at the house, hovering 24/7—he was feeling bighearted, and he'd take responsibility if this helped in any way. Still, Charles had not committed any crime, and even the Chelsea Beach police had to concede this with his clean release, as there was nothing actually illegal about behaving like a jackass or even throwing up on a cop.

Still, he got that Leah was mad at him, and if it helped the situation, he'd let her gloat with her lousy two-point lead. He watched his wife line up her shot at the tee. She pulled back the putter as if she was about to tap the little blue ball, but then she stopped short of connecting and paused to reassess. That had evidently been a practice swing. She now pulled out her cell phone and checked the screen.

"Any word yet?" he asked.

"Nada," said Leah. "No messages, no missed calls. Nothing." Pat had promised to have Jordan call as soon as they made contact.

Leah reappraised the geography of the green, widened the space between her feet, and repositioned her weight. But then, instead of taking the shot, she put the putter down, took the elastic band from around her wrist, and used it to pull her hair into a ponytail.

"Jesus Christ, Leah. This isn't the U.S. Open. Just hit the bloody thing."

"My hair was falling in my face. I couldn't see properly. You don't need to be so rude."

"All I'm saying is it's just a game. Just go ahead and hit the ball. There are people behind us, waiting."

She turned to face him, hands poised tightly on the club like the potential weapon that it was. He couldn't see her eyes, which were shrouded by sunglasses, but he knew exactly what they said. They said there was a long history here. They said that he had no standing to criticize her sporting behavior. They said, improbably, that if she wanted to beat him at mini golf, she could, and maybe she even would. Perhaps he was just disoriented by this latest, possibly irreversible shift of power in their household now that he had screwed up big-time. He was feeling a little vulnerable, and he found himself entertaining the slim possibility that Leah might have been able to beat him all along in anything she chose. He knew that sometimes Leah and Jordan even conspired to allow him to win, just to make him happy. He still felt a little twinge of guilt when he recalled the time his wife and daughter let him get away with the assertion that rice was a vegetable in a word game they were playing. He later looked it up and could see that they'd been right when they had tried, gently, to convince him otherwise: rice was a *grain*, although in their house, they continued to pretend otherwise.

Leah turned back to the green and continued in her quest for some sort of perfect Zen alignment with the ball. It was June at the beach—peak season for mini golf—and there was a group of impatient golfers behind them, hovering close to the tee. Charles took a deep breath and urged himself to remain calm.

She took a swing at last. The ball rolled slowly toward the nick in the wall, hit it at the sweet spot, and with a perfect trajectory glided between the V in the mermaid's tail just as it was in the ascendant position and landed in the cup: a hole in one. He could have predicted this. He could have seen this coming as far back as yesterday, or whenever it was that he had made his daring escape to the beach.

It was hot out here—too hot for mini golf. And he was more than a bit rank. Even though he hadn't had a shower since leaving home, he'd at least been able to change into the clothes he'd bought on the boardwalk just a few minutes earlier. They didn't have his size, so he'd squeezed into a too-small Chelsea Beach T-shirt that was making him uncomfortable, choking him at the neck. Not surprisingly, they didn't have underwear for sale on the boardwalk, so he'd bought himself bathing trunks instead, hideous psychedelic, baggy bathing trunks emblazoned with peace signs, something a stoner kid would wear. At least they were clean.

But here they were, baking sun or not, and they might as well make the best of it and try to have a little fun, especially since it was hard to see much in the way of amusement ahead. Once Pat returned with Jordan, they would go back to the original Beach Week house and pick up the Honda; then they'd sort out the situation with Leah's Subaru, and with the apparently totaled rental car, after which they would drive back home and . . . *and what?* Live happily ever after somehow? Or not. One day at a time. *"If you've got the time, we've got the beer."*

"Nice shot," he said to Leah. The generosity of his compliment went unacknowledged.

They had agreed to play the game taking turns at putts instead of having one player just shoot through to completion. He stepped up to the green nonchalantly, and without making a big production out of it, he tapped his orange ball gently. Too gently, as it happened; it rolled up the hill and then, just before hitting the corner where the nick was, lost momentum and began to roll backward again, hitting his foot. "Goddamn it," he said. The mother in line behind him shot him an angry look as her three small children stared at him, fidgeting impatiently with their little putters.

"Sorry," he mumbled. He avoided looking at Leah this time as he lined the ball up and tried again. Four strokes later he was in the hole, one over par. Part of the problem here almost certainly had to do with this extremely annoying mechanical mermaid; another culprit was the orange of the ball. Who could concentrate with this clashing cacophony of color? He had wanted the blue ball, but Leah had grabbed it first, and under the circumstances, it had seemed unwise to argue. That

there were no other options struck Charles as odd. "Where's
the green?" he'd asked when they signed up to play. "The yellow? The plain old white? What kind of mini golf establish-
ment is this? Color is critical!"

"It's been a busy day," the kid behind the counter had said.

As he walked away, Charles heard the kid mutter under his
breath, "What the hell is wrong with that guy?"

By the twelfth hole, he was trailing Leah by an unprece-
dented six points.

Leah pulled the scorecard out of her pocket and recorded
their latest stats, then put it back without speaking and lined
up her ball at the tee again. Hole number thirteen was decep-
tive. While less gimmicky—there were no moving parts, no
aquatic-themed creatures involved—Charles quickly ascertained that this one was going to require some strategic planning. You wanted to hit the right wall hard enough that the ball
would bounce back and hit the opposite wall and then turn the
corner, heading straight to the next turn, and . . . well, it
seemed pretty close to impossible to get a hole in one here,
which he needed to do on at least a couple of the forthcoming
greens in order to tighten up the game. He'd always taken a
perverse pride in his natural golfing abilities, particularly since,
as a kid, he'd taught himself to play on a scruffy public course.
He wondered sometimes whether he might even have had the
talent to go pro if he'd had a different, Martin Krazinski sort of
life. Yet here he was losing to his wife, who wouldn't even
know which kind of club to use to break the window of an
SUV.

Leah reconfigured herself again, preening a bit, reorganizing her hair for the umpeenth time, as if this were a modeling
shoot. Now here she was, stepping back and putting her sunglasses on top of her head, then squatting, squinting. What was

she doing? Surveying the green, evidently. Was she going to take out a tape measure next? After what seemed an interminably long time, she finally took her shot. The ball rolled slowly, banking off the wall at the intended spot, then stopping just a few inches away from the hole, nicely positioned for an easy putt on the next turn. A two was about the best you could hope for on this hole, barring divine intervention. Charles put his ugly orange ball on the tee, pulled back the club, and made contact. Golfing 101. Except that was a little different from Miniature Golfing 101, and he supposed he might have put a little too much muscle into it. He hadn't meant to whack Leah's ball so hard that it took flight, barely missing the head of a small child as it soared up and then over the fence of the park.

"Whoops," Charles said. "Sorry!"

The child's mother ran over and began screaming at him. "What are you *drunk* or something? This is mini golf. There are little kids here!"

"Sorry," he repeated.

"Sorry? I've got a mind to call the police."

"Truly, it was an accident. Can I make it up to you, buy your kid an ice cream or something?" Charles looked toward Leah, hoping she'd intervene somehow. She was good at talking people down in these kinds of situations, and this was one of the many things he loved about her. People liked her, she knew how to put them at ease, and when he did dumb things like this, she made him a better person by proxy. He appreciated this, perhaps even relied on it to an extent he'd not previously realized. He was about to tell her as much, but when he turned toward her, she appeared to be crying.

The mother wasn't finished with him yet. "You stay away from my kid," she said, as if he were a sexual predator in addition to just having a mean mini golf swing.

"Not a problem," said Charles in admittedly not the most conciliatory tone. He was just about at his limit. Now Leah was walking away. He called her name, and she just kept going.

It took him a few minutes to find her. She was inside the video arcade, sitting in the dark behind the rifle of one of those 3-D deer-hunting games. Given the range of more benign amusement options—she could have chosen to position herself beside one of those goofy, smiling hippo games, for example—this seemed meaningful, and he didn't want to read too much into the fact that she appeared to be fondling the trigger. She saw Charles and turned her face away, pulling a tissue from her pocket and blowing her nose with a ferocity that suggested the trickle of mini golf tears had now turned into full-force weeping. It was hard to tell in this light, especially with the sunglasses back on her face.

"What in God's name is wrong with you?" she asked.

"Nothing, really. Nothing at all! We're just having an intense game of miniature golf! You're completely overreacting."

"Don't tell *me* I'm overreacting. You just about killed a child out there."

"Well, technically that was your ball. And you're exaggerating." He wasn't so sure this was true; he knew he'd whacked that ball pretty hard. He was aware that he was doing some semi-deliberate regressing here, like he was testing things, trying to blow up his life and his marriage by pretending to be fifteen again. Maybe Leah loved the man he was today, but would she have loved him in eighth grade?

"Okay, look, Leah. You're right. That was obnoxious of me, I confess. I'm completely guilty. It's been a god-awful couple of days. A god-awful couple of years really, but I'm completely at fault for the last twenty-four hours or however long it's been. It's no excuse, and I know you've been under just as much pressure, but it's like I've been trying so hard to hold it together for so long, all this time, trying to just keep going, to provide for you and Jordan, trying to dig us out of this hole and—"

"Don't start with the whole caveman hunting and providing thing—"

"No, no. I mean, I can see that there's more going on here. It's like I've been wound so tight lately . . . I don't know, I admit this has been ridiculous, appalling behavior. Here I am at forty-five and sometimes I fear that I'll get through this phase of adulthood without ever getting it right . . ."

"Hey, are you guys playing the game or are you just sitting there talking?" said a skinny kid with baggy trousers and a spider tattoo on his neck. He looked too young to have a tattoo, a thought that made Charles start to panic again about Jordan. If the police knew where she was, he wondered why it was taking so long to retrieve her.

"Come on, Leah," Charles said, reaching for her hand, which she offered reluctantly. "Let's let this guy shoot some deer. It's too depressing in here anyway. I see some benches outside. Maybe we can have a snack." He led her toward the concession stand.

"What would you like?" He looked at the menu and could see that this was one more installment in a days-long, or maybe years-long, series of bad ideas. The food looked so vile that even he, a consumer of pickle relish straight up, was reluctant to eat any of it. The pizza looked like oozing grease on soggy cardboard, the hamburgers like something you might be asked to eat on a dare on that *Fear Factor* reality show. Amazingly, there did appear to be one healthy entry on the menu. "Look, Leah. They have a veggie burger on a whole wheat bun."

She stared at the concession stand a long, long time, as if she were making the decision of a lifetime. Her answer seemed to imply that she was. "Get me a hot dog, please," she said. "With onions, relish, mustard . . . and, oh wow, are those cheesy fries? I haven't had those in years. And a Diet Pepsi."

Charles didn't want to overinterpret, but this could only be good. Unless it was bad. So bad that she was eating suicidally. But he was by nature an optimist, and the thought that his wife might be turning the corner into a happier, more nutritionally challenged, chemical-friendly place seemed to him to bode well—for the immediate future of their marriage, anyway, if not necessarily for Leah's artery-clogged senior years.

20

. . . . .

Noah was mid–guessing game when he saw the police car, which was hard to miss on account of the blaring siren in the middle of the day. There were a lot of police cars in Chelsea Beach, especially in the summer, but you rarely saw one like this, a peacock with its feathers spread, ablaze and on full alert. The girl looked a little worried.

Surely this was overkill. Nothing could have happened at midday, right here, without him knowing about it. He kept a watchful eye over this stretch of beach, and he'd been on shift since opening Joseph's at 10:00 a.m. The most interesting thing he had to report was that one of the lifeguards had left his perch for more than an hour and was over at the smoothie stand, flirting with the girl who worked there. The only other thing of note was that a very pregnant woman had been walking barefoot down the boardwalk and had stepped on a piece of glass. It seemed unlikely that either of these things explained why the police were drawing near.

He turned his attention back to the girl. She didn't look too well. She had very thin red hair, with matching eyebrows and so many freckles that Noah found it hard not to stare. She seemed too young to be wandering around on her own, but it turned out she was at least a little older than she looked. She'd just turned sixteen, she said, and she was here at Beach Week with her boyfriend, who was a graduating senior from a private school. Where was the boyfriend now? Noah asked. She said he was back at the house; when she'd left, he was still passed out. She was actually a little bit worried, since she couldn't rouse him, but a couple of other kids had gone over and put their ears to his chest and felt his pulse, and they seemed to reach a general consensus that he was alive and just needed to sleep it off. Noah wondered if this might explain all the police siren hysteria—maybe they were coming to tell her the boyfriend was dead.

A few minutes earlier he'd asked this girl what her favorite flavor of taffy was, and she said she didn't have one. This seemed frankly not a believable answer, so he asked her a bunch of other questions to get a baseline for her level of truth telling. Where was she from, in what city was she born, what did her parents do for a living, that sort of thing. Her answers got increasingly evasive, and now all of a sudden there was a policewoman walking over, her badge gleaming in the sun. Was it a crime to ask a girl questions? he wondered.

"Hey, Noah," said the policewoman, like they were old friends. He'd never seen her before and was surprised that she even knew his name. She had long hair worn in a tight braid, which was not how he pictured your typical cop. She also had freckles, which made Noah wonder what was going on, whether he was in the middle of some freckle conspiracy.

The girl froze, panicked. Perhaps she hadn't been straight

with her story and had drugs in her pockets or had run away from home.

"You okay?" the policewoman asked her.

She nodded tentatively.

"This perv do anything to you?"

"No. I mean we were just talking. He gave me a piece of taffy." Now the girl looked so frightened that Noah wondered if he had actually done something wrong.

"What?" Noah said. "You can't give out taffy at a saltwater taffy stand?"

"Just keep your hands to yourself," the policewoman said irrationally, since he wasn't doing anything with his hands.

"I'm gonna go now, if that's okay," the girl finally said. "I see some of my friends down there on the beach." She motioned vaguely toward the ocean.

"Here, take my card, just in case there's something you want to tell me later," the policewoman said. The girl took the card and stared at it for what seemed longer than necessary.

"I'm here until five if you change your mind and decide you want some candy," Noah said. "And also if you figure out what your favorite flavor is. I'd really like to know."

The cop shot him an angry look, which made him remember that Jill had told him that for some reason he was supposed to stop asking this question.

"Where is she?" the cop said. "We heard she was here."

"Who?"

"You know who. The missing girl."

Noah looked toward the beach and saw nothing but girls. Were they missing? He thought of that dog book Oliver loved. Big girls, little girls, brown girls, yellow girls. Girls in bikinis and girls in summer dresses. Girls who were lost, and girls who were found. Jesus Christ, there was even a girl in a black burka

down there at the edge of the ocean, the hem of her robe getting sprayed by a wave. Even her head was covered, except for
some netting around the mouth, which made her look like a
beekeeper. He was assuming it was a girl, although it could be
a grandmother for all he knew, or an alien or a whale. A whale
of a girl or an actual whale standing on its flippers. He began to
laugh at the thought of a whale in a burka walking around on
flippers, and it seemed like the beginning of a joke. A whale in
a burka walks into a bar . . . He wasn't completely sure where
you would go from there, but he started to crack up all the
same.

"There's nothing funny about this, my friend. The parents
are here, and I told them I'd be back in an hour with their
daughter. I've already had a call from a reporter, and at this
rate it's going to be all over the local news in about half a
minute, especially since someone just told me that your wife
already wrote a book about you being a perv. That's gonna
make a great tie-in. Then everyone will read about you. So you
might want to stop laughing and help me figure out where this
girl is."

"I wasn't laughing about the girl. I was laughing about the
girl in the burka . . ." He stopped talking; he could tell this was
going to be difficult to explain. "Are you looking for Harriet?"
he asked instead.

"No, Noah. The girl who was staying in your house. Who is
now missing."

"Yeah. The one from Dr. Pu-Pu's."

"Dr. Who's?"

"She asked if I still had my MRIs, and in fact I do, I have
them here, in the filing cabinet. So I showed those to her. She
left about an hour ago."

"I don't quite get what you're saying."

"We knew each other. I knew that I knew her the first time I looked in the window and saw her taking pictures of my pictures . . ."

"I'm not so sure. The girl I'm looking for, no one said anything about her being sick."

"She's not sick anymore, but she was. That's how we met. I knew I knew her, and she knew there was a connection, too, but she wasn't sure why at first."

The policewoman took out her phone and started to make a call, but then she stopped, like she'd just had some better idea.

"Tell me exactly what happened—when was she here? When did she leave? Was she with anyone? Do you have any idea where she was headed? Can I take a look around?"

Noah lifted the counter to create an entrance and waved her in. "There isn't much to see, but sure, come on in. It's just a couple of rooms. The office is to your left; on the right is the stockroom. Look around all you want."

She took her time doing weird things, like she knocked on the walls, and then she took out her wooden baton and tapped at the floorboards.

"Show me exactly where the two of you were when she was here."

"Well, mostly we were in front. We sat right here, on top of the counter, and talked. But that was after. First she wanted to see pictures of Oliver. And also, I wanted to show her my films. They're in the filing cabinet." He led the cop to the office and pulled open the top drawer and retrieved a large envelope. He pulled out the film and spread it on the desk. "Here, you can see the small crack in my skull, from when I fell. There was a bit of swelling to the brain, but . . . well, it's easier to see in the light."

She wasn't even feigning interest. "How long was she in here?" She tapped at the other wall now.

"What, do you think I buried her or something? Do you think I've got a trapdoor in here? I'm telling you the truth. I showed her my MRIs, and we talked about how, apart from the small crack, there was nothing to see, how you couldn't see the supposed memory loss or the so-called paranoia and all that other stuff my ex-wife goes on about in her stupid book. And the girl said she totally understood, that the absence of something is even harder to comprehend than the presence, like in her case . . ."

"Look, I'm not interested in your medical bullshit," the cop said. "I just want to know where the girl is. I told her parents I'd be bringing her back."

"I'm telling you the truth. She was wandering down the boardwalk and she recognized me, so she stopped. We wound up having a lot to talk about, and she was here for a couple of hours. Then she left."

"Where'd she go?"

"She walked away, up the beach, that way," Noah said, pointing north. "She said she had to go get her car or something. She might have even been going back to my house. I threw them all out, you know. The new Mitch Mingus said that was okay—it was actually his idea, as they were violating terms and all that."

Noah couldn't tell if she'd heard this or not, but she pulled out her phone again, and this time she actually did make a call: "The perv says they just talked for a while and then she walked north . . . yes, about an hour ago . . . right. She may have gone back to the house on Ocean Breeze."

"It's true," said Noah, even though the cop didn't seem to be asking for verification.

"And I'm not a perv," he said. But she'd already turned and was walking away.

The first thing Noah told Jordan when he saw her on the beach was that he'd known from the start she was different, the way she sat there so quietly, so self-composed, at Dr. Pu-Pu's office, reading her textbooks for school or just looking around and taking it all in while others were twirling their hair or shaking their legs with nervous energy or flipping through the pages of old magazines. There was always someone who was crying, too, at the neurologist's office. Maybe not conspicuously, or even really noticeably, but Noah had a keen eye for people unraveling, and he could usually tell, even if they were trying to be discreet.

She said this wasn't so good—it wasn't necessarily what she'd been going for, being different. What she wanted at this point was to just be the same—not the new girl at school, not the girl who'd created a big drama on the soccer field. Not the girl with freaky headaches, and definitely not the girl who lost it over a jerk like Khalid.

"Who's Khalid?" he asked.

"It's a long story, but he's no one really. Just some jerk I was kind of obsessed with, and I thought I still was. Actually, I half figured I was going to break down and call him from Beach Week. I was kind of waiting for an excuse, and there it was, with the whole lobster business. I mean that's really dumb, but I've done dumber. But I didn't call him. And that's good."

"That's good," he agreed. He wasn't completely sure what was good, but he knew from when he'd been married that when in doubt, agree.

"I don't know what that was all about, really. I mean, was it just random? Could it have been any guy standing there at the party that night?"

"Could have been," Noah said, still clueless. Here was another backward conversation, another person he'd gotten to know in reverse. She just kept talking, without any prompting.

"That was the whole thing with Khalid. I was assuming it was some great operatic love affair or something. I was thinking that I needed to be special, to be different. Like I couldn't just go off to Beach Week or have a normal graduation party like everyone else. I guess I kind of felt like this whole experience with the concussion made me different and that I needed to be different. But really what I think I need is to be ordinary. That's so dumb.

"I think maybe I was also . . . it's terrible to say and I don't really even want to think about it too much, but like, maybe I was also trying to upset my mother . . ."

Noah so wanted to help this girl, but what she was talking about was pretty much beyond him. He thought he'd try to ground this in something he could understand.

"Do you like taffy?" he asked.

"Of course I do. Who doesn't?"

"It's true—not that many people don't. It's one of those things, you know, that's kind of universal. It brings people together. Of course that's not totally true, because one thing you do find is that some people worry about their dental work. And what I try to explain to them is that this taffy is not that sticky. It's not like the junk you buy in the grocery store. That stuff will rip your fillings out. But this is nice and soft."

"Is it? I had some at your house . . . I hope it's okay, I didn't mean to just take it or anything, but there were a couple boxes sitting there and I figured you wouldn't mind. But it wasn't that great. It was hard to chew."

"You can't judge it by that—it was old. I saw you trying to chew and I wanted to tell you not to, and I almost did but . . ."

"But what?"

"But I'm not supposed to be looking in windows. Or even talking about taffy. Although you tell me, what's so bad about talking about taffy?"

She shrugged her shoulders. "Not sure. I guess it's kind of about context?"

"What do you mean, context?"

"I just mean it's not so much about asking people about taffy, it's more about *why* you ask them."

"I just want to know what people's favorite flavors are. What kind of assortments they choose. I'm just trying to *understand*. You know, like maybe there's some way to get a little insight into human behavior by keeping a log of what makes people the same and different. Like, what's your favorite flavor taffy?"

"What's my favorite flavor taffy? Jeez, that's the weirdest question anyone's asked me in a while . . ."

"It's not really that weird. Just think about it for a minute."

"Um . . . I'm not really sure I've had enough taffy in my life to know the answer!"

"That's good, actually. I've always wanted someone to experiment on," he said.

"What do you mean? That sounds a little creepy. No offense . . ."

"Here, come sit," he said, pointing to the counter.

They pulled themselves up and positioned themselves with their backs against opposite walls so they were facing each other like they were going to play a game of jacks. He handed her a fistful of taffy and watched as she unwrapped each piece slowly and chewed. Sometimes she'd start laughing, but she did seem to be concentrating, taking the survey seriously. She unwrapped a piece of banana, and there was the sudden appearance of yellow.

"I thought I was trying to prevent a murder," he said.

"A murder?" She looked startled.

"Back in Verona. When they said I was peeping. I was just trying to make sure Mrs. Bergstrom was okay."

"What do you mean, exactly?"

"I heard her," he said. He explained the walkie-talkie intercept and the words he had heard: " 'You've got to get out of that house. He's killing you.' Or was that it? It's killing you. You're killing me? Actually I'm not sure I remember what I heard exactly, but it seemed like someone was killing someone else."

"Whoever said that might not have meant it literally."

"What do you mean?"

"Like maybe something in the house was kind of eating at her—not, like, murder?"

"You mean like a fungus or something?"

"No. I mean like a . . . okay, well maybe like a *psychological* fungus."

He was not following this at all.

"Maybe there was something going on in her life that she couldn't live with."

This made complete sense. "You mean like not being allowed to see Oliver anymore?"

"I don't know about that, but maybe."

"I see what you're saying, but that couldn't be it, because there was all this other evidence. Like Mrs. B. was always getting packages. So I thought maybe there was some drug thing going on."

"Well, maybe she was doing a lot of online shopping!"

"Like a shopping addict or something? She was always at her computer, that's true. But there was more. Like the curtains on the basement windows were always closed. So I was kind of thinking maybe there was a meth lab down there, or . . ."

"That's kind of a big leap. Maybe that's what was going on, who knows, but it seems pretty extreme given that there are lots of other more plausible possibilities."

"Yeah, well, the obvious one might be the most plausible, too. Sometimes a person goes pretty far out of the way to make up excuses for what must seem like a no-brainer. Like me, trying to figure out why Clara was always crying. She was always crying because she was unhappy."

"Sorry to hear that. I don't mean to change the subject, but I'm kind of not sure what we're talking about anymore, plus I have an answer for you: vanilla."

"That's incorrect."

"You're so weird!" she said, but in a nice way, like they were friends and she wasn't afraid to say the wrong thing. "You asked me a question, and I just sat here and chewed like a zillion pieces of candy, and now you're telling me that my answer's *wrong*?"

"It's just that that's such a predictable answer. Most people like vanilla, and you aren't like most people."

"You mean, that's a totally boring, normal answer?"

"Yes. You seem like you'd like . . . I don't know—hardly anyone likes banana."

"Banana saltwater taffy? Yuck!"

"So you're a boring vanilla," Noah said.

"Well, maybe that's good. I think I just need some boring vanilla in my life. And I also think I don't want to go straight to college. I want to take a gap year, maybe go to someplace like India."

"That's sort of the opposite of boring, isn't it? This is one of my more complicated surveys. Usually it's pretty straightforward. Do you mind if I ask you a few personal questions, just for my records? I'm doing this a little backwards, but if you wouldn't mind filling in a few statistical gaps . . ."

"I'd be happy to. Do you suppose you could do me a favor, though?"

"What's that?"

"I'd like to bring a box of taffy home for my parents, just to thank them for putting up with me lately. But someone took my wallet."

"What kind would you like? We've got long sticks and kisses, sugar and sugar-free, boxes of assortments or single flavors, or even individually selected mixes . . . you can pick chocolate, molasses, vanilla, orange, lime, banana, cherry, peppermint, strawberry, lemon, licorice, spearmint, or peanut butter."

She hesitated for a moment, then asked for assorted taffy kisses.

"That's also totally boring and predictable," Noah said.

"It is?" she asked cheerfully. She smiled and reached for the box.

21

* * * * *

Leah saw Jordan as soon as the car turned the corner. She felt
an instant release, like steam escaping a boiling kettle. It didn't
matter that they were still a good quarter of a mile from the
house or that Jordan was facing the other direction; Leah knew
who it was. You could show her any portion of her daughter—
an elbow, an ear, a sliver of an eyebrow—and she'd recognize
Jordan. Unlike Charles, who had at times lately seemed one
new quirk away from becoming someone she no longer knew,
her daughter could transform into another being entirely, she
could be turned by a witch into a newt or a bat, and Leah was
pretty sure she'd still be able to pick her out of a lineup.

Jordan was leaning against a shabby house that looked
like . . . well, actually there was no better way to say it other
than it looked like a house at Beach Week the morning after a
party. Except surely that couldn't be the right house. Maybe
the numbers had become transposed with the one next door.
There was trash all over the place, and a sad, deflated dinosaur

stretched across the entirety of the lawn. There was a sign slapped on the front door that said EVICTION NOTICE, and below it a padlock. Jordan had her face pressed to a window.

"Jordan," Leah shouted, flinging open the door of the police car before it had even come to a full stop. She ran toward the house. "Oh my God, you have no idea how worried we were!"

Leah realized as she said this that she hadn't allowed herself to feel the full weight of her concern until this very moment. The thought that something might have actually happened to Jordan was so terrifying that she'd suppressed it all into a seething ball of rage aimed at the little cup on the green of the Putt-Putt course—or, maybe more accurately, aimed at Charles. Which was not to say he didn't deserve at least a little of her wrath.

She pulled Jordan into a tight embrace and held her for the longest time that she could recall since her daughter was an infant; remarkably, Jordan didn't push her away.

Charles emerged from the car and gave Jordan a hug, too. Then he hugged Leah. Then they were in the midst of another three-way embrace, which by now Jordan was trying to wriggle out of. Leah had almost forgotten that they were with a policewoman, who was walking around the perimeter of the house and had just appeared beside them.

"What were you looking at, darling?" she asked Jordan. "Are you a peeper now, too?" She said this in an atonal way that was hard to interpret but seemed mostly to convey annoyance about the whole ordeal.

Jordan motioned toward the window, and the three of them pressed their faces to the glass. Some boy Leah had never seen before was lying naked on the floor. Another boy was standing in front of the television, fake strumming.

"What's he doing?" Leah asked.

"He's playing Guitar Hero."

"What's that?"

"Are you kidding, Mom? You've never heard of Guitar Hero?"

"Oh, I've always wanted to play that!" said Charles.

"You're not allowed any games for a while," Leah said. "You're on probation."

"What if we play together? On the same team?"

"That would be a novelty." She hadn't meant to sound so mean. This was perhaps Charles's version of an olive branch.

Officer Pat started banging on the door. "You're not supposed to be in here. You guys are officially out," she yelled. "Evicted. Can't you read?" No one moved from inside, and Leah could see that the boy strumming the fake guitar was wearing headphones.

"How did they even get in," Leah asked, "if there's a padlock on the door?"

"Probably they never even left," Jordan said. "People started hiding all over the place when we got busted. I just came back to get my stuff . . . it's still upstairs. And my car keys . . . Dad's car keys, I mean . . . are in my bag."

"Gotcha," said the policewoman, "but for now, what I'm gonna recommend is you guys just go down to the beach for a little while and let me sort out these boys. This one isn't quite . . . presentable." She motioned toward the guy on the floor. "I'm not sure your parents really want to see how this goes down."

"I'm really sorry, Mom," Jordan said as they sat on the hot sand. Someone had left a half-finished sand castle nearby, as well as a bunch of pails and shovels and a few toddler toys. Jordan was absentmindedly doing a little renovation, connecting two of the towers with a moat, adding on a new wing. They didn't have any beach gear with them, but Charles had his new bathing trunks on, and he'd run straight into the surf.

"I know I've been horrible."

"You didn't do anything that awful," Leah said. "You've been through a lot . . ." She stopped herself from running through the list, unsure of whether they were talking about the last two years or just the last two days. The distinction hardly mattered. "Here, that part of the castle, right there, I think it needs a flag."

"Do you think? It's not really a castle it's . . . a grocery store."

"A grocery store in the sand? That may be a first. So what's that, there?" Leah asked, pointing toward another cluster of smaller sand structures.

"That's . . . um . . . affordable housing. I don't know, Mom, normal teenage stuff is going to tanning salons for six weeks to get ready for Beach Week, then getting shit-faced and hooking up with random boys."

"Affordable housing?"

"You know, like for teachers and police and stuff, who might otherwise be priced out of the community."

"That's so considerate of you . . . and what's this?" Leah asked, pointing to the new wing. "Wait, did you just say hooking up with random boys? And tanning salons? Are your friends really doing that? Oh my God—sorry! Never mind! I didn't mean to say that . . ."

"It's okay, Mom. That's . . . a twelve-screen movie theater. And that's an elementary school."

"I know, but I'm trying to let go a bit more. I know you're

sensible, and I'm working at changing. I even ate a hot dog for lunch, and believe it or not, I had a Diet Pepsi."

"That's huge, Mom. Although, actually, I'm thinking I might become a vegetarian, after seeing all those hamburgers, and then the lobsters . . . oh my God, Mom, you should have seen them. Khalid would've . . . Never mind."

"What? Khalid would've what? You never even really told me anything about him."

"There's no point. It was stupid. I turned what should have been a one-night stand into some . . . Never mind. I don't want to talk about Khalid anymore. I don't even want to think about him."

Leah forced herself to let the one-night stand reference go, too, which wasn't easy. "Okay. What should we talk about, then?"

"Can we talk about India?"

Leah wondered at what point, precisely, this whole mothering thing was going to start to get easier, although she supposed a year off before beginning college wasn't the worst thing in the world. "Yes, we can talk about that," she said. "But let's wait for Dad . . . What's that you're doing now?" she asked. Jordan was scooping sand with her hand, making a loop around the cluster of buildings.

"That's the tunnel for the Metro."

"So the zoning board approved the Cobalt Line?"

"They did! They met last night and agreed it made sense, you know, to ease congestion. And they agreed that this is exactly where the stop should go. So now we can break ground."

Jordan took one of the pails that was filled with water and poured it into the center.

"What are you doing now? Destroying Downtown?"

"No, not at all. I'm enhancing. We're putting an ocean in the middle. It will be even better than a pool."

"Brilliant!"

"Yeah. Let's show Dad."

"Where *is* Dad?" Leah asked. She put her hand to her forehead to shield the sun from her eyes and looked out toward the ocean. A bunch of people were standing on the shoreline, and there seemed to be some commotion. She scanned the horizon, and there was nothing but a vast, quivering blue that stretched as far as she could see.

It was mind-boggling to think of all that was out there, other worlds beyond and even beneath, to imagine that a person could just swim out there, find a sea cave or a portal into some other life. She supposed that's what her daughter was after in her search for something different, to explore the world, to decide randomly that she wanted to go to India or lose herself in some boy named Khalid.

Leah could use a bit of blowing things up herself, although she supposed there was something to be said for just giving what she had a good tweak. And where, exactly, was the object of the tweak? Again she looked out toward the spot where she had last seen him bobbing in the water, but she saw no sign of him.

"It looks like maybe something's happened out there," Leah said. "Let's walk up to the water and see what's going on."

"Yeah. Actually I see a couple of people from our school . . . Oh, there's Courtney Moore! They moved into the house just a block away. And one of those kids, he's the neighbor's son. Ben, I think. I wonder what's going on."

. . .

A shark sighting was what was going on, and still no sign of Charles.

"I was out there, about a hundred yards from here," said the kid Jordan had identified as Ben, "and I saw it. I'm sure of it. I felt this weird churning in the water and I saw this massive white thing just below the surface. I mean you hear about these things, but you never actually think . . ." He was visibly trembling, and someone handed him a towel.

A group had formed around him, and now everyone was talking about his own near brush with the shark. Someone claimed to have nearly lost a leg, another an arm. The stories were getting wilder, more animated, less believable with each recitation.

Leah looked back out toward the horizon and still no sign of Charles. She felt terrified—and terrible. She couldn't deny harboring uncharitable thoughts toward him, one as recently as a minute ago when Jordan reminded her of the Downtown debacle. Even in her darkest moments, though, she had never wished him any harm. No matter how mad at him she might have been, she had never once fantasized about her husband being eaten by a shark. She wondered if, on Judgment Day, this would earn her any points.

Of course there were other, less fantastic dangers posed by the sea. He might simply have swum out too far, and in his exhausted, stressed-out, hung-over condition he might not have had the strength to swim back in. The strong wave of emotion that accompanied this thought took her by surprise. Was it possible that she was underestimating the strength of their connectedness? That over the course of all these years he'd become a part of her that was just as inseparable as Jordan? This had to be the case because she felt an ache as deep as anything she'd ever known when she contemplated the idea of Charles drowning or progressing through the intestines of a great white shark.

"Where's the lifeguard, for God's sake?" someone yelled.

They all looked toward the lifeguard station, but the chair was empty.

"Is that him out there?" Jordan asked, pointing toward the horizon near a small fishing vessel. They both stared in that direction for a moment, until they lost sight of the speck they had seen.

"What about over there?" Leah asked, pointing toward another object off in the middle distance. But that figure rose with the next wave on top of a surfboard, wearing a bikini.

Leah was startled by the slap of a wet, cold hand on her back, and then an equally wet sandy embrace from behind. It was Charles, and he seemed even more startled to have Leah turn toward him and take him into her arms in his soaking-wet condition.

"Are you okay?" he asked, even though she was the one who was supposed to be asking this question.

"I was worried about you!" she said.

"No need to worry about me," he said. "I've just had a great swim. So refreshing! It really cleared my head, and it did wonders for my back. We should really come to the beach more often. Maybe that's why we're all walking around half dead in the suburbs . . . I don't know, maybe they should do a study on the state of mind of people who live at the ocean and see if there's as high a rate of depression, alienation, even as high an incidence of the common cold . . ."

He was getting very excited in the old Charles-like way that she hadn't seen since they'd left Omaha.

"I agree, Dad," said Jordan. "In fact, come see what I've done to Downtown."

"What do you mean?"

"Come see." She took Charles's hand and led him back up the beach.

He looked at her sand development and smiled proudly, as if she'd just won a spelling bee.

"It's a wonder, although I'm not sure that I follow exactly . . . what's this?" He pointed to the tunnel.

"That's the Metro."

"Ah, you're quite the optimist, aren't you!"

"Well, when the zoning board understands that you're going to put an ocean in, they'll approve the Metro, no problem."

"The ocean?"

"Yeah, Dad, why not? I mean, they put a fake wave machine in one of the stores at the mall. So why not a fake ocean?"

"You know, you may be onto something. I did read about a project like that in Japan. I think they actually did it, with sand, salt water, a retractable roof . . ."

Again, Leah bit her tongue. As if you could drop an ocean into Verona County. But she was no longer the naysayer.

"Could you put in a boardwalk?" Leah asked.

"For you, I would put in a boardwalk," he said.

"Maybe you could have some seafood restaurants . . . one that serves crabs, with Old Bay seasoning."

"And for you, we will have crabs with Old Bay seasoning."

"What about fish and stuff, Dad?"

"I don't know. We'll have to look into that."

"But let's not have any sharks," Leah said.

"For my lovely wife, we will not have any sharks."

"Actually, let's get rid of the deer and bears, too."

"No, no. You need wildlife, some sense of danger. You need to keep people on their toes. But now that you mention it, we could do without owls."

"This is so silly, Dad."

"Of course it is. But you know what they say: Big dreams lead to big things."

"Who said that, Dad? Einstein?"

"You know, I'm not completely sure," he said, "but I think it might have been Snoopy."

"Snoopy? You're looking to Snoopy for inspiration now?" Leah said. But maybe this wasn't the worst place to turn.

Jordan picked up Charles's Chelsea Beach T-shirt and was just about to hand it to him, but she thought better of it and began to race down the beach, taunting him, laughing. Leah thought that the storybook ending here would be for her and Charles to chase after Jordan, laughing, hair blowing in the wind, but they were both exhausted from their own little mayhem at Beach Week, and instead they collapsed in the sand and watched Jordan run.

EPILOGUE

* * * * *

Leah started crying the moment she heard the first refrain of "Pomp and Circumstance." She turned toward Charles and could see he'd teared up, too. When Jordan stepped across the stage to accept her diploma, Charles reached for Leah's hand and squeezed it tight.

Jordan looked radiant. It seemed the humidity and salt had done something magical to her hair. It looked like it had grown another inch since Beach Week, which in the Adler house was now known as Beach *Day.* It splayed radiantly from beneath the mortarboard. Leah thought she ought to clip a piece and put it in her pocket, a talisman of health and good fortune.

After the ceremony and the dinner out, Jordan agreed to a little party in the backyard. Leah's parents had flown in from Des Moines, and although it was a marginal call whether or not to bring Florence, Jordan wanted all of the family there. Besides, Florence continued to be surprisingly cheered by all things related to high school. Leah could only hope that if she got stuck in a particular groove in her later years, it would include this one. This very moment was one she'd want to relive, and she supposed she could even manage in perpetuity the rough parts of the last few years; but Beach Week she could do without.

They'd been gone all day—graduation was held in an auditorium downtown, and the expedition had required major logistical planning in order to park and get the grandparents situated, and then they'd fought rush-hour traffic to get back to the restaurant where they'd reserved a table.

Leah had just corralled everyone into the backyard for cake when Charles appeared at the patio door, his face pale. In his hand were several envelopes that he'd evidently just collected from the box on the front porch.

"What is it?" Leah asked, waving the match in the air to put out the flame.

"Nothing. It can wait."

"You look pretty upset, Dad. What is it? We can handle it."

"Probably best not to do that right now."

Jordan went over and grabbed one of the envelopes from his hand. It was thin, like a college rejection letter, except that the return address said "Department of Justice, Chelsea Beach, Delaware." The other envelopes all had the same return address.

"Charles?" Leah asked tentatively.

Jordan ripped open the letter. "It's a summons. They want me to appear as a witness in the case of *State v. Cherie Long* and"—she opened the other envelopes—"as a witness in the case of *State v. Dorrie Glover* and in the case of *State v. Courtney Greene* . . . and in the—"

"We get the idea," said Leah.

"When is all this?"

Charles grabbed the papers from Jordan. "One on August eighth, another on August ninth . . . August tenth, August eleventh . . ."

"All week?" Leah asked. "Are they insane? There must be some way to get out of this. It's an unreasonable burden. How can Jordan be expected to be there for an entire week?"

"I've heard it's easy to wriggle out of, Mom. And probably all the charges will be dropped by then anyway, what with everyone having their lawyers and stuff."

"I think we should make the best of this," said Charles. "Let's embrace this thing and stop fighting it."

"What do you mean?"

"I mean let's go to the beach. Let's have our own Beach Week."

"I don't know, Dad. Your behavior wasn't exactly exemplary."

"Hey, I just got caught up in the moment. I mean, have you ever played beer pong? I got a little carried away, but—"

"You played beer pong, Dad?" Jordan asked, incredulous.

"What's beer pong?" asked Leah.

"We can play at the beach. I'll teach you."

"Dad, I don't see that happening, somehow."

The phone rang from inside.

"Let it go," said Leah. "We're just about to have cake." But her mother had already answered it and was calling to her.

"Take a message, Mom," Leah said.

"I did," her mother said, returning to the patio. "It was some woman named Janet Glover. She said there's a meeting tomorrow night at the home of Alice Long . . . something to do with Beach Week? Collecting checks to pay a lawyer or something? I said you'd call her back."

"Speaking of checks," said Charles. "Did you ever get—"

"Please let's not go there right now," said Leah. "Let's just enjoy this moment."

ACKNOWLEDGMENTS

• • • • •

Heartfelt thanks to Melanie Jackson and Sarah Crichton, as well as to Kathy Daneman, Dan Piepenbring, and everyone at FSG. Thanks also to the members of my writing group: Kitty Davis, Ann McLaughlin, Leslie Pietrzyk, Carolyn Parkhurst Rosser, Amy Stolls, and Paula Whyman. And to Linda Greider, Jean Heilprin Diehl, Julie Langsdorf, Trustman Senger, Ally Coll, Emma Coll, and Max Coll for reading sections of this manuscript. Thanks, too, to Sam "Magic" Johnson for participating in the beer pong tutorial. And to Steve Hull, at *Bethesda Magazine*, for being a true friend of fiction. As always, enormous gratitude to my husband, Steve Coll, for his encouragement and steadfast support.

A Note About the Author

Susan Coll is the author of the novels *Acceptance* (Sarah Crichton Books, 2007), *karlmarx.com*, and *Rockville Pike*. A film adaptation of *Acceptance*, starring Joan Cusack, aired on the Lifetime television network in 2009. Coll lives in Washington, D.C., and New York City with her husband, the writer Steve Coll. She is a three-time Beach Week survivor.